THE TREE OF LIFE
(A NOVEL)
AND SHORT STORIES

THE TREE OF LIFE
(A NOVEL)
AND SHORT STORIES

TRANSLATED FROM THE TELUGU SAMSAARA VRIKSHAM

R.S. SUDARSHANAM

ATLANTIC PUBLISHERS AND DISTRIBUTORS

Published by
ATLANTIC PUBLISHERS AND DISTRIBUTORS
B-2, Vishal Enclave, Opp. Rajouri Garden, New Delhi-27
Phones : 5413460, 5429987

Sales Office
4215/1, Ansari Road, Darya Ganj, New Delhi-110 002
Phones : 3273880, 3285873, 3280451
Fax : 91-11-3285873
web: www.atlanticbooks.com
e-mail : info@atlanticbooks.com

ISBN 81-269-0026-1

Typeset at
APD Computer Graphics, Delhi
Printed in India at
Mehra Offset Press, Delhi

THE TREE OF LIFE

"They speak of an imperishable Asvatha Tree with its root above and branches below. Its leaves are the Vedas; who knows it is the knower of the Vedas."

Ch XV, Verse 1,
The Bhagavadgita

"...One space spreads through all creatures equally, inner-world space. Birds quietly flying go through us. O, I that want to grow, the tree I look outside at's growing in me!"

Rainer Meria Rilke

INTRODUCTION

Samsara Vriksham or *Tree of Life* is the fourth novel of R.S. Sudarshanam, a well-known critic, novelist and short story writer in Telugu. *Anubandhalu* (Attachments) *Mallee Vasantham* (Return of the Spring) and *Asura Sandhya* (Dusk of the Devil) are his other novels. *Tree of Life* was published in 1976 in Telugu.

In Sudarshanam's other stories such as "Burden of Ash," "Blood-red," The Clone," and "Sea" we find the same philosophical quest — man in search of his soul, in search of the fundamental truth which will explain the ultimate meaning of life. Is human life purely materialistic or is there anything otherworldly about it?

The intricacies of human relationships have always been a major concern of Sudarshanam. He tries to place them in a philosophical perspective in his novels and stories. In *Tree of Life* there are two main characters — one is a materialist and rationalist, the other, who also happens to be the narrator, is an idealist. They argue endlessly about the meaning of human existence. Both seem to be correct from their respective philosophical standpoints.

Sudarshanam has made a thorough study of the Indian and Western philosophical traditions and creatively juxtaposed them in his fiction. He always tries to explain various commissions and omissions of his characters from the philosophical point of view. He is an advocate of the existentialist philosophy of Kierkegaard and Jean Paul Sartre. He has also been greatly influenced by Adi Sankara's advaita philosophy. He tries to bring about a synthesis between Sankara's advaita philosophy and Sartre's existentialism. Thus, by extension he tries to bring about a fusion of Indian and Western thought. Advaita philosophy is a synthesis between materialism and idealism, according to him. In *Tree of Life* we find the same philosophy expressed in the form of a novel.

Sudarshanam's short story "Madhura Meenakshi" (The Fish-eyed Goddess") is an example of this synthesis between Western and Indian thought. The protagonist of this story finds similarity between the goddess Meenakshi of Madurai and his lady love Meenakshi. Ultimately, he realises that both are the same.

In Sudarshanam's other stories such as "Loneliness," "The Immortal Red," "Reflection," and "Union with the Sea" we find the same philosophical quest — man in search of his soul, in search of the meaning of life, in search of synthesis between various contradictory points of view. Advaita philosophy is the ultimate message of all his short stories. There are no two truths but only one truth. Materialism and idealism do not contradict each other; they are one and the same. Man has to find this truth with his own experience and experiments and during his own life time. Nothing is predetermined. There is nothing like fate or destiny. Man is the master of his life; he is responsible for everything he does. There is nothing like force of circumstances or social compulsions. These are only excuses that man invents to escape reality. Man is condemned to be free. How he is going to use this freedom is left entirely to himself. Freedom entails responsibility. Every man must create meaning for his own life and strive to realise it. These are some of the ideas that Sudarshanam cherishes and codifies in his fiction. His stories are basically stories of ideas. After going through them, readers often find life itself in new light. Life can never be the same after reading Sudarshanam's fiction.

RAJESHWAR MITTAPALLI

CONTENTS

SHORT STORIES

PART I

"Rice and lime, they look all the same,
Eat you rice, all the same!"

It was Sunday afternoon. Lying in my bed I was wide awake. I didn't feel like reading a book. Children were playing and talking outside. Suddenly they started clapping hands rhythmically and singing a song.

I knew the song in my childhood, but had not heard it in recent times. I wondered wherefrom these children had got it. Inquisitively I came on the verandah. I saw Viswam, Gopi and Radha under the peepal tree. Viswam was in the seventh class. The other two were much younger and had just started going to school. I beckoned them.

"Where did you learn the song?"

"Yesterday my teacher sang it in the class," said Viswam.

"Did he really sing like this and ask you to join?"

"Not like that. He told us the story of Rantidev. In the story he mentioned the song briefly..."

"And then?"

He said that Rantidev's story did not make sense. To go hungry and yet feed someone with the food available may be shown as a great act of sacrifice. But it is just a wonderful story and nothing else. One should eat and also feed others. That is socialism. If one eats denying others their share, then that is capitalism. He said many other things too. IIc talks a lot."

"You couldn't follow all that! Your teacher seems to be quite a fellow!"

"Sadhus and sannyasins are cheats, when they say that rice and lime are one; a fistful of earth or gold has no difference in value. But they are really after good food like fruits and sweets, and look for a chance to steal money and gold. Saying that, he mentioned this song."

"If he told you about sannyasins, who are cheats, then he must have told you about the real ones too. Did he describe them?"

"No. All of them are cheats only."

"Very good. What is the teacher's name?"

"Shyamsundar."

Radha whispered something into Gopi's ear. Gopi, pulling at Viswam's shirt, said : "Look, it has come." Viswam looked out and asked the children to remain in the verandah. He hurriedly left saying :" I'll go and inform the doctor, you wait."

"What is it, Viswam?" I queried.

"A mad dog. It's just gone behind the tree."

I stood up and looked. An emaciated dog, suffering from skin disease was about to lie down under the tree. The vacant site opposite my house was meant as a children's park, but remained undeveloped. The peepul tree had been there even before the area was colonized. Children gathered round the tree to play. Now dogs seemed to have migrated from the heart of the town. The one I was looking at was definitely not a rabid dog, but a diseased one. It was a pitiful sight.

Gopi and Radha were keenly observing the dog's movements.

Eight year old Gopi, and five year old Radha were my friend Bhavanarayana's children. Viswam aged twelve, their next door neighbour's only son, had none of his age group close by to mix with and drew these two children into his company.

"Radhamma, come to me," I said. Radha, a sweet child was my wife's favourite too. As we had no children of our own, we treated her with special affection. Gopi went inside the house to drink a cup of water.

"Are you scared of the dog?" I asked Radha. She nodded her pretty head in assent. She was not the chattering type. She spoke a word or two only when it was absolutely necessary. She sat in my lap and we both gazed at the tree and the dog, which by now had curled up at the base of the tree.

Viswam and the doctor who lived next door came on the road. The sudden firing of a gun startled little Radha in my lap, and my heart gave a jump. I stood up and saw a pistol in the doctor's hand! He had aimed at the dog and had killed it. He quietly retired into his house saying something to Viswam.

Only by his act now, I realized that the doctor had a pistol. A few months ago, the doctor had come to this town on transfer. I did not know him except for a nodding acquaintance. That a doctor would resort to preemptory shooting of pariah dog was unimaginable for me.

Radha spoke to me with some glee : "The mad dog is dead. The doctor killed it, uncle!"

My wife Savitri and Gopi came on the verandah, having heard the pistol-shot.

"What happened?" my wife queried.

"The doctor has taken the life of a fully alive creature."

"That is it! A good thing! A wonderful man, this doctor, has done just the right thing. These dogs have become a great nuisance of late. Mad ones, eczema ones, barking and quarrelling...the municipality doesn't care. Nobody cares. People like you are simply incapable and indifferent."

"Well, I cannot kill."

"You can neither kill, nor give life. You can talk Vedanta."

I fell back into my chair and said :

"When one is capable of talk only, why not talk good things and avoid others? 'Rice and lime, they look the same, eat you rice all the same' the children sang a little while ago."

"You can afford to spend your time talking, as you have landed property, and there are elders, who would send you rice. Ordinary folk can get neither rice nor lime. They die of hunger and disease like the dog we see under the tree. Anyway this particular dog must have good *karma** to its credit. The doctor gave it *moksha***."

The reference to *karma* and *moksha* was a gibe at me.

Viswam came back even as Savitri continued her lecture. He said triumphantly : "The mad dog is dead." I tried to intervene to say that it was not a mad dog, but he ignored me and continued to give the doctor's message to his listeners, "Unless these useless dogs are done away with, they become a big health hazard. As soon as the servant comes in the evening, the doctor is going to get the corpse buried in his yard as fertilizer for the palm tree."

When Savitri was about to comment on it, I said to her : "Don't you think it is time for some tea?"

Savitri looked despairingly at me and went inside.

Viswam and the children went to have a look at the dead dog.

I thought there was something unusual about the doctor. He had taken out a government licence to keep a pistol and ammunition ready with him. A policeman wears arms by virtue of his occupation. In certain areas of the state, civilians too have them for reasons of security. Unless one was threatened by enemies, or was placed in special circumstances, one did not require fire-arms. A doctor is looked upon as a benefactor of society. It was extra-ordinary for him to think of self-defence. In America even teen-agers sport guns, but in this country we hadn't progressed as far as that. This had been Gandhi's land till yesterday!

---

* *Karma* means the effect of one's deeds in past lives.

** *Moksha* means soul's liberation after death from rebirth.

Savitri came back with tea and biscuits. She beckoned the children to join us. Viswam said, "Bye-bye" and went home. The youngsters came up.

While I sipped tea, Savitri said to me : "You've completely forgotten our Raja. The dog hasn't touched food. I thought you would inquire and perhaps take a few biscuits to offer him personally. You are indifferent; really incapable of affection."

Raja our pet dog, all white in colour had a distinguished look. I was ignorant of his breed and pedigree. He had come to us as gift from a friend of Savitri's.

Raja was now in his third year. An adolescent dog, he liked to wander about. He didn't obey orders. If he was chained, he would raise a hell of a cry till he was released. He knew no fear and refused to be intimidated. When Savitri tried to discipline him, he showed his teeth and sulked. He ran after all the street bitches. He became a problem. My friend Bhavanarayana observed : "You cannot manage, because neither of you has the temperament to discipline the dog. The best thing to do is to get him castrated by the vet. Or you have to provide a suitable partner for him. Even then who can be sure of his behaviour? Taking him to the vet appears to be the only solution to your problem. When his balls are gone, the dog will remain confined to the house and will improve physically too. He will develop into a proper watch-dog."

I didn't give the matter any further thought. Savitri too encouraged me. I got the operation done at the local veterinary hospital. On return from the hospital, the dog looked downcast and helpless. The look he gave me sent a pang through my heart.

Savitri offered him milk, which he accepted. I kept him chained in the bathroom at the back of the house. The leash was fairly long and allowed him free movement. The dog licked his wound, made circular movements to settle down, but was restless for a while and gave little cries of pain. Afterwards he was quiet and I forgot about him. I had not inquired whether Raja had his lunch or not.

"Giving lunch, milk, or biscuits, being your privilege, Savitri, I didn't make any inquiries. Such an inquiry would have been an insult to your mother's heart!"

"Is that an insult or a compliment now? A childless person like me, how come I have a mother's heart? You aren't a man but a stone!"

Savitri hit back at me, but her eyes brimmed with tears. In a sudden movement she gathered the tea-things and went inside. I had not meant to hurt her. It was a casual remark meant to defend myself from her accusation that I did not care for Raja. Eight years after marriage, we remained childless. She worried more about it than I did. Of late it had become a frequent irritant between us. In bringing up Raja, in the affection we showed towards Radha and Gopi, we seemed to seek some compensation.

Perhaps I wanted to impress upon her that I was least worried and on my account she shouldn't have regrets. If it was only her mother-instinct that bothered her, I couldn't help it. Detachment and an objective attitude were dear to me as guiding principles. I deliberately cultivated them in every matter. Not because it was preached in the *Gita**, and had become a tradition, but because it happened to be my temperament too, I had shaped myself in that mould.

I loved Raja and the two childdren as much as Savitri did; but I never allowed that love to be mixed up with the thought of our childlessness. Savitri failed to understand this. She called me a 'stone'. Observing my silence perhaps, Gopi took Radha by hand and said : "Uncle, we are going home." I nodded assent and watched them go. Then I got up and went in the direction of the bathroom.

Savitri was in the kitchen. I gently stepped into the bathroom, washed myself and entered the attached room, where Raja was lying. The smell of dettol greeted me. Raja lifted his head and

---

* The *Bhagavatgita*

sniffed in my direction. He had eaten the biscuits but not touched the milk.

"Raja," I spoke to him. His eyes moved with the ears held back.

"How are you, my dear fellow? Sip the milk, my good boy, you'll be all right." I pushed the milk-bowl a little towards him. Raja stood up, stepped towards me, and moving his tail a little, licked my foot. My heart responded, may be with love, friendship, or pity. I touched his head and soothingly uttered, "Raja, Raja." After those moments of absorption, I was thrown back into my normal state of mind, and came the thought that everything was meaningless. "Raja is an animal. I am a human being. His karma and my karma. This had to happen through me!"

There was nothing unusual about getting a dog castrated. It was justifiable as a rational act. Some dog-owners cut off the tail, just for the sake of fancy or for a superstition. If a dog's tail curves over into a full circle like a zero, it is believed that the movement of flies through the circle would being poverty and disaster to the owner. Could there be any end to such beliefs? In my childhood, whenever I made noise with the loose-end of the door-bolt, my grandmother would reprimand me saying that would cause poverty and misery. I did not behave superstitiously in the case of Raja. It no doubt caused him suffering. Life is inconceivable without suffering and pain.

Raja might have lost his manhood. But he would lead a disciplined life hereafter. And that would mean happiness. I should think that there had been no mindless violence in what I had done.

Along with the evolution of society, man's rationality had shaped nature according to his needs and purposes. Castration of animals and killing them, and things like birth-control, abortion, class-struggle, the atom bomb and the bid for world peace, all of them were actions, attempts, struggles and movements to achieve happiness for man *en masse*, though a few of them were mutually contradictory. I could not condemn any of them!

When Savitri accused me of being stone-hearted, I felt guilty for a while. When I saw Raja suffer pain, I had for a moment some moral doubt. Similarly when the doctor killed the dog, I wondered whether he did the right thing. All these doubts and questions arose as a part of the culture and tradition I had imbibed from childhood. I considered myself a rationalist and an advaitin. My reason must help me to get rid of the influence of imbibed ideas, and lead me to objectivity and equanimity. That was my *sadhana* or spiritual endeavour. Accordingly my feelings and doubts were but an illusion and showed that my attitude of detachment hadn't become stable and firm yet.

In cultivating detachment I had not yet become a man of action. Till Savitri persuaded me, I had procrastinated in taking Raja to the vet. But Savitri contradicted herself frequently. She made me do it and yet accuses me of being stone-hearted.

"The doctor is at it. He is getting the dog's corpse buried under the palm tree. Come and have a look. You can see it from our back-yard," said Savitri, standing at the door of my study.

"Let it be. I am plagued by dogs from this morning till now. They have become a problem."

"Well, imagine killing a live creature without a moment's hesitation. Unless one has that hardness, one cannot be a surgeon!"

"What do you mean by that? You approve, or disapprove!"

"What do you mean by that? You approve, or disapprove!"

"Such a deliberate act of taking life is perhaps a sin."

"Savitri, you are impulsive. A little while ago you said that he had done the right thing. Now you say it is a sin! There is neither sin nor merit, please go about your work."

Savitri left in a huff. She must be very angry, too angry to hit back with some retort or other.

PART II

The perception of a thing varies on a person's sensibility and imagination. There are descriptions of Nature by the English poets and by the Indian poets. When Shelley talks about the West wind, the culture of Greece is evident. When Rabindranath Tagore describes the wind, the Vaishnavite culture shows. A modern poet of the Progressive Movement would put into it the class-antagonism and the relentless struggle. For the Revolutionary poet that becomes a cyclone. A man's perception in every instance is coloured by his cultural background and bringing up.

The peepul tree standing opposite my house till that Sunday had been only a peepul tree. On that Sunday, when Raja was castrated, and the sick dog was shot dead by the doctor next door, on that very night I had a strange dream.

I dreamt that the peepul tree was burning. I was seeing it burning from my verandah. Black clouds of smoke rose and spread across the sky. Then there was a down-pour. Heavy cascades of water, gleaming and shining flooded the ground. As the streams of water raced along, some appeared to be snakes with fascinating zig-zag movements. One among them came up the stairs of my verandah. I flinched back a few steps. I closed my eyes out of fear. There was laughter. I opened my eyes. Before me stood an entrancingly beautiful woman smiling and fixing me with her eyes.

"Your curse had turned me into the tree. I am now released, I am going."

"Don't go, Hema, please...don't...."

I wanted to say something. But she was gone. Then I woke up. Well, it was Hema! Hemasundari in a violet sari, resplendently charming! Hema was Bhavanarayan's sister. It was a year since I had seen her.

What must be the association between the peepul tree and Hemasundari? Many a time she had stood in the verandah talking with me for long spells, and I had glanced at the peepul tree on those occasions. The tree had become a part of my consciousness, along with Hema's face. The truth hidden from me till then became known after the dream. In the morning when I went out and had a look at the tree, indeed it appeared differently as if Hema stood there and smiled at me in the form of the tree.

I remembered what she said in the dream : "Your curse turned me into the tree." Did I cause so much anguish? But Hema never showed it, never gave me an inkling of it!

Well, she must have got over it during the past one year. Would that be my supposition only? Should the friendship between us be considered a curse? Had she been standing before me for one whole year in the form of a tree suffering that curse? Well, if that was over now, then she must have succeeded in forgetting me!

The bonds of love and friendship would not obey our rules and dictums. They transcend our intentions. I couldn't accept Hema, and invite her into my life. How could I? What would become of Savitri? Would the excuse that Savitri was childless be a valid one to give her up? That had not been my complaint at all! It had been her complaint and grievance. In the face of that truth, any legal grounds for divorce acceptable to law were not acceptable to me. I wouldn't have liked to build my love on the basis of falsehood, and I didn't want to distance myself from Savitri, whether I loved her or not.

It was really strange to think how in the course of three months Hema had come close to my heart! If only chance had not brought us together, we could have as well avoided all this anguish! Life meandered, and nobody knew why.

I spoke in a similar vein to Hema bidding her farewell. "Suppose we had never met. Suppose your brother lived and worked in another town. This relationship wouldn't have been there. Let us forget it now. That is our present duty, duty to ourselves and our people. Thoughtlessly we have drifted and it has become a problem. We have been very free and gave our hearts and minds to each other. Well, it appears that isn't a good thing always! Having arrived here, I don't see any way further. You have to excuse me." Hema had remained silent throughout. She left without a word and we never met after that.

Hema joined as a school-teacher and lived in Kurnool. I sent her my good wishes. There was no response.

The dream changed my perception of the peepul tree. I became aware of a wound in my heart. It had been easy for me to indulge in a glib philosophical sort of explanation and bid her farewell, but I had not realized how strongly I had been bound in the matter. A sense of restraint and moral duty was uppermost in my mind.

Hema was fifteen years my junior. She had the dash of youth, and looked up to me...I thought it was wrong to take advantage of the situation, forgetting my relationship with Savitri.

That this sense of moral duty must have been awake and operative in the beginning itself, would be a legitimate criticism. But should I stop talking to young women as a rule, fearing that my loyalty to my wife would be jeopardised? Hema was a graduate preparing to become a teacher. It was the most natural thing for her to meet me and discuss books with me, when our two families happened to be close friends. Hema's intellectual clarity and flair for ideas drew me to her and attracted me more than her charm as a woman. In the matter of just two months we had become friends. Savitri never cast any doubt at any stage. She had left us free and alone. She would never intervene or monitor.

It would be unjust and unnatural to condemn, with hind sight, a relationship that had developed innocently without any motivation. It might have stretched emotionally to a state socially not viable, but that would not make it wrong. It did not allow it to become a problem and grow to unmanageable dimensions. My detachment saved me, I thought. Hema got a job and left the place. The bond of friendship had to end. Though she came up to my mind quite a few times during the past year, I always recalled what I had said to her finally, and never had any second thoughts.

The dream had opened a door within me. I could not rationally comprehend my inner state of mind. The glimpse of a complex reality baffled me. The cycle of births, and the existence of autonomous spheres or levels of experience with differing time-sequences filled my thoughts. As I sat in the verandah, Bhavanarayana came up. He was an officer in the government department of agriculture. In the course of our rambling conversation, I mentioned to him the dream I had had, without identifying the woman in the dream. I said she was an ethereal being. I asked him to offer his comments on the significance of the dream.

"Well, it is not born of indigestion, nor is it just a fancy. It appears to have a profound significance. My prediction is that very soon a daughter, ethereally beautiful like the one in the dream, will be born to you. And that would mean literally a release for both of you from the curse of childlessness," said Bhavanarayana.

"What is the authority for your interpretation? Is that indicated in any of our ancient texts?"

"Why go to any specific text? Our culture itself is a big treasury of wisdom and reference. The peepul tree is renowned as the child-giving tree. For an angel to emerge from that tree signifies your future child. She is sure to become a distinguished person. Then the serpent is equally associated with child-birth, as it is a practice among women to worship the serpent and pray for off spring.... Because of the combination of the peepul tree and the serpent as dual symbols, I think it is an auspicious dream promising you a child."

I laughed within myself at this new interpretation. Every man is an island. Every man's mind is a castle, impenetrable to others. If he were to know what had transpired between me and Hema one year ago, would he have given this meaning to the dream? If Savitri had dreamt something similar, the interpretation of coming childbirth might have been appropriate. I had no strong desire for a child.

"Why bother about children?" I queried.

"Well, it is a part of our dharma."

"Doesn't dharma change with times? When we are worried about population explosion, what kind of a dharma or duty is it to add to the population. In the present age, in our country it is certainly a non-dharma, even adharma!"

"That applies to those who have already produced offspring and not to you."

I had to remain silent, as I was not free to disclose my personal secret. I changed the subject, and we were discussing politics when Savitri came on the scene. Bhavanarayana immediately addressed himself to her :

"Please listen to my advice and worship the peepul tree for a while. And then let us go to 'Vidura Asvatham" a well-known place nearby, which gets its name because of the famous peepul tree there visited by hundreds of childless women. It has a reputation of granting women their wishes for children."

"I have heard of it. We must go sometime."

"No vagueness about it. I'll programme it for you one of these days."

"You know what my husband is like! He won't move easily."

"Hema will be here next week on a visit. We'll go on a picnic."

I felt excited at the news. But why? I asked myself. Where was my detachment?

After Savitri's exit, I said : "Well, you know the saying...after leading a glorious life, the man dies in the backyard! Even so, forgetful of thousands of years of human progress, we get back to the primitive cult of worshipping trees and stones. That is what your advice implies."

"The Asvatha tree is mentioned in the *Bhagavadgita* and you accept the authority of the *Gita.* The Lord says that He is the Asvatha among trees!"

"The Asvatha is a symbol, but not literally the Supreme Lord. This is the unfortunate confusion widely prevalent. It is the incrustation of ignorance and superstition. Our metaphysics and symbolism reached the highest levels the human mind is capable of reaching. But that was in the past. We turned all that into the grossest forms of beliefs and a variety of idols and call that our religion today."

"But you witnessed in your dream the Asvatha turning into a cloud and then a serpent emerging out of it. That was not superstitious belief, but a vision and a revelation!"

"It is true that we may perceive certain things through symbols. Intimations may come that way. But there is no justification for attributing divinity to them and to start blindly worshipping those symbols. That is not true religion."

"Well, I think we should not reduce symbols into bare ideas and feel smug about it. There is more than philosophy in symbols. What the intellect and discursive thinking cannot reach forth to, that knowledge or experience or revelation, whatever you may call it, is embedded in symbols. They come by themselves and not as substitute signs as in algebra. While I agree that a symbol should not be turned into God and worshipped, I must say that a symbol like the one we are talking about must be considered as having some power, magic or suprarational quality of influencing things and events."

"If you make every object into a symbol that way, how can you think and act rationally? Science developed only when we stripped things of their magical attributes. We now control and manipulate nature for our needs. We could make a bid for freedom. Freedom from slavery to nature. That is the achievement of civilized man. If the mind and the objective world had remained as one entity in man's consciousness, he would have been no better than other animals. Just as mobility differentiates an animal from a plant, even so analytical thought makes man superior to the animal. The capacity to separate thought from the object gave man an advantage putting him one step up on the ladder of evolution. From this point of view, your plea that we should accept the world of objects as the world of magic symbols putting aside discursive thought is to get back to our primitive state."

"What is the goal of progress of evolution? Should we not get back from division to unity?"

"Yes. But that must be a step forward from where we have arrived now. It is for that reason I plead for socialism and communism as a step forward from individualism. Man's integration as a personality and the future integration of humanity should go hand in hand. I don't accept materialism. What does it matter whether man came from mind or matter? We should not concern ourselves with the origins of life. Today matter and mind act upon and influence each other.... And mind is the observer undoubtedly. Therefore, today man's mind is of paramount importance. I am neither a materialist nor an idealist. I am a humanist."

PART III

Not to Vidura Asvatham but to Nallacheruvu, a village near Kadiri, I was asked to join the group consisting of Bhavanarayana, the doctor my neighbour and the doctor's friend a businessman, who were all going to meet a swamiji camping at Nallacheruvu. Dr. Veerabhadra Rao, my neighbour was properly introduced to me by Bhavanarayana. I was surprised to see that Bhavanarayana, without ever giving an inkling of it to me, had become a good friend of the doctor within a short period. The doctor was introduced to me as an intellectual with progressive ideas. I nodded with a smile and observed, shaking hands with the doctor : "Oh, yes. I saw him shoot a paraiah dog under the peepul tree some days ago, and utilize its carcass as a fertilizer."

"A sharp young man, sharp like a knife," said Bhavanarayana.

"A progressive intellectual going to see a swamiji! It surprises me," I said.

"He has no prejudices. He would rely on his own experience. He doesn't believe in setting limits to his knowledge."

The doctor intervened to say : "There should be no inhibitions to experience and to judge for oneself."

We were already in the car, driven by the businessman, who owned the car. I was seated by the doctor in the back seat.

"Man's capabilities are limited. Even if one wishes to be without limits, one is restricted by what nature has endowed on oneself," I remarked.

"Man's natural endowments should be looked upon as opportunities and not as restrictions. They are actually the means of experience. And the different ways in which they can be used arc really limitless, which we should recognize as the creativity of man. The story of man's progress establishes that. Then there are inhibitions, which religion, custom, ethics and such other mental blocks have created over the years. Take the principle of Ahimsa or Non-violence. At one time that was made into a political weapon. Soon vested interests turned it into an obstruction to change and progress. Besides its misuse, the principle is inherently, that is metaphysically invalid. Both for revolution and for individual experience it is an inhibition and a limit to be set aside without hesitation...."

"In killing the diseased dog, were you trying to prove it?" I asked.

"You're right. Revolution and a special experience are both implied in it."

"Of late, I have heard of the slogan : armed revolution. But I've understood that to be an exceptional means in desperate circumstances. What could be the speciality of experience in killing a miserable dog?"

"Well, what is the goal of life? Death. In fact man is struggling with death every moment of his existence. The pleasure in living is derived from this struggle with death. To save a living thing from death is a joyous experience. There is joy too in dealing death, when it becomes a necessity."

"I cannot believe that there could be joy in dealing death! Even to imagine it is difficult for me. Vengeance, anger or craziness might drive a man to deal death, but how could we call that a joyous state of mind?"

"Who are you to assert that it is not joy? To perceive and name the state of mind of another individual is not possible for any man. It will be a presumption only. Please tell mc whether any man can live in an absolutely non-violent way? Ask those who are pestered by mosquitos and bed-bugs, and they will describe to you what joy there is in killing each one of them. Similarly to put an end to a poisonous snake, a hopelessly infected dog, a traitor to society, an enemy of the people, or any thing of the sort, gives joy and pleasure, which you cannot deny. If you deny it, it only shows you up as an inhibited individual, one who has erected walls in his mind and become a prisoner in a self-made jail. Look at the children, who still have free minds. The walls of prison have not yet closed on them. They pursue butterflies, catch hold of ants and play with them. The play deals death and involves prolonged violence to those creatures, doesn't it? But that is the way of natural instincts. You cannot deny that experience as joy, experience sanctioned by nature. Refusing to see it that way is refusing to face truth."

"You want man to cultivate violence? Then what is the meaning and purpose of the culture and civilization man has built up over thousands of years? "

"Who is there to dictate to man what he must do, or to predict what he will do in future? Every man must decide for himself. There is no need of inhibitions to wield violence as a means when there is occasion for it. And dealing violence is certainly a special experience and a natural one too. That is what I want to point out. What you call culture and civilization have not been achieved without the use of violence in history. Battles and wars, exercise of power and authority by the king and by religious institutions even the modern state, every single thing of civilization without exception is violence. That human society is built on non-violence is a myth. Well, if you would call it a half-truth, I have no objection, because dualities constitute life. To the extent you emphasize non-violence and love, you have to concede violence and enmity also to the same extent. Police firing, lathi-charge, imprisonment and execution, are they not necessary to hold society together and safe?"

"Necessary evils there have been and still there are. We don't consider our society perfect. To eschew violence must be the goal and aim of our progress : to make a doctrine out of the very evil that humanity should strive against, appears to me strange and perverse."

"My dear Sir, the conditions now prevailing very much warrant it. A time has come to arrive at a correct understanding of the nature of violence, particularly in this country. Those who are for change and revolution should exercise their minds about it, very much because Gandhi influenced us in the past."

I concluded that the doctor was a naxalite, and stopped arguing further. But I was intrigued why the naxalite doctor had agreed to meet the swamiji.

At Nallacheruvu we were told that the swamiji was put up in a cottage situated in a mango-grove, which was the property of a rich landowner, Narayana Reddi. We went to see Narayana Reddi first.

A plumpish elderly man of medium height, ruddy complexion, honey-coloured eyes, and a gentle demeanour. He was soft-spoken and started talking about himself and his family. Narayana Reddi for a while forgot the purpose for which we were visiting him. Bhavanarayana reminded him twice : "Now let us go and meet swamiji." "Not yet. He will be in meditation. There's no hurry. Take some food. Even if we go now, we'll have to wait there. I am sending a boy to find out whether swamiji is ready..." Narayana Reddi continued to talk.

He was sixty now. Fifteen years ago Narayana Reddi was brought to Nallacheruvu by a quirk of circumstances. He had no children of his own. He had adopted a girl, his sister's daughter. The girl's father, his brother-in-law died suddenly and there was nobody to manage his sister's affairs and property at Nallacheruvu. Narayana Reddi came to live in Nallacheruvu and two years later his wife died. Having sold his property at his native village, Narayana Reddi became the guardian of his sister's two children and settled at Nallacheruvu. He did not remarry. He was the trustee and trusteeship he looked upon as something God had assigned as a duty to be performed selflessly. Indeed he had turned his thoughts towards God even while he managed the property competently.

"You see, the path shown by Ramakrishna Paramahamsa and Vivekananda is the right path. Kings and kingdoms do not last. As the poet Potana says : "Were they able to take their wealth with them, when the time came for them to go? I strive to the best of my ability. When I happen to meet a spiritual man like this swamiji, I invite him to spend sometime with me. The children have come of age. They won't need my service much longer. I am waiting for the call, and then I may go away, far far away, never to return."

"Where did you meet this swamiji?" I queried.

"I had a marriage to attend at Tirupati. I spent three days on the hills. On the third day, I walked alone towards Papavinasam water-falls. I met him on the way. As it had been my practice to contact sadhus and sannyasins, I went to the swamiji and sat silent facing him. After half-an-hour or so, he smiled and looked at me. "What are you asking my son? You want to know how long it will take? Not long, I may tell you." Truly it was the thought upper-most in my mind at the moment. I wanted to know when I would be able to set aside my worldy burden. He gave me the answer. "Please show me the way for the final release," I said. "You are going on the right path," he replied. I wept like a child. Swamiji asked me to move near him. He took my hand in his and shut my fingers into a fist and left it. There was something solid in my hand. It was a rudraksha. He asked me to wear it round my neck by a thread or a chain. Then I invited him to Nallacheruvu and be my guest. He went into meditation. I waited for about an hour. He agreed, and I brought him along with me.

"I got the cottage used by the watchman, cleaned and suitably equipped as required by the swamiji for his stay. He hasn't told me how long he intends to stay. It's two months now. His needs are very few. He takes food only once a day. That may be rice with curd or only fruit. He washes his own clothes. Between eleven and one during midday, and four and six in the afternoon, he will be available for darshan. He generally remains silent, but may occasionally speak to an individual a word or two directly relevant to that individual. He gave rudrakshas to one or two as he did to me. Sometimes he gives vibhudi too."

"He gives rudrakshas from his own stock?" I asked.

"No stock. He puts his empty hand into the person's, as he did in my own case, then closes the receiver's fingers into a fist and then leaves off. On opening the fist, the rudraksha is found. The rudraksha materializes from nowhere."

"Then he is capable of miracles."

"No other miracle whatsoever till now." If you ask him, there would be no reply.

He is unpredictable that way. Two days ago a married woman came to see him. Her husband had gone to another village to buy bullocks. The swamiji said to her suddenly : "There is nothing for you here. You should feed the person who is waiting at home for your return and not waste your time here." She went home and found her husband famished and eagerly awaiting her. The interesting point about this episode is that the woman has all along neglected the needs of her husband, a person well-known for his tolerant nature. The woman known for her aggressiveness, would always make herself busy with religious rituals and with visits to temples and holy men. The swamiji can easily see through a person and read the character as in a mirror.

We went into the mango-grove. Under the shade of trees in front of the swamiji's cottage, arrangements were made for us to be seated on country mats. There was a little mud platform covered with a rug for the swamiji to sit and receive us. The swamiji came out and sat before us after we had been seated for sometime. He had a black beard and long hair and looked like the poet Rabindranath Tagore as we find him in the popular photos. Dressed in a short-sleeved shirt and dhoti of ochre colour he was recognizable as a sannyasin. He did not wear anything round his neck, and no *kumkum* or *vibhudi* on his forehead. He was about fifty years of age and looked healthy and strong. After he came and sat, he closed his eyes. His legs were stretched down the mud platform as he sat on its verge. The villagers who were there and Narayana Reddi, one after another quietly approached him and bowed low touching his feet. We did not make any gesture. When the swamiji finally opened his eyes, and folded up his legs, we were introduced to him by Narayana Reddi. Then we were invited to sit in his proximity albeit on the ground. We sat in a semi-circle facing the swamiji. He looked at me and then at the doctor and said : "I love to listen to your debate. Please proceed."

I was taken aback and asked : "Debate on what?"

"On violence and non-violence. On limits and opportunities."

"It looks you have overhead our conversation during the journey. Please let us have your opinion."

"Truth is not in opinions. It lies in experience."

The doctor intervened : "If truth does not lie in opinions, then why should people like you go about brain-washing others with your opinions about God and His existence?" He was harsh and critical in his tone.

"Every person is entitled to talk about his experience," the swamiji replied.

"Does it mean that everybody is talking about his experience? Do all these sadhus, sannyasins and preachers of religion speak from their experience of God? Don't they repeat sacred texts parrot-like?"

"I agree that there is difficulty in recognizing the nature of experience for what it is. Experience is one, but opinions vary. That is why I say that truth does not lie in opinions. Whatever one may talk, that doesn't matter."

The doctor said : "I cannot understand the statement that experience is one. When there are personal differences in experience quite obvious to me, how can I accept your view?"

The swamiji turned to Narayana Reddi and pointing to the doctor and to me, said : "The doctor and the lawyer are one, their experience is one, but they will never agree!"

I said : "Kindly clarify how we are one. Please say a little more."

The swamiji took a mango-leaf lying there and tore it across into two. Holding the two pieces in each hand and bringing them together close to their original position, the swamiji said : "Like this. The jagged curves fit into each other. This is unity in diversity, in contradiction."

Doctor : "It means there is symmetry in nature. There is a certain balance, and one thing compensates another. Is that what you mean?"

Swamiji : "That is not what I mean. It is something higher and more complex than mere speculation or deductive thinking. You will not come to understand it through explanation. When the right moment comes, that will come as experience and not as thought."

Bhavanarayana : "Swamiji your perception reaches beyond the limitations of time. Kindly let us know whether we have a happy future."

The swamiji asked Bhavanarayana to come up to him, and taking his hand closed the fingers into a fist and let it go. When Bhavanarayana returned to my side, there was a big size rudraksha in his palm. We examined it and returned it to him. Narayana Reddi advised Bhavanarayana to wear it round the neck afterwards.

I asked the swamiji : "You haven't replied to his query."

Swamiji : "What is it?"

I said : "About the future and the question of happiness?"

Swamiji : "What is meant by happiness."

"Fulfilment of one's desires."

Swamiji : "Desire may get fulfilled, but not in the way you expect it to be fulfilled."

"What is the difference?"

Swamiji : "Say, you want to eat mangoes. You expect Narayana Reddi to send the mangoes. It may turn out to be someone else and not Narayana Reddi who sends them. Your desire of course will be fulfilled, but your expectation would go wrong."

Narayana Reddi : "Swamiji, is there such a thing as series of births?"

Swamiji : "It is and it is not. It depends on how one views it. We are assembled here as separate individuals. Are we really separate? You may say yes, and I may hold the view contrary to it. As I mentioned earlier, experience is one, but opinions are many...."

I said : "That advaitic state of non-dualism, that all experience is one, can I hope to attain to in my life?"

The swamiji looked at me intently. I looked back into his eyes and waited for an answer. A wave of joy swept my heart. I thought that was the answer to my question, an unspoken answer communicated directly. That must be the level of experience transcending the thought and speech of mind. I still waited for his word.

Swamiji : "Not through social progress. It is not in evolution. Not through change of thought and opinion, as you seem to hope. The world and the mind mirror each other. It appears as though they are interacting and struggling against each other. Of the two which is reality and which is shadow, the question itself is meaningless. They are one. Their appearance as two is an illusion. Variety, change, conflict and contradiction are characteristics of this one reality. Therefore, the advaitic state is not of the mind.

but is beyond the mind. If any one longs for it ardently, it will surely take him in."

"When it is attained, does the mind become quiet, does it cease to exist? By its descent, as Shri Aurobindo envisages, doesn't human society get transformed into a heaven? What is the future of mankind?" I asked him.

Swamiji : "I don't know him. I am not a learned person. The very characteristic of mind is movement. How can it be ever perfectly quiet? If one succeeds in concentrating the mind on a point and by force of will holds it there for a while, that cannot result in a change of its character, it will be only one of the innumerable changes and movements it is capable of. And that is not advaitic state. The one who has attained to the advaitic state would not worry over the movements of the mind. He would not be anxious about the changes in society too. He will not think of the future."

Doctor : "Then what is your opinion about social revolution?"

Swamiji : "I have no opinion."

Doctor : "I think you are evasive. When you have expressed so many ideas and opinions, how come you don't have any opinion on revolution and society?"

Swamiji : "Well, as I am a man like you, certainly I have opinions. But I don't have opinions on revolutions and vegetables for soup."

Doctor : "You put revolutions and vegetables in the same category?"

Swamiji : "I certainly do. Some people like the bitter-gourd, and some do not. As a sannyasin I have no preferences. I accept whatever is to be."

The swamiji stood up.

It was one O'clock. We had lunch with Narayana Reddi at his house. He arranged couches and pillows for our afternoon rest. Comfortably relaxing and chewing pan, we were recalling our interview with the swamiji. The touch of bliss bestowed on my heart by the swamiji was still there, and I was mindful of it.

Doctor : "Opinions and ideas don't matter. Experience is one. Rice and lime look alike, but eat rice all the same. Well, it is this philosophy that leads to actual scarcity of rice. Lack of social consciousness and right ideas will have disastrous consequence. Of course, the swamiji has no responsibility to society. He owns to no such thing. For him revolution and bitter-gourd fall in the same category. But can we afford to be indifferent like him?"

Nobody cared to comment on it. I too kept silent. Suddenly recollecting the song, I said : "Didn't you get that song about rice and lime, from Viswam?"

"Yes, the children as well as the adults seem to sing the same song of merry indifference. Which, I say, is sheer selfishness."

"Well, I am for change and progress. But we don't seem to agree philosophically and politically. We could adjust our differences for progressive political action. We could leave the question of experience aside and discuss progress to come to an agreement."

"No, we seem to disagree on the concept of progress. How can we discuss and sort out things? Through mere talk we will never achieve progress. He says that experience is something beyond the mind. Isn't that a new definition? If it is not the mind then what is it that experiences? If that is such an incomprehensible and inaccessible thing, then what is its use for an ordinary man? I couldn't make head or tail of what the man said!"

"If it isn't incomprehensible, how did the rudraksha materialize in my palm?" said Bhavanarayana and added : "He does read our thoughts like a book. Because there is something that transcends the mind, he is able to see things as one from a state above ours. He also indicates by that that it is possible for others too to reach that state. Should this not be the true path of man's progress in the future?"

Doctor : "Look at this concept of progress! All right, let it be conceded that he has attained to certain mental powers unusual and extraordinary, but how can that be considered as going beyond the mind? That is obviously an achievement of the mind!"

Bhavanarayana : "The saying is that unless one plunges into the waters, one cannot ascertain the depth. There is no use of idle criticism. When a path has been indicated, one should go along, and find out for oneself where it leads to finally...."

Doctor : "Well, that is not a path useful to society. I am not able to see through the trick, but it is surely a waste of energy and time to get a rudraksha that way. Can't we get it in a shop? What is this secret and complicated way to obtain an ordinary thing? All this is symptomatic of a decadent culture."

I found our companion the businessman silent all through and so prodded him : "You didn't ask the swamiji anything, now what is your opinion about these matters, we have been discussing?"

He said : "Well, really I don't know. I accompanied you for the pleasure of it. There are great men of all sorts. When I come across them, I offer a reverential bow, and then mind my own business. That is my way. Reddi gave us a nice lunch. I am just thinking of a short nap. That is my habit, if you don't mind."

All of us accepted his suggestion.

After evening tea, we returned to the mango-grove. That was at the instance of Narayana Reddi. He insisted that we should see him before we left the place. There was a larger group now sitting round the swamiji. As soon as he saw us, the swamiji got up and came towards us. He took Bhavanarayana alone into the cottage, and returned after a while to bid us forewell. With folded hands I said : Thank you, Swamiji, it has been great meeting you." He touched my hands. Bhavanarayana prostrated before him. The businessman said : "Namasthe." The doctor waved his hand and said : "Good-bye."

We thanked Narayana Reddi and got into the car. I asked Bhavanarayana seated by my side : "What happened when you were taken inside the cottage?" He said that the swamiji had whispered a mantra into his ear and had advised him to repeat it while he sat in meditation. The doctor in the front seat turned round and asked : "What is that mantra?"

Bhavanarayana : "It's a god's name. I am not supposed to reveal it to others."

"Why should it be kept secret?" asked the doctor.

Bhavanarayana had no answer. I too could not think of a possible answer. There must be some reason for it.

Doctor : "Any way he treated you in a special manner and won your confidence."

Bhavanarayana : "I came to him to ask for something. He said that my wish will be fulfilled, and gave the mantra as a bonus."

The doctor then asked me what was the 'great' thing I had got out of my meeting with the swamiji.

"When I asked him about the advaitic state, he bestowed on me a look straight into my eyes, which sent through my heart, a wave of bliss. I thought that that was his gift to me. He is certainly a special person. His words revealed his spiritual status. Yet he had had no formal education."

Doctor : "Shall I tell you my reaction to the man? If I had my pistol with me, I would have liked to shoot him down on the spot. What are we going to do with these ante-deluvian creatures? They have no place in modern society."

When the doctor spoke those words, and he did it with some vehemence, I felt as though a pistol shot pierced through my heart. The touch of bliss bestowed by the swamiji, its remnant appeared to vanish completely and leave my heart empty. It was like being shaken out of a nice dream because of a sudden fall from the cot on to the ground. Unable to understand this sudden change within me, I kept gazing at the fast moving trees and other objects, almost dumbly questioning them about the sudden void I found in my heart.

On return, I wrote in my diary : "Your desire will be fulfilled but not in the manner of your expectation....Experience is one, opinions vary....The advaitic state is beyond the mind. If you long for it ardently enough it would receive you...."

PART IV

Hema had arrived. She did not call on us even after ten days. Meanwhile Savitri visited her three times. I kept aloof. Though I very much wanted to see her, I didn't go to Bhavanarayana's.

That afternoon I returned from the Court earlier than usual. Hema was in conversation with Savitri. As soon as I entered the sitting-room, she got up to go.

She was in a violet coloured sari!

"Why Hema, what is the hurry? He is not new to you. Please sit down. I'll get some coffee for you," said Savitri.

"No, I've to go. There's an urgent letter to be sent to the post-office. The office-attender will be coming to take it. Or I'll send it through Viswam."

"Just ten minutes. When you were here, you used to spend hours with us. Now you have hardly stepped in, and you want to leave! Please wait till I get you some coffee..." requested Savitri, and turning to me said : "Please talk to her for a while." Then she made her exit.

"Is she the same Hemasundari, the woman who appeared in a violet sari in my dream to tell me that she had been released from a curse! Isn't it strange that she should stand before me in a violet sari now in reality!" I kept thinking as I sat down in a chair. There was silence between us. Abruptly Hema got up and walked away! I wondered whether her behaviour was not in conformity with what she had said in the dream-appearance.

Then Savitri brought in coffee....

When she got up, Hema had gone into the kitchen to tell Savitri that she was going without waiting for the coffee.

"Well, what has happened between you two? She hardly spoke a word to you. Have you quarrelled?" asked Savitri.

"I don't know! When did we quarrel? We hardly saw each other this time. And one year ago, when she was here, there was no quarrel I can remember. She is a busy, working-woman now. There appears some change in her."

"Whatever may be the change in status, one doesn't behave differently with old friends, unless there is sufficient reason for it."

"You should have asked her about it!"

I've been observing ever since I met her this time. She tries to be on her normal behaviour with me. But when I mention you, there is a change in her. Being innocent, she is incapable of hiding anything. She cannot dissimulate. I asked her straight now in the kitchen, whether she had quarrelled with you. Her eyes brimmed with tears, and she remained silent. Finally, she said :

'I'll talk to you tomorrow' and left. I feel bad about it. You must tell me."

I was in a fix. I was thinking about it while I sipped the coffee. I didn't know what to say.

"Savitri, where is Raja?"

"Must be somewhere in the house. First tell me about Hema."

"I have saved a little coffee. Unless I give it to him, I won't feel satisfied."

"All right !...Raja, Raja !!"

The dog came and lapped the coffee.

"Now tell me. Please don't try to evade. And don't weave a nice story either."

"Savitri, you are unfair to me. I hate lying. One of the reasons why I am not successful as a lawyer. One should not insist on the truth being told on all kinds of occasions. One should be satisfied that no falsehood is spoken and leave the matter at that."

"I don't like such reservations between husband and wife. The awareness that something is being held as a secret will lead to speculation and suspicions of all kinds. So better make a clean breast of the whole thing."

"All right, since you insist. My friendship with Hema led us both into a more serious relationship. In time I called a full stop to it."

"Well, well, you behaved like a typical male! I cannot think of you being romantic and all that! Tell the truth. She rejected your advances and humbled you, didn't she?"

"I have told you the truth and nothing but the truth. It is for you to imagine whatever you want."

After the first shock, there appeared in Savitri's face a variety of quick emotions...anger, jealousy, and then an affectionate concern.... I don't know what she saw in my face, as I watched her with detachment, but she suddenly burst into laughter.

"No, I can't believe that any woman can fall in love with you, of all people! You are a granite statue! I don't believe it. I'll get it from Hema herself. Then I'll know what exactly happened between you."

I was offended. I said : "What are you going to ask her? And how? The whole thing is ridiculous. Would she be able to tell you the truth? One should have the sense of leaving it there, for whatever happened is over and done with. It is the past and must be forgotten and buried."

"Why, why should I bury it? You talk of good sense; what happened to it when you enacted the romantic role of a lover? I have every right to question in my own way and find out what happened. It is my personal matter. I'll find out for myself where Hema gets off!"

I left her to herself.

The next night, I brought up the matter myself.

"Did you ask Hema about that?"

"Why? Why are you inquisitive? What is your interest?"

"You might have created a scene."

"No, not a scene. That was a test for her. I should say that she is a very nice girl. She has the courage to tell the truth. And she told me the truth. I just asked her what was the quarrel about between you two. She held my hands in her's and said pleadingly, 'No quarrel. You have to excuse me for overstepping my limits. I never had any intention of taking your place in his affections. Without anticipating any thing, we had become friends and when we realized our mistake, we just withdrew from each other. A mistake, I assure you, that will not be repeated. We should continue to be sisters as before.' I said yes. If she had taken a different line, trying to tell me that you had made advances and she had to teach you a lesson and all that, I would have judged her differently."

I hugged Savitri tightly and gave her a hearty kiss. Because of her faith in me, and love for me, she was able to deal with Hema in the way she had done. I was also pleased with Hema's transparent goodness and honesty. The question is not fulfilment of one's desires and hopes. That is not important. The question is whether one has the strength of character to be honest and truthful. For that alone can bring persons together and constitute true friendship.

"Did you kiss Hema similarly?" said Savitri

"Not so hard."

"Is she so delicate?"

"Let us forget her now."

"Nothing doing. Don't you think you should marry her, as I have no children?"

"I've told you a hundred times, that I don't regret being childless. That is no problem between us. I would request you earnestly not to play the role of an ideal wife of the epics, say Savitri your namesake or Sumati. And please don't even talk like that."

"But a child is absolutely necessary. Otherwise it would be a grave injustice to you and your family tree. I don't like to be responsible and be a hurdle."

Who taught you this ethics? The defect may lie with me. Suppose I remarry and beget no children. What are you going to do? Why should you worry about something that doesn't concern me personally in the least?

"Because it happens to be my personal concern. Very much so. Why didn't you ask the swamiji about it?"

"Well, I didn't think of it. When you are mine and I am yours, why think of a child?"

"Please take me to the swamiji at Nallacheruvu. Let us go. I want to meet him." I said yes pressing her close to my heart.

Before I could plan a second visit to the swamiji, news arrived that Narayana Reddi had passed away on the day of the winter solstice. His sister's son brought the news to Bhavanarayana. He had a heart-attack. The swamiji was by his side. There was no time to call a doctor from Anantapur. The swamiji administered sacred water into his throat as a last rite. Looking into the eyes of the swamiji Narayana Reddi passed into eternal peace. A pious man, a gentle soul. All the villagers had praised him. The cremation was over late in the evening. The next morning the swamiji had gone. Nobody had seen him going. Even the watchman at the mango-grove could not say anything. He must have been there for the last two months only to keep company with Narayana Reddi during his last days. A rare act of significance, so people described it. It was some sort of a spiritual bond between the two reaching forth from a previous birth to this one. That was the common belief among the people.

As I sat listening to Bhavanarayana informing me of these details, I noticed some-one, having gathered the dry leaves of the peepul tree, set fire to them in a heap; and the flames and the smoke looked like Narayana Reddi's burning pyre.

In the Bhagavadgita, the Asvatha tree is described as the Tree of life. But it stands upside down. The roots are in heaven. The branches and leaves are spread into this world. With the sword of *Asangatva* or detachment, one has to cut the branches and reach forth to the roots. The way is up and it is through surrender to Him. A beautiful picture. Narayana Reddi did precisely that. His life was an illustration, a remarkable instance. The family for which he laboured was not his; the children whom he brought up were not his own. He had kept his sword of detachment bright and shining. He had always looked up; and in his last days he did come to him in the form of a swamiji to lead him by the hand!

The winter-sun. The shade in the mango-grove. The silver haired Narayana Reddi with half-closed eyes and a lovable face filled with the bliss of faith in the presence of the swamiji. The memories of yesterday were pleasing and most satisfying to recall. We were nothing to him, but he treated us as his own kith and kin. He talked to us intimately about his life. He asked the swamiji only one question : "Is there a series of lives for a soul?" And then death followed.

Is this a decadent, degenerate culture?" I asked the doctor a few days later when we met and talked about Narayana Reddi.

I won't say it is degenerate, but it is certainly decadent. The system of society based on private property is not going to survive for long hereafter. When private property is abolished, persons like Narayana Reddi will have no importance. Their leadership and so-called virtues will have no value. Competence and competitiveness will be important in the new society. Everybody assumes that the new society will be a worker's society. But that is its outward, external form. Inwardly it will be based on competitiveness. And competition implies violence, violence in a myriad forms.

"You will not find all this in Marxist books. In that society everyone will work. All are workers. The necessities will be provided. But competitiveness and self-aggrandizement will motivate the individual.... How else could one aspire for leadership, power and privilege? Don't tell me they will not be there. They will be very much there. In a feudal society they came through the ownership of land, in a capitalist society they came through money and wealth; and in a workers' society, they will come through competitiveness. And competitiveness, as in an educational institution will not express itself through creative abilities and talent only, demanding recognition. It will express itself through self-aggrandizement and concomitant violence in all possible ways. Please remember that a man with landed property or with wealth can afford to be generous, charitable, loving and non-violent; a man with talent has to compete and cannot afford those virtues. The state cannot abolish competetiveness. It will mean curbing creative talent. It would lead all work and progress to a grinding halt. There can be no society without hierarchy, and a society based on the hierarchy of talent is as much dependent on violence as any other. More so, man in society has to wield violence and suffer violence. There is no way out of it. The history of communist societies in Russia, China and elsewhere illustrates this. The future in India is not going to be different. A cultural revolution is very much on the cards. The old culture is on its way out. Let us realize this."

"I thought you belonged to the Communist Marxist party, and were sympathetic to the Naxalites.... But you don't seem to agree with either group."

"I have gone deeper into the question. I go beyond today's politics. But I have been acquainted with the two groups."

"Why not socialism through democracy?"

"Well, democracy has become an instrument of the capitalists. Today in this country what matters is not vote-power but money-power. Votes can be purchased and manipulated. Money of the black-marketeers and the smugglers is getting a strangle-hold on the politicians. If by some chance a true progressive comes to power and strikes out against the money-bags, there will be cries of repression, violence and dictatorial methods. Violence in fact is going to be the very basis of a future society. No progressive would avow it now openly. The instrument of violence, whether it is going to be wielded by those in power, by the government, or by those in opposition, the Naxalites, is a historic necessity. Who will succeed in using it effectively, we have to wait and see. There can be no such thing as pure non-violence or undiluted democracy. It is a dream. The political manifestation of capitalism is democracy. The political manifestation of communism is totalitarianism. One party dictatorship. The basis and nature of that party is violence. If you delve deep into the matter you will find that violence and non-violence are present in any system of society. But the manifestations differ. In the bourgeois society, violence wears nice masks. Its existence is ignored, or given fine names. In the coming society it must be recognized and regulated. That will be the essence of the new culture. The culture that idealized non-violence and non-attachment and looked up to God and Heaven is a decadent culture. It is on its way out...."

"If violence as you have described is to be the basis of society, then how can one feel happy? Will there be joy in living?"

"Not happiness or joy but intensity of experience. Certainly the state of mind will be different. Wielding violence and suffering violence are not alien to human nature. Anything in its extremities becomes intolerable. It is so with violence too. The happiness and joy you speak of are associated with the aloneness of the individual and the state of detachment from life. It is symptomatic of the attitude that one can live without being related to others, that one can live outside society or as a non-social being. In a world where society is stronger than ever before and population is increasing by leaps and bounds, the density and pressure of social life produces tension which is the experience of violence. It has to be recognized and channelized. The attunement of mind to it will result in the new culture of the new society. If you have objections to the use of the word violence, because of its past associations, we could call it, say 'pressure' or 'tension'. We have expressions like 'the play of the cat' when it teases the mouse it has caught as prey. Isn't that play by the cat an expression of violence? We already employ a number of words which conceal violence. It depends on how we view things."

Dr. Veerabhadra Rao's line of thought, and his analysis came as a surprise to me. Without being casual or excited by argument, he was trying to give me an exposition of his philosophy. He seemed to put into his words the very essence of his personality. He spoke with conviction. He was not a person to be reckoned lightly. Just as Gandhiji had fashioned a science and a weapon out of non-violence, the doctor was making violence the centre of life and man's future.

That was a Sunday and we had gone to see a movie. Like a majority of Telugu movies, this one was also full of sex and violence. Long fights and leisurely rape scenes formed the staple content, rounded off with bloodshed and vengeance. I wondered whether the words spoken by the doctor about the coming society were not being enacted before my eyes. Were the makers of these movies acting like the precursors of the new culture envisaged by the doctor? But could they understand the doctor's philosophy?

"Perhaps the future society will be like this?" I said.

"This is a mindless distortion of violence. Things like rape and revenge associated with sadism and violence really belong to the old culture. As in a magnifying glass they are portrayed here, indicating the decadence of the old culture. Chase and pursuit in sex, hostility and vengeance are natural to life, but not in this crude manifestation as shown here."

I became curious to know about Dr. Veerabhadra Rao's past. "Are you associated with the Naxalite movement at present?" I asked him.

"If I am, would I tell you?"

"Perhaps you are a former member! If you really were, my surprise is how you could get out of their grip! Your intellect might have come to your aid. Being capable of independent thinking, and being wary even during your membership, you must have avoided or escaped their stranglehold from the beginning."

"I wanted to continue as a member and activist. But the completion of my professional education got the priority; and then I thought I should personally study life and society before getting back. You're right; I am very much an independent thinker. There is a good deal of self-training that is necessary. Without that one cannot develop and cultivate new values necessary in the new society. That doesn't come about by studying Cheguvera or some foreign revolutionary. Revolution is a creative act. That cannot come through imitation."

"But by the time your self-training it completed, the political situation may change and opportunities for the kind of action you get ready may be lost for ever...."

"Revolution cannot be a matter of a few opportunities only. Getting ready for it involves the perception of what a real opportunity is and what is not. Without gaining such a perception, it is futile to plunge into action."

"How and why did you get into a government job?"

"I was posted in one of the Telengana rural vacancies. A temporary appointment. I spent three years there. It was then easy to get a posting like that. It is not so now. Then I was transferred here."

"What about your parents?"

"My father was an officer in the army. He died when I was twelve years of age. My uncle financed my education. My mother is here with me. Haven't you seen her? I am the only son. I have no sisters."

"That's why you have been able to shape your life freely according to your will and pleasure. Though we differ in our ideas, as a person I respect you...."

"Thanks."

On my return from the theatre that evening Savitri informed me that Hema had left for Kurnool.

"Is that some news worthy of special mention?" I said.

"Mr. Bhavanarayana was here in the evening."

"What does he say?"

"He is in search of a bridegroom for Hema."

I did not react to it.

"Why are you silent? Shall I propose you for her? If not now, it may be too late afterwards."

"Please put a stop to your joking."

"He told me that there are two proposals under consideration. One is a college lecturer and the other is the doctor, our next door neighbour."

"Dr. Veerabhadra Rao? I wonder whether he will marry her!"

"Why do you say that?"

"He is a peculiar man.... You have seen him with the pistol."

"What does it matter? He is self-assertive and dignified. Today I saw you talking with him for a long while, and then you went out together. What is he saying?"

"Violence. He will use violence."

"Against whom? Against his patients or his wife?"

"Everybody. With whomever he is related in society."

"Don't be so enigmatic. Please explain."

"You cannot understand, even if I trouble myself to explain all that! I am sleepy."

In fact I lost my sleep. My thoughts were roused about Hema marrying Dr. Veerabhadra Rao. It was really food for thought. I told myself finally that cultivating non-attachment was not an easy thing!

PART V

Savitri had a troublesome cough during nights. It was a hindrance to our sleep in the nights. In daytime it did not very much show itself up. I took her to the government hospital. A blood-test was taken. Dr. Veerabhadra Rao said he would get me the result in the evening and would give a prescription at his residence.

A course of arsenic injections was advised by him for 'esnophilia' and I went along with Savitri for her first injection. The doctor treated some patients at his residence in the evenings. He had a moderate private practice. There was a ten-minute wait before we could be called in.

The doctor got the syringe ready and Savitri went behind the screen with the doctor. After a while she returned and the doctor said : "Better she sits down for few minutes, to watch whether there will be some reaction." But Savitri said : "let us go home. It's only next door. We can come back if necessary."

The doctor agreed. "You may go now. I'll look in later and find out."

On returning home I asked Savitri : "Why were you in a hurry? After all, the doctor is a friend and we could spend some time talking to him there itself."

"I don't know. I think I was a little frightened."

"Frightened? What for?"

"When he held me by hand firmly, I felt a mild shock; and then he pierced me with the needle with some cruelty so to say.

Perhaps the needle was not sharp enough, or the look in his eyes might have made the difference. I didn't want to stay there a moment longer than necessary."

"All that is your fancy. It's a long time since you had an injection, and you must have forgotten how it feels to be pricked by a needle."

Savitri became thoughtful and then smiled : "You said he swears by violence. I think he takes pleasure in it."

Meanwhile the doctor called and I came on the verandah.

"How is she?" the doctor inquired.

"She said the injection was painful. But there is no other reaction noticeable."

"Let her have fomentation in the night. She must have another injection two days later, and a full course of five at similar intervals. Then we could go in for a blood-test again."

The doctor sat down. I remembered that Savitri had informed me that he was a prospective bridegroom for Hema. As I had not met Bhavanarayana, I had not verified or discussed the matter with him. I became inquisitive to explore the doctor's personality afresh in the light of the information. As we talked about certain diseases for a while, Savitri brought coffee for the doctor.

"How are you?" he said.

"I'm all right," she said and looked at me.

"He advises you to have fomentation in the night," I said.

Savitri went inside.

"You haven't thought of marrying yet?" I said to him.

"For want of a suitable match."

"Then you aren't against marriage? What are your views on marriage from your revolutionary point of view?"

"Marriage should not become a hangman's rope round one's neck. Both man and woman should have personal freedom. I mean it should be a natural relationship between two persons, and not a convention or a bondage."

"That much is now conceded by everyone."

"Who concedes it? You see, a partner who is physically satisfying, that is in sex, may not be suitable temperamentally, as an intellectual companion. An intellectually accomplished person may not be sexually attractive. A person who is attractive both ways is something of a rarity. And a rare person like that may not click both ways with the partner, and the relationship may be based only on one of the two aspects. This is the situation commonly found in marriages. Therefore sometime or other there is scope for the entrance of a third person in that marriage. The unsatisfied, unrelated aspect of a person may be drawn to another person other than the marriage partner. Is such extra-marital relationship sympathetically understood or conceded now?"

As the doctor talked about this, I was immediately reminded of my affair with Hema. Savitri is a sexually satisfying partner to me. But intellectually I was drawn to Hema.

I said : "Intellectual attraction is understandable, but it does not stop there. That would lead in most cases to sexual relationship too. And that is the snag."

"Naturally! It is very difficult to differentiate and identify between the two. Though one may know it subjectively, the onlookers, the society cannot make the distinction. It is therein a wife or a husband should better understand and sympathise with the other's behaviour. If possible a place should be found for the third person within the marriage frame-work...."

"What happens to the idealism of marriage? The sanctity of the bond will be lost. It could pave the way to confusion and erratic behaviour finally destroying the marriage institution itself."

No. It wouldn't destroy the institution, it would change the shape and form of the institution, giving it a new dynamism.

The limits of conduct and behaviour within marriage will depend on the individual and not on a preset condition. There's not very much new in what I am proposing. Traditionally a man has been marrying two or more wives. Both the Hindus and the Muslims accepted the practice. Even among them it has not been a universal practice, though permitted by custom. But this privilege was never granted to woman. The institution of Devadasis had for its basis the same psychology I mentioned in the relationship between man and woman. But in the old order woman was a possession and looked upon as a slave. She did not have equal rights. The Hindu Code Bill took into account the Christian tradition and thought it to be modern. For the new society, provision for divorce will not be enough. It will be a negative approach. A marriage with three or four partners is conceivable and feasible.

"What about romantic love? And the ideal of one man for one woman made for each other? Unless love and marriage are concentrated in a couple, they will be bereft of meaning and sanctity."

"The nature of love is freedom, and love cannot be restricted and channelled to a single person of the opposite sex to the end of one's life. Making romantic love found in poetry and fable, the very basis of the marriage institution is nothing but stupid confusion on the part of the bourgeoisie. Romantic love is essentially love and worship in the absence of the desired person, a deep longing for the inaccessible beloved. It is a psychological aberration, made much of in poetry. In the meeting of a man and woman, the mutual confrontation with looks and gesture and language decides instantly whether they are sexually acceptable to each other or not. It is a true meeting of two persons; and the meeting implies what I call violence or intensity. It may unfold or develop into an erotic hide-and-seek, or chase one by the other. Now what you call shyness or modesty in a girl, when she exhibits a certain reluctance to look straight or talk straight to a man she is attracted to, all that goes by the name of feminine grace and virtue in our society. The side-glances and secret desires and fancies are approved of. And we give it the name of love between the youngsters. Worse than this is the way youngsters worship and eroticise over the photographs of film-stars in privacy.... Romantic love is an accepted perversion in our civilization. It is unfortunate that it is so. After marriage, where is the chance to worship the wife? All the glamour and fancy will be gone when they start living together. Every person's experience shows that romantic love is a mirage, and a new day-to-day relationship, person to person becomes established after the marriage.... But nobody talks about it. Sex-attraction starts and gets decided in the encounter between man and woman as persons. Sexual love is dynamic, and its course cannot be pre-determined.... Single partnership cannot be a focal point or a static centre for it. That is what I mean by freedom in marriage...."

"Is this view acceptable to all the revolutionaries?"

"They give priority to politics, and political and economic issues. They don't like to spell out their views on marriage to avoid controversy among themselves. Among the naxalite leaders there are a few who have married two or three women. The conventional Marxists have found fault with them. They subscribe to the existing monogamy ideal, I may say, in spite of Marx's own sexual life! And the general membership of the naxalites too considers such cases as exceptions due to circumstantial pressures; they do not see the psychological truth behind the formation of such relationships when bestowing thought on the future of marriage...."

"I take it that you will select your marriage partner in a face to face confrontation."

"Well, that will be so sexually. But then sex is not all. Marriage being a partnership and a coexistence, the aspects of personality will also come under consideration.... Intelligence and education are basic. The quality of being intellectual or creative is different and cannot be included among basic requirements."

"Haven't you found a suitable partner in sex so far?"

"I might or might not have. That is strictly personal, but all such encounters cannot lead up to marriage. But one thing is true. I don't like cowardice or timidity in sex. I am not attracted by a sweet or a moony face."

I laughed. The doctor appeared to me in a new light.

That night when Savitri was using the hot-water bottle for fomentation, I offered to help her. Even when she said "It's getting too hot, please move," I didn't comply just for the fun of it. She snatched the bottle from me saying : "Many thanks. Now you please mind your business."

"How is my violence?" I said.

"I see. The doctor's influence has started working on you!"

"Do you know what the doctor said about marriage?"

"What? Has he accepted Hema?"

"He would marry not only Hema but also you and me all together."

"Please stop being enigmatic and let me have facts."

"I'll explain what the doctor means. For being childless in marriage, you asked me to marry Hema. That would make it three in a marriage. Then the doctor joins, that would be four in one."

"How can the doctor join?"

"Well, I marry Hema. For acheiving equality of status, you will marry the doctor. Even then if we remain childless, neither you nor I bringing forth a child, then Hema and the doctor will marry, making it a foursome, and I am sure that will certainly yield a child."

"How disgusting! Please stop joking and tell me the facts."

"All this is not joking, darling! If such freedom is not provided for, then marriage is not a suitable or meaningful institution, according to him."

"How could you permit such a frivolous talk, involving women? He should have proper respect for women. Why did you sit listening quietly to all that drivel?"

"He never mentioned Hema or any proposal. All this was general and theoretical. I don't think Bhavanarayana has yet approached him. He said he would get married if a suitable match came up. Then we were discussing the future shape of society, and the question of feminism and equality between the sexes. All these ideas came up regarding the future shape of marriage."

"Equality and all that nonsense will not carry matters to that absurd and ridiculous extent. Neither woman nor man would stand for such developments. It's against human nature."

Savitri was categorical in her assertion and she left with the hot-water bottle calling a stop to further discussion.

I was left to my own counsel. What is human nature? Has anybody defined it? What are its parameters? The human society has evolved, and circumstantial changes have been many, and have varied from country to country. Through behavioural patterns over a length of time, custom, practice and institution among people have taken strong hold, giving the impression that human nature is thus defined and settled. But human nature is not predetermined.

Two days later, in the evening by the time I returned from my work, Savitri had kept my coffee ready and was dressed up to go out. She was wearing her favourite Venkatagiri gold-bordered sari. I asked her : "What is special?"

"I've to take the second injection today."

"It's only next door."

"Distance doesn't matter. The doctor appears to be a snob. You see, I've to maintain my dignity. After all, we have some status. I don't like going there without being properly dressed."

"You didn't seem to be aware of all these things on the first occasion?"

"I thought that it was just like visiting Bhavanarayana's. There's a lot of difference. I spoke to the doctor's mother yesterday. They are snobs."

We both went to the doctor. After the injection was given, I inquired of Savitri how she felt.

She said : "No pain. I'll just go in and have a word with the doctor's mother. Are you going home, or would sit here for a while?"

The doctor was very busy with his patients. I went home. A little later Bhavanarayana called on me.

I said : "Were you aware of official camp or what? I didn't see you for quite a while."

"Yeah. I had been to Sarpavaram, my native village."

"Your parents are dead. Who are the relatives worthy of a visit?"

"Only cousins. I have three acres of cultivable land. I've put it up for sale. You see I've to perform Hema's marriage. That's my responsibility as a brother. I gave word to my mother."

"If you sell away all the immovable property in this manner, what will you do for Gopi and Radha? You saw Hema through college. She got a professional qualification and is now employed. When she is self-reliant, where's the hurry to marry her off?"

"You talk of hurry. It's a matter of age, and in our society girls cannot be expected to choose their partners and settle in marriage by themselves. A lot of money is involved, and without my financing it, the marriage cannot take place. And then about individual choice, I may tell you Hema is still a child. It will be for her good that I take the matter into my hands. About the future of my children, I'm not worried. I trust in God. My wife has some landed property."

"It seems you mentioned one or two probable matches to Savitri, before you left for your native village."

"Yeah. There's a college lecturer. He wants a dowry of fifteen thousand rupees. He is a little younger than the doctor, your neighbour. I've thought of the doctor too. Maybe the dowry will be more than fifteen. The doctor's age is nearer thirty.... I don't think I can go beyond the fifteen thousand I've mentioned."

"Who said the doctor would demand a dowry? Did you ask him?"

"I guessed it, after an informal talk with his mother."

My wife's impression too was the same. There's been no direct approach. When I'm not financially upto it, I thought I shouldn't risk a no from him, especially as he happens to be a friend. Of course I thought of you to sound the doctor and know his mind. In any case I thought I should get the money ready first. Now, would you mind ascertaining the doctor's idea about dowry?

"You introduced him to me as a progressive, didn't you? If he is particular about dowry, then how do call him a progressive? Where's the revolution he speaks of? Why do you doubt his integrity?"

"Well, that's what we observe of your young men. They talk ideals. But when it comes to brass tacks, he may hide behind his mother, and leave everything to her."

"I don't think he is like that. You needn't worry that he will demand dowry. The question is not one of dowry. As a person he is different and you have to be wary about that. First he should meet Hema and decide. Then what he will make of that marriage, we cannot be certain, in the conventional manner of speaking. His ideas and attitudes are not easy to grasp or guess."

"That will not matter. She is also an educated girl and modern enough. If you could find out whether he is particular about dowry, and how much he expects, I'm willing to go ahead. In fact I came to make this request to you to act on our behalf."

I said I would play my part, but cautioned Bhavanarayana to think over the ideas about marriage which the doctor had already expressed to me.

"All that is nothing but youthfulness. In my student days, we used to read Chalam and very much fancy free-love and the reform of marriage.... "

"But the despair that our generation failed to achieve those ends seems to turn the new generation into desperate experimenters and revolutionaries. The indications are quite a few."

"Well, he is already nearing thirty. What is it that he has achieved? Marriage will set him right. Till then these romantic ideas will continue to plague him."

I could see the ground truth and common sense in what Bhavanarayana said. I looked at myself. Perhaps because I had no responsibility of bringing up children, and was placed financially in a comfortable position, I too remained a dreamer, and an inveterate intellectual. Bhavanarayana with his burden of supporting a family and carrying on official duties, has lost the sheen of youthful idealism! Further he had developed a lot of enthusiasm for our culture, and faith in our ancient texts and the theory of 'karma'. A parallel development in me, if it could be called that, was my interest in the *Bhagavadgita* and the advaita philosophy. I believed in advaita not so much as a philosophy but as an experience I should attain to. I saw no contradiction between the teaching of the *Gita* and modern ideas. I was trying to build a bridge between the two within myself. It was a personal quest. I had given up faith in ritual worship.

It was for that reason I could not accompany Savitri to Vidura Asvatham, when finally the trip materialized. Bhavanarayana kept his word given long ago to Savitri and organized the trip. His wife and children, Savitri and the doctor's mother formed the party. An office subordinate of Bhavanarayana's was put in charge of all arrangements. There was also a motive involved : when I failed immediately to make a direct approach to the doctor about the marriage proposal, Bhavanarayana put it to his wife and Savitri to sound the doctor's mother during the trip in the course of general conversation. Indeed it was an excellent strategy. Any compromise of family dignity and the risk of a negative reaction were avoided.

But on the very day the ladies went to Vidura Asvatham, I got the chance to discuss in a general way the issue of dowry with the doctor.

"The custom of giving or taking dowry is repellent to my mind. But the bride should not be deprived of her legitimate share in the family property or wealth. Whatever she is entitled to, she must receive, and it should remain her personal possession...."

"Bhavanarayana wants to make a proposal. You know he has a sister employed as a teacher. He wants to offer her in marriage to you."

"I've seen her, but not met her. Bhavanarayana knows me well. Why should he put the proposal through you?"

"Well, he thought it to be a delicate matter between friends. He asked me to find out your inclination in the matter."

"Even now I have to meet her and then decide. There's the risk of my saying no. About views in general, I have never been in agreement with Bhavanarayana on several things. In particular his behaviour before the swamiji at Nallacheruvu. I disliked it. It was neither devotion nor reverence, absolute slavery, and blind faith.... Chi...."

The doctor surprised me. He disliked Bhavanarayana, and yet had no objection to meet his sister and marry her! How would this alliance between two families turn out finally? Meanwhile, the doctor himself added : "But that doesn't matter. I am going to marry his sister and not Bhavanarayana."

"But things have to go through him."

"Let them. I won't pick up a quarrel with him. I don't see any reason for it. As long as he deals straight with me, I'll have no objection to deal with him."

"Bhavanarayana has a pleasant demeanour, a good heart, and he keeps his word."

"Is that his weakness?"

"Why do you say that?"

"A good heart and a pleasant demeanour mean nothing. What is required is honesty and integrity of character. He should have the courage to meet a person as a person, without these masks...."

"Well, he has that honesty and that integrity. I don't think there was any impropriety or evasion in requesting me to put the marriage proposal to you, as I am a trusted friend of the family. All the three of us are good friends. The matter is under discussion among us only. If you want to count me out, I'll gladly step aside."

The doctor looked into my eyes for a moment and said : "Yes, that'll be the right thing to do. You step out." The doctor's saying it, shocked me. I couldn't understand the man. I got up and said good-bye.

On return from the excursion to Vidura Asvatham, Savitri informed me that the doctor's mother was in favour of the match. "However the final decision rests with him. My opinion is of no importance," she was reported to have said. About the dowry also she left the matter to her son's discretion entirely. But she hinted that there was still an outstanding debt of twelve thousand rupees incurred for the purpose of his education, and the property was under mortgage. "I wish to make all things plain and clear. My son wants it to be so."

"Whatever it may be, the doctor told me plainly that our mediation in the matter will be unwarranted....," I said.

"He is quite a tough guy," said Savitri and added : "In any case his virtue shows in not demanding a dowry."

What could I say to that assessment of the man? Both Bhavanarayana and Savitri amazed me with their judgment of men and matters, especially in dealing with the doctor, and I started wondering whether I was not impractical and useless in worldly affairs! They paid the least attention to the doctor's outlook on life and the orientation of his personality. Such things hardly made an impression on them. Their greatest satisfaction was that the question of dowry did not come up. I was primarily worried about the personality and character. I thought he was a naxalite; I thought of him as a neo-Marxist; then I saw him as an advocate of free-love. He might be all these and yet not really any one of them! He was an intriguing personality to me. For the others this was no problem at all. They were only bent upon getting Hema married to him. He would be the most desirable person to them till their purpose was achieved. But what would he turn out to be after the event?

The next day Savitri was ready for the third injection, and had been waiting for my return from work.

I said I was not going with her. She could go alone.

"You seem to have taken offence at his words?"

"Till the affair gets settled between the doctor and Bhavanarayana, I think it is prudent I don't talk to the doctor. Why should I spoil it inadvertently?"

"I hope there is no objection to my talking to the mother?"

"Better use your discretion and decide for yourself."

As Savitri sallied forth towards my neighbour's, I stood watching her from the verandah. I saw a new confidence in her. After our relationship started with the doctor, I found Savitri never pensive. I caught glimpses of a new enthusiasm in her.

PART VI

In the third week of February, the marriage talk finally assumed a concrete shape. Hema arrived of a four-day visit. Bhavanarayana arranged for a meeting between her and the doctor. I was never told of the details of what transpired at the meeting or encounter, as the doctor would call it, but I was informed that the two had agreed to become husband and wife. I maintained, throughout, my non-attachment towards what was going on. I never visited or met the doctor. And I never kept company with Bhavanarayana even when he invited me to accompany him in the marriage-talks. Through some excuse or other I managed to keep aloof.

I asked Savitri whether the doctor had told Hema all his revolutionary ideas about the institution of marriage, and whether she had approved of them. "How can a girl discuss such things with her prospective groom? Was it an academic discussion or what? You seem to have no comprehension of these matters. He might have said a few things, and she would have meekly listened to him. All that is a sort of formality. Do you mean to say that every word spoken on the occasion would be remembered and literally observed? The crux of the matter is one looks at the other to ascertain whether they like each other or not. After that, things take their own course. Each adjusts with the other. Nobody theorizes in advance. Life is not acting out our ideas. It is your special privilege to talk and theorize. Others may talk but they don't confuse it with life and living."

"What do you mean by that? Where am I found wanting? I live my life according to my lights. "

"I you want to know I'll tell you. We should have got our municipal water-connection six months ago; why has it been delayed? Everyone pays off the concerned engineer what he is accustomed to receive, but you won't. Your principles have stood in the way. Fortunately we have a well in the backyard, and I'm managing. If it had been otherwise, what would you have done?"

"He said I would have to wait for my turn. Waiting for one's turn is social morality. There's no philosophy involved in it.... We have to observe certain norms in society...."

"In dire necessity people behave differently. Quite a few got the water-connection even out of turn by paying off the engineer. As we are in a position to wait, we can talk of principles. No doubt they are important, if things go well. It's not only Hema's marriage, but also every blessed thing in society, it must be first accomplished, then theories and principles will follow the event."

I had no reply. Her pragmatism, I don't know whether it could be rightly called that, simply amazed me. There could be no arguing with that.

A few days later I had to go to Hyderabad. At the railway-station the doctor and his mother were waiting for the Guntur train. She told me she was going to her native village to look to certain property matters and also invite all her relatives for the wedding function and celebrations. After a long interval I had the opportunity of speaking to the doctor. And it was the first time ever I had talked to his mother.... Her happiness that her son was getting settled was very much in evidence in the way she talked.

That meeting was significant because that happened to be the last occasion of my meeting with her, as later events turned out. When I returned from Hyderabad five days later, things not only took a drastic turn but influenced my life too. And that is the story I have to tell.

On return, I found Savitri a very sick person, scared and looking haggard. I was shocked by the change in her. She told me what had happened during my absence.

Two days after my departure, she had her afternoon nap as usual in our bedroom, and after that carefully closed the windows and doors, and went to visit Bhavanarayana's family. She returned home along with Radha, Gopi and Viswam, at six in the evening. She opened the bedroom to take out a book required by Viswam. When she switched on the light, she found a cobra lying on her bed. Scared to death, she immediately closed the bedroom door and ran out in fright not knowing what to do. Viswam ran to the doctor next door and informed him. The doctor arrived with his pistol, opened the door carefully and shot the serpent dead!

The discovery that it was a vicious cobra, and the thought that it should have entered the bedroom in the afternoon itself, when Savitri had been taking her nap, almost maddened Savitri with fear of what might have happened, and the fact that she had been very close to death upset her completely. There were a few flower-creepers and certain trees near the window and the adjacent yard. The serpent must have entered through the window; and done so while Savitri was still asleep on the bed. After she was up, she moved about in the room and closed the window, and any of these movements could have provoked the serpent to attack her. It was a miracle that it did not, and Savitri escaped death.

But Savitri refused to rejoice on her escape. She regretted that the snake was killed. The doctor didn't consult her whether he should kill it or do something else. Hardly was there any time for it. And her state of mind, one could easily imagine it, was such that she was almost incapacitated with scare. Things happened quickly. Savitri would refuse to accept the inevitability of it, ponder over it again and again, and she foresaw evil consequences to flow from the killing of the cobra in her bedroom. It signified for her childlessness not only in this life, but in the future incarnations too. That led to deep mental depression. I tried to tell her that since the killer was the doctor, the result of the karma should go to him and she was not accountable in any way. She argued that as a saviour of her life, the doctor had earned merit, but the cobra having been killed on her bed, would wreak vengeance in future lives and would not forgive her. There could be no conclusions and no meeting ground on such highly emotive and superstitious issues. The question was one of restoring mental peace to her.

Bhavanarayana and his wife, being tradition bound, thought on the same lines as Savitri did, and added to her illness. They were emphatic that the event had been very inauspicious, and insisted that some kind of propitiatory rites should be performed to counter the possible evil effects. They prescribed to us pilgrimage to certain holy places, as one of the ways. I was in a fix and did not know what to do. Pilgrimage or not, Savitri was ruining her health, as she even neglected proper intake of food. The doctor had given her sedatives. He had visited her frequently before my arrival and had spoken sensibly to remove her fears and to strengthen her mentally. I felt grateful to him.

I asked Savitri about the doctor's views. He had exhorted her to treat the death of the serpent as the death of an ingrained superstition in her, and accordingly her mind liberated. This being a good development in her life, she should look upon the event as the starting point for many good things to come and not otherwise. For the present she might be uneasy and confused, but she would soon gain in confidence and courage, and a new enthusiasm in life would appear. The cobra was nothing but a poisonous reptile, and it should not be given more significance than what natural science gave it. It appeared that the doctor had taken charge of the carcass of the serpent and handed it over to someone to skin it, and he would make a nice wallet with the skin, so that it may remain a souvenir of the event!

I was glad that the doctor could make some impression on her to allay her fears. But she confided in me that she sometimes got the feeling, looking into the eyes of the doctor, that the doctor himself represented the spirit and soul of the cobra. And when she thought of it, a thrill and a shiver went through her, down the spine. He had held her hands in his own tightly and had instilled courage into her. He had given her an injection too.

I had to face the situation in the best way I could. I asked her to take an objective view of things : "We are not in control of happenings, and we should be glad that no harm has befallen and all the worry was over a traditional, a cultural belief, and it should not confound us. Suppose it had happened to a foreigner, would he worry about it? What might or might not happen tomorrow, could not be grasped by man's mind. Except our belief about the normal course of events day after day, there is neither certainty nor assurance from any source that one's life life would run such and such a course. Trying to look into the future, craving for security and certainty, we become easy prey to fanciful thought. That way thought corrupts our joy in life. Life must be looked upon as an adventure, and every day should come as fresh and new."

Explanations and exhortations cannot change in a day a person's mental orientation and cultural background. Savitri was not rid of her apprehensions. I discussed the matter with the doctor. He offered to help her with his psychoanalytical therapy. He had studied it with special interest, though he had not taken a diploma in it. He met her half-a-dozen times in the course of two weeks and listened to her free-association talk sympathetically and leisurely. I was thankful to him for the help, as Savitri showed signs of cheerfulness and normalcy, may be as a result of her interaction with a friendly person. How much scientific method there was in it, I could not say, but an intelligent listener is a good therapist in such cases. During those six occasions, the doctor had either lunch or dinner with us. In any case his mother was away and it suited him.

The doctor was now in the position of a close friend of our family. Though Savitri treated him as a brother, he never called her 'sister' and preferred to address her by her name.

I cannot pin-point the precise occasion or time when I started feeling uneasy about the relationship between the doctor and Savitri, but I did not relish the manifest affection and partiality she started evincing towards him after sometime. It became a sort of concern whenever I was alone with myself, and my principle of non-attachment could not help, though I frequently invoked it, to overcome what I would name as my 'jealousy.'

Savitri once said to him in my presence : "Imagine all the fuss and confusion this gentleman would have created, if he had found the serpent in that position. Even then finally you should have been called for our rescue. He can talk philosophy endlessly, but in moment of crisis, I know, he cannot act decisively one way or other."

Savitri would press him to eat more, saying : "You aren't getting any fee from us in the form of money. How can I pay you for saving my life, but by pressing on you to eat more?"

"No. You are mistaken! I did not save your life, but took away the life of the serpent, and I very much enjoyed doing it! I didn't miss my aim, you know. Therefore there is no indebtedness on your part." That was the doctor's rejoinder.

"Brave people, men of action talk like that!!" Savitri's face lit up with appreciation and joy.

"Without courage and bravery, there is no meaning in life, Savitriji. You should first be rid of superstitions and customary inhibitions, and set your mind free. That will show itself as courage and bravery in action," said the doctor indicating that to be his achievement.

In Savitri's estimation and esteem, the doctor assumed the dimensions of a hero and a knight of the medieval times. No doubt the traditional background and hold of superstitions weakened, and she became mentally healthier and confident. But the result of the doctor being deified in her imagination was not to my liking.

I grew anxious to get rid of the doctor. But I didn't know how to do it.

Though it was already six weeks, the doctor's mother had not returned from her visit. Then a letter arrived. She would be back in a week, after concluding the affairs there. I heaved a sigh of relief. That might minimize the doctor's visits to my house!

Then it was a telegram, saying that the doctor's mother had died of a sudden heart-attack!

The doctor's stoicism and restraint of grief took me by surprise. He hardly spoke a word, and silently with a brief indication to us, he left in a friend's car for his native village.

Bhavanarayana was in a fix. He didn't know whether it would be proper for him to accompany the doctor or not to his native village. If he had been only a friend, he would have certainly kept company. Now that the marriage had been settled, the sudden death of the prospective groom's mother would be customarily attributed as an inauspicious result following the announcement of the son's engagement to a particular girl, the girl being Hema. And for the girl's brother to appear in the village with the groom, would certainly be an embarrassment to both the sides. Bhavanarayana was apprehensive of the comments and remarks the doctor's relations might indulge in, and the insults they might hurl at him. On the other hand he was anxious that the doctor's mind might change and some close relative might advise him to drop the girl, who had brought misfortune at the very first instance. Finally Bhavanarayana left the future in the hands of the God he trusted, and decided to await the doctor's return.

The doctor's absence no doubt provided me relief from my concern about Savitri's undue attention on him. A lurking thought was there that my intense wish for the exit of the doctor might have been in some way responsible for the doctor's misfortune! I felt ashamed of myself. Was it egotism about my mental powers, or was it devilry gloating at another's misfortune? In what way could I be responsible? I was amazed at my irrationality! Rational thinking, as I knew it, appeared quite helpless against the vagaries of the mind. Indeed I had a long way to go in objective thinking and in attaining non-attachment!

Tradition and superstition have a certain established logic and theories of cause and effect, which are not easy to counter.... Apprehensive of what the doctor's relations might say about the death of the doctor's mother, Bhavanarayana and his wife started saying that the doctor's sudden misfortune was all because of his sin in killing the cobra. His arrogance, recklessness and disregard of cultural beliefs had led him astray and he had abandoned all compunction in murdering the cobra, an object of reverence and worship in our culture. The counter propaganda they started in this vein shocked me, and I felt disgusted!

Their motivation was clear to me. They wanted to defend Hema even before a real necessity arose for it. Before the doctor's relations or somebody else could brand Hema with inauspiciousness, they carried out an offensive against the doctor without waiting to know the doctor's attitude to the matter. It was nothing but their refusal to understand the doctor as an individual with a mind of his own.

I could not agree with Bhavanarayana. I told him so and requested him not to give further currency to his view. Though I felt jealous and uneasy about the doctor, I could not turn round to accuse him as a sinner, when he had rendered the greatest good service in a moment of peril. He had certainly saved Savitri at the critical moment. He had saved her from future fears about the return of the serpent, by putting an end to it, and not merely driving it away. That would have put Savitri and me in a situation of living death!

I could perceive that Bhavanarayana and his wife had given up hope about the wedding coming off, and it was that disappointment and despair that had turned them to this line of propaganda. A good match, with no specific stipulation about dowry had slipped from their hands. That thought made them reckless.

But I didn't believe that the match was off. From what I had known of the doctor's mind and actions, he would not yield to influence from relations, but would be guided by his own judgment. If anything, he was certainly not superstitious to reject the girl of his choice, as Bhavanarayana feared. But it was not easy to convince Bhavanarayana about it. With Savitri I think he counted upon me as an impractical person ignorant of worldly ways....

Savitri was the only person who believed in the doctor, and had developed a genuine affection and admiration for him. She just dismissed the misgivings expressed by Bhavanarayana.

I looked into myself. Savitri's affection for the doctor and the doctor's familiarity with her were not to my liking. But I was helpless. Social decency and my own norms of fairness and personal freedom stood in my way of ordering the doctor to keep away. I only wished that the doctor would soon marry Hema! And what a wish!! A little while ago I had looked upon Hema as my private possession and imagined I had some right over her as a friend. Now I was worried about losing Savitri, though she was my wedded wife! Several times in the past I had shown indifference towards her, and had thought that she was not adequate intellectually. But now all my concern appeared to be to keep her as my own! The vagaries of my own mind puzzled me!

A letter arrived from the doctor, addressed to me and Savitri, that he would return in two days. He didn't inform Bhavanarayana. He didn't even mention his name in the letter. But I thought it my duty to convey the news to Bhavanarayana. His reaction took me by surprise.

"He is coming back after performing the funeral rites for his mother. How can we perform the marriage now? He will have to wait for an year."

I thought this too was a defensive position being taken by Bhavanarayana, as he did not trust the doctor. Perhaps he felt hurt that the doctor had not written to him. In reality, my own reading of Bhavanarayana was that he wouldn't be much of a stickler after orthodoxy. And ways always could be found, if a thing had to be done. I was amused to note that there was a lot in our culture and customs which could be used both ways. A sword sharp both ways, as the saying goes! It could be used both for defense and offense.

"Wouldn't you like to talk to him about the marriage and ascertain his views, as soon as he arrives?"

"I think you or your wife can do that. You are better placed for that in your relationship with him."

"Suppose he says that he wants the wedding immediately?"

"Let him say that. We'll think over and find a way to convince him or satisfy him."

I thought I had understood Bhavanarayana's position correctly.

On arrival, the doctor came straight to my house and stayed with us for five days, during which period he got his house cleaned, white-washed (as is the custom when a death occurs in the family) and rearranged, and also engaged a person to cook for him and do the house-keeping. I noted that none of his relatives had accompanied him on his return, contrary to what Bhavanarayana had expected.

He became even more friendly and voluble with Savitri, and the two spent a lot of time together, while my presence brought restraint to his tongue. He also evaded with me discussions of the kind, which had first brought us together. I couldn't understand the change and said the same thing to Savitri.

"He is in deep sorrow and grief. He is childlike and he has nobody to talk to freely. All the time he keeps recalling his childhood memories. He cannot talk in that vein with you or in your presence. He seems to have had a fight with his relations there. He refused to perform the prescribed funeral rites, and his relations were shocked by his refusal and roundly abused him. They had created difficulties in property matters even in dealing with his mother, and that brought on the heart-attack, he says.

Therefore, he somehow settled the affairs with them, and finally broke off from them, returning here to us. To whom could he confide all these things?"

"It seems that he could find only one person, and that is Savitri, in the entire world! He could talk to me also about those things. Why this differentiation?"

"Well, that is that. I need not tell you again that you are stone-hearted and cannot understand others!" She laughed the matter away.

"Look here, Savitri, this doctor is not an ordinary person.... If he loves his mother so much, why did he not perform her funeral rites? No worse form of disrespect one can imagine towards a mother! How come you have become the only confidant for him! I want you to be on your caution, you're playing with a snake."

"No fear. I think I know this snake well!"

"It's not a joke. You are not aware of the change that has come over you. He is not related to you. You don't know him. You haven't even defined for yourself what he is to you. How could you be so intimate with him. I don't like it."

Savitri was hurt and angry.

"I need not define any relationship with him. What is felt and known inwardly is sufficient. He is my unborn son, my non-existent brother. Call him whatever you like. But please don't pass orders on how I should conduct myself. Now I've lost my fear of serpents. If I am to die because of my trust, well, I'll die only once, you know. With fear and distrust of people around me, I cannot make my life a continuous dying!"

While we stood talking, I noticed the doctor pass from the bathroom towards the front room. He might have heard a part of our conversation, though we became silent when we saw him. This happened on the fourth day of his stay with us. I regretted that I had been in a hurry to express my misgivings to Savitri. Then the doctor went back to his residence.

But I could not put any restraint on Savitri. She would go to his house freely, and would give instructions to the cook, and give numerous suggestions about house-keeping and sundry matters.... Observing all that, I was practising non-attachment.

About his marriage with Hema, Savitri herself sounded the doctor instead of my doing so at the instance of Bhavanarayana. The doctor wanted the date to be fixed. Then Bhavanarayana and I went to see the doctor. Bhavanarayana asked him about the rites to be performed in due time for his dead moiher.

"I don't believe in all that, and I am not going to observe any of them," he said.

"Well, if that is your decision, then one hurdle is crossed. But do you have faith in the marriage rites?" Bhavanarayana asked him.

"It is not a question of my belief. If you desire that the rites have to be gone through, for your sake I have no objection. But let me tell you that faith and trust between persons cannot depend on rites. Only if you trust me as a person, you go ahead with the wedding, otherwise, please don't do it...." Then turning to me he asked me : "At least do you trust me?" In the manner he put that query to me, I thought he was aware of my jealousy. I simply smiled in reply.

The wedding was fixed for June, and the formality of getting the date and time verified and set down on paper in the presence of a priest was gone through. The doctor said : "Don't expect any of my relations to attend the wedding."

I was amused to find that Bhavanarayana's objections on the basis of custom and religion which he had previously expressed, never came up finally. They had achieved their objective and Bhavanarayana was happy that he was discharging his duty by his sister and his mother's soul would rest in peace.

When I thought over all the fuss created by Bhavanarayana and his family prior to the finalization of Hema's wedding, I had a feeling of distaste and disappointment about their changing attitudes and erratic thinking. Bhavanarayana's acquaintance with the doctor started much earlier than mine, and he decided for himself that the doctor would be a suitable match for his sister, and yet he could not develop any genuine relationship of affection and trust with the doctor. He tried to take advantage of the progressive views of the doctor, but never had any real respect for those views. The fact that the doctor would not demand a dowry, the doctor's rejection of the Hindu rites for the dead, the doctor's quarrel with his relations, everything worked out in favour of Hema's marriage. But what happened to the professed values of culture and tradition, of which Bhavanarayana never tired of talking? It amazed me! However Bhavanarayana was not an exception.... He represented the vast majority, who did not live by what they professed! For them beliefs, tradition, or progress, nothing really mattered. Because they were bereft of commitment, they also did not value personal relationships. They were incapable and indifferent to judge for themselves the worthiness or otherwise of an individual. In Bhavanarayana's mind, hereafter, the doctor would be labelled as "sister's husband," but could never acquire the status of a person known, regarded and related to oneself as a person. I consider this lack of personal regard and relationship among people in our society, as the greatest single misfortune, and responsible for our ills. A firm cultural background, in which people not only profess belief, but by which they could form individual relationships of trust and affection appears to be absolutely necessary, for the progress of our country. It need not be singular, based on one religion or one ideology. We take pride in pluralism, tolerance and syncretism. But without the individual's firm commitment to one framework of values, all that is utter nonsense.... Neither progress nor socialism can become meaningful unless the individual believes in himself and believes in others as individuals. How will it come about? Through education? What kind of education? Perhaps it will come about through a violent revolution, as the doctor believes! In a sense what the doctor talks about as violence is just another side of the coin, the other side being suffering, and individual suffering is known as 'tapasya,' when it is consciously and willingly gone through...I was lost in speculation and thought.

PART VII

I had to go to my native village in Cuddapah District. I was the youngest of three brothers, and five years ago I had divided my property, landed and otherwise with the two elder brothers, who lived in the village. My share of the agricultural land was under the management and cultivation of my second brother. My eldest brother had three sons and my second brother two sons. We had no daughters in the family.

A few days ago, my eldest brother had fallen seriously ill and had been taken for treatment to the Christian Mission Hospital at Vellore. He had returned to the village now. He had been prescribed a regulated diet along with medication for hypertension and diabetes. He wrote to me asking me to go and see him. Accordingly I went. But I would lodge with my second brother only. Our joint family broke up and property was divided because of my first sister-in-law, the wife of my eldest brother. She didn't much care to maintain good relationship with my second sister-in-law or with my wife. Therefore, I preferred to be the guest of my second brother and his wife, though I went to see my eldest brother.

My eldest brother lived not only by cultivation, as our ancestors did, but also had in recent years entered business in partnership with his wife's brother. In fact this venture of his was the point of separation among the brothers. It took me two days to understand why my eldest brother had called me to the village. He told me that his health was in a poor state and he wanted my assistance in some matters. As I had remained childless, I was advised to adopt his last boy, now ten years old, and take charge of him fully. That would not only lessen his burden, but also put our brotherly relationship on a firm foundation for the future. The eldest son aged twenty was aligned with his maternal uncle and was looking after the business side of the family involvements. He stopped school after the tenth class. The second son, who did not proceed further than the eighth grade, was getting involved in agriculture. Now it was the third and the last boy, he was worried about. If I adopted him and put him to school in Anantapur, my brother said, he would enjoy peace of mind, and perhaps would live a little longer than he otherwise was destined to in view of his shattered health.

When I mentioned all this to my second brother, he saw nothing but a sort of political manouvering on the part of my eldest brother and his wife. The immediate result of it all would be to take away my part of the agricultural land for cultivation by my first brother from the second one. He pointed out that the best adviser and the most important care-taker was the businessman brother-in-law, and he would most certainly be in charge of all the affairs, and he could arrange for the education of the last boy also. In a situation like that my role was bound to be unimportant. It was only a strategy to take control of my landed property. He added : "You and your wife are still young enough to bear children. Why should you think of adoption now? Where is the urgency?"

There was a lot of commonsense in the comments made by my second brother. I could perceive his own self-interest in it. Not only were my lands under his cultivation now, which he was loath to give up, but also was the unexpressed wish that for adoption he too could spare his second son, if indeed I went for adoption as a last measure for want of an heir. However, the motivation might be, it was a fact that he was dealing fairly with me in respect of my lands till now, and his wife treated my wife with affection and regard. How could I disregard their view point and act according to my first brother's wishes? But a reply was due from me.

I said : "Let me have time to think over. On my next visit Savitri too will be here. I'll explain to her all things, the way you wish them to be. Then we can decide."

"That's right. But I don't want things to be postponed indefinitely, considering my health. So be sure that you will be here with Savitri in a fortnight's time. I must have peace of mind. And that will be possible, if these matters are settled to my satisfaction. The doctor advises that I should not entertain anxieties and worries, and that alone will keep my condition stable. I have left the eldest boy to my brother-in-law's care. He will safeguard his interests. But will he do the same thing in the case of my other two sons? He may, but there will always be a difference, as he wants to make the eldest boy his son-in-law by marrying his daughter to him. That would certainly make a difference. That is the reason why I want to entrust the last boy to you. Then you will also have a say in the affairs of the three brothers, not my brother-in-law alone." That was my eldest brother's plea to me.

There was a genuine concern in what he said. It was impossible to assess the condition of his health. I didn't want to be hurried and hustled into an arrangement which might not work out. Of course I was mentally ready to assist my first brother, if any contingency arose. But I didn't like to commit myself one way or another right at the moment.

I was firmly set against adoption. I was almost certain that Savitri too did not very much relish the idea. The question would arise seriously, if it were to be established beyond doubt that we were incapable of having children at any time in the future. Even so, Savitri alone should decide about adoption and who should be adopted. On return home I did not inform Savitri about my eldest brother's proposal. I told her only about his poor health. But I came to a decision that I should get tested for fertility without any delay. Till now all tests were gone through by Savitri and I had never subjected myself to fertility test. Savitri had not been declared totally infertile, and in my case it simply had not occurred to either of us. It only goes to show how man's egotism and prestige prevail in our social set-up.

Without informing Savitri about my decision to get tested, I approached Dr. Virabhadra Rao to have me tested. The knowledge that the doctor was a progressive made me feel at ease. Another doctor might have laughed at me, or talked about it in his circle of friends. This doctor had become an intimate friend to both of us.

"How has it become important right now? You are anxious for an heir to your property?" he said.

"I am not bothered about the heir. Becoming a mother is very important to Savitri. If the question is settled, she could at least adopt a child and gratify her mother instinct. It is absolutely necessary she should have someone to mother. I find her very much frustrated."

"You're right," said the doctor and was thoughtful for a while. Then he added : "One of the legal provisions for divorce is the incapacity of the wife to bear children. When the wife intensely longs for a child, and the husband is not impotent, but is proven infertile, why should not that be a ground for divorcing the husband? The law-makers do not seem to have contemplated such a situation. What is your opinion?"

"Yes, equality between the sexes demands such a provision, but how many women in our society would like to enforce such a provision? The emancipated women fighting for equal rights are not enamoured of motherhood. They consider that as a special disability to be somehow overcome, and not a special privilege."

"Let us leave the emancipated women aside for a moment. If your wife wants to do it, how would you react?"

"No doubt I'll be ready for it. But Savitri will never take such a step."

"So that is your confidence! You're a wonderful man! " The doctor laughed and added : "You have a lot of vested interest in the present set-up. And yet you are always talking of a new society!"

"I may envisage a new society and talk about it, but when the changes do come, I cannot say that I won't be emotionally affected by them. A bitter pill will surely taste bitter, even if it is intended to cure a disease. It is difficult for a person to transcend his personal limitations, though changes may be for the general good. If my wife is legally enabled to divorce me, I may accept it as justice, but I cannot stop my grief and prevent my feeling hurt as a person."

"You know the profession of a doctor is to administer bitter pills. He takes pleasure in it, and a revolutionary is thus in the role of a doctor. He likes to administer to the ills of society."

I visited the hospital, where the laboratory facilities were available and gave a sample of my semen for test under the supervision of Dr. Virabhadra Rao.

That evening the doctor brought me the result. He said : "Sorry to disappoint you. The result is negative. You have no chance of begetting an heir."

"Is that a temporary disorder, or a permanent disability."

"I am not sure. I think it's something congenital."

I was dumbfounded. I was depressed.

"Are you shocked with disappointment?"

"Well, I don't mind it. I am thinking of Savitri. What would it mean to her?"

"True. She might even get hysterical. She is just now recovering from the serpent's scare."

"What do you advise me to do?"

"You needn't convey the bad news to her immediately. You can bide your time. Even you need never tell her. The necessity may not arise. Sometime later you may adopt a child, when you come upon a suitable orphan or someone like that."

There is no link between fertility and sexual potency. But lack of procreative faculty somehow appeared to me as a deficiency to be regretted. In what way did it affect me as a person? I didn't long for an heir; nor was I particularly fond of children. Why had nature crippled me in this special way? There are human beings born deaf, dumb or blind, and how unfortunate they are! My disability was not apparent to the world to see, and I could well conceal it, being born a man, which itself was a privileged position compared to that of woman. All the same it was a fact which I could not conceal from myself. And for the present I might keep it away from Savitri, but how long could I do it without affecting the truth of our relationship. To dub her as a barren woman, to maintain a self-respect and prestige known to me as false, just because I would maintain my position as a husband, was unthinkable and alien to my very nature, and to the goal of life I had set before myself, which was the pursuit of truth at all costs. That was untenable. I would wait for a suitable time and tell her. Unless I made that promise to myself, I could not feel at ease in my relationship with Savitri. And I did make that promise to myself.

To think of the consequences of such a revelation whenever the time might come, was also a very painful process for me. I was not particular about begetting children, but I looked upon married life as a beautiful and glorious experience. Because it was a realization of love. Sex was an expression of that love, a private language between me and Savitri. I prized it for its own sake. Savitri looked upon it as a means to an end. Her goal was motherhood.... Her love for me, her sex with me were only means to an end in her view. When the moment arrived for her to know that the means had failed her, then it was possible that she might renounce both love and sex in our relationship. That was my nightmare. Could I face it? She might not go to the extent of abandoning me or divorcing me, and even agree to adopt a child, but all that would be a hopeless compromise, and neither of us would be the same again.

If only Savitri were modern enough not to value motherhood as the highest purpose, but gave at least equal value to sex and personal relationship, I would not be faced with this dilemma. Savitri's personality and cultural background happened to be different. Was it my good fortune or bad luck?...

"What is the matter with you? You are always brooding and look pensive. After your return from the village, you are not your old self. It's now almost a week, and you haven't got rid of the mood with which you seem to have returned," said Savitri. I was seated in the verandah as usual. My depression and melancholy were noticeable, I thought, from Savitri's comments. What should I say to her? Till now there had never been any reservations between us. We had always spoken whatever was uppermost in our mind. Now I had to improvise.

"Look at that tree, what do you call it?"

"Why? Have you been meditating on the peepul tree?"

"It's a peepul tree all right, but how do you see it?"

"I see it as a tree!"

"It is a family-tree for you. Symbolizing progeny. To me it is a worldly tree, symbolizing worldly attachments. In the Bhagavadgita, it is so described. While you desire progeny, I am bent upon cutting my worldly attachments with the sword of non-attachment and achieving a liberated state. How can our two views be reconciled, that's what I have been thinking about."

"Well, both views can be reconciled. First progeny, and then spiritual liberation. There's time for bringing up progeny, and there's an apropriate time to sit in meditation of God."

"You have not grasped what I'm saying. The relationship or bond through which you desire children, from that very relationship I wish to attain liberation."

"Does it mean that you want sannyasa immediately? Well, if you so much want it, go for it! Where is the need to think or ponder over the matter? I like the tongue-in-cheek manner of your talking. Really!" She was laughing.

"Non-attachment or renunciation doesn't mean wearing ochre robes, shaving one's head after going through a certain ritual. It's spiritual and mental; going through life's experience, one has to become totally non-attached. Like the water-drop on the lotus leaf, being on it and not of it."

"Even now your attitude is the same, isn't it? You have no financial worries, and you spend all your time talking philosophy.... Well, let us go to the movies and relax."

We returned from the movies in a jovial mood.

Dressed in a milk-white sari Savitri was a cup of nectar I enjoyed that night. The scent of jasmines from her coiffure pervaded and intoxicated me, and all the melancholy was drowned in an ecstasy of love. Time and Savitri would not standstill. But it was a golden moment. A new, momentary awareness sharpened my desire.

That was an unusual union. The discovery of a new experience, the discovery of my being myself. The usual thing was different. There's a pond. When one is fully immersed in the water, one is aware of the water and nothing else. The extent of the water and the pond's limits disappear. For one, who holds his head above the surface, they are distinct and visible. My experience that night was neither of the two kinds. I was immersed fully, but I was not lost. I was myself and discovered myself in that experience, being one with it.

What is the 'self?'

The self is not this body. It is not the pleasure I had. The body and the pleasure both belong to me. I am attached to them. Being attached is different from identity. Through the experience and its unique quality, however, I had discovered the true self. What does that mean? It means that death (the decay of the body), and love (the pleasure of sex and intimacy) remain as my attributes only and cannot destroy me, the self.

The self cannot be described or defined through any of these attributes. It is beyond them, beyond time and space and activity and remains a witness! And yet it is involved too!

The next day, I asked the doctor, because I respected his intellect :

"Did you at any moment realize that you the self is different from the body, not through thinking, but as an experience?"

"Never, because that is wrong thinking. It is just an illusion helping one to run away from reality. Apart from this body and its activity, myself and my life cannot exist separately. It just doesn't make sense."

"This insignificant body and this limited life, how could they afford any satisfaction or fulfilment?"

"Well, by assuming that the self is not this body one would not get much satisfaction either. In fact being dissatisfied is the very quality of life, its very essence."

"If the self is not different from the body, the self dies, one dies with the death of the body. To believe that there is a self, a soul beyond the body and it is deathless, isn't that a great satisfaction?"

"It is precisely for that reason I call it escapism. A mere assumption or belief will not result in the conquest of death. One should fight against death, carry on the struggle against it. That is the purpose of life. Death makes life meaningful, and constitutes its goal and its fulfillment."

"The experience, not the thought or assumption, that the self is apart and different from the body, do you consider that as an illusion?"

"When one is faced with a critical situation, an unresolvable difficulty, the mind is capable of creating for itself many subterfuges, and I would say it is one of them."

"What would you say to the teaching in the *Bhagavadgita*, that the soul does not die, it's only the body that dies? The body is cast off like the clothes one wears and so on."

"Well, it can be argued both ways, you know. Since the soul is deathless, it doesn't matter if the body dies, and therefore fight in the battle. That is one way of saying it. If the self and the body are one and the same, the body is bound to die some time or other, and therefore is it not preferable to fight and die instead of being a coward afraid of death? That is another way of saying it. The point is one should fight and not run away. Because of the general fear of death, because of the general dislike for it, a philosophy, a metaphysics based on the first way of argument was built up. A deathless soul was created for the purpose. There is no need of such an assumption for facing life. There is no life without death, fighting against death is life, therefore accept death totally. From this point of view, the body and the self are one and the same."

"Have you personally to accepted death? You have no fear of death ? What happened when your mother died? Did you not react with grief and anguish?"

The doctor took in his palm the sponge on the table and making a tight fist, he squeezed all the water out of it and said : "I am trying to squeeze out like this all my memories, and yet some wetness remains. I'm not terribly grieved that my mother is gone. Death is natural. But some memories and habits of mind cause sadness of mind. To get rid of them is also part of the struggle that goes on between life and death."

"How do you get rid of memories? They don't obey orders."

"To invite fresh experiences is the way."

Perhaps his coming marriage with Hema will be one, I told myself. What a man! I could not get at the total picture of his culture. Even after many conversations with him and a number of discussions, I was not certain I understood him!

My perceptions of life and men were inevitably coloured by my cultural background and the imagination pertaining to it. The doctor's personality could not be figured out by them. He was still an enigma, and the glimpses I could get of him only puzzled me instead of enlightening me. In a way he had become a challenge to my view of life and my beliefs. Even so he did not put me off. He aroused in me curiosity and attraction, which I had no way to resist.

One morning I was driving a nail into the wall and inadvertently hit my left thumb. I went to the doctor to get it cleaned and dressed. He hadn't yet opened the clinic, but attended to the wound and offered me coffee.

"Who was responsible for this clumsiness in driving the nail? Your soul or your body?" he asked me with a smile.

"The soul is only a witness. The responsibility belongs to the body," I responded.

"Then as a soul you are totally irresponsible."

"It has its responsibility. The soul is the supervisor. It is the protector, and it is the punisher too."

"When you hit yourself on the thumb, was there an instant cry of pain or not?"

"Yes, there was."

"Did you at that moment have the awareness of the difference between the soul and the body? Please try to remember and tell me, was it the soul or body that reacted with the cry?"

"There is no way to say that."

"You see what happens to the mind when the intensity of experience is on the rise. If the intensity of pain is greater than what you experienced, you would become unconscious. Then what happens to this witness you mention? Some people may practice tolerance of pain. But even so cannot go beyond certain limits. All this pertains to the body and the nervous system. I would say that based on the training of the mind and the hardening of the will, one may have the illusion of a soul apart from the body. Beyond the body and its adjunct the mind, there is no such thing as a soul."

I had no immediate reply. I was thinking. The coffee cups were on the table. There was another sally from the doctor.

"You said that the soul is a supervisor, a protector and a punisher. What was the wrong done by the body to invite this punishment from the soul?" I thought over the matter further, and after a while said this :

"I am indeed grateful for your criticism. The experience that the self is separate from the body, to the extent that it is a mental perception, is not the true self-knowledge. As you have pointed out, it is a certain mental state only. But I don't agree with your saying that when a man becomes unconscious, there is nothing beyond the body and the mind. The soul exists. How does one know it? That is the question. You said that my body has been punished. My mind at the moment doesn't know the reason for the punishment. It is not in a position to know right now. But the soul knows it, and that knowledge in due course will be imparted to the mind too. In the course of one's life, things unexpected happen just as things expected and desired may not come to pass. We just call it chance. But this realm of chance, not within the grasp of the mind, truly belongs to the soul. The soul has its reasoning different from that of the mind and the body. When the mind is opened up to the soul and gets attuned to it, then the mind too will receive that knowledge. The meaning and purpose of a man's life, which cannot be figured out by the mind in its ego state, can be figured out by reaching forth to the soul. If you dismiss the proposition of the existence of the soul, life will always be fragmented, and your philosophy of death will reign supreme, treating life as meaningless and drab."

"What is the self right here and right now? A self that is not operational now, but is to be hopefully realized sometime in future, is really of no use for living. It is a philosophy of the other world.

How is it better than my philosophy of struggle and acceptance of death?"

"The self that operates right now is the ego. It is made up of a body-mind continuum and consists of memories and desires. The true selftranscends the ego limits and restrictions, brings in the oneness of all life and the bliss of existence. Man's struggle is to transcend the ego limits towards liberation."

"All this is pure speculation and fantasizing. You are now talking about fanciful things instead of experience. Not as a faith or an ideal state to be achieved, but as an experience and a reality here and now if you talk about the soul, there will be meaning and purpose in it. Otherwise it is useless like religion as far as I am concerned. You say that my philosophy is meaningless and drab. To understand society and the changes occurring in human relationships in my time I require a fresh and dynamic point of view shorn of all past shibboleths and superstitions, of which the concept of soul is one. Every experience of the body is significant and meaningful, if you care to understand. One need not go beyond the mind to perceive the meaning."

"What is the significance of this hurt to my thumb?"

"Doesn't it show that you are not skillful with your body? Better ask someone else to drive nails for you to save your thumb. Isn't that a good and purposeful lesson in itself?"

"What does my infertility mean?"

The question that had been the focus of all my recent moods, I could not help blurting out, curious to know how his line of thinking would find an answer.

The doctor laughed. I wondered for a moment whether he was laughing at me!

"It will be no loss to society if you don't bring forth children. It shows that your Vedantic philosophy has no revolutionary potency, it is just barren. Any number of social implications and indications...."

"But they don't mean anything to me as an individual. Any revolution in society is no revolution at all unless it can make the individual happy, unless it involves and ensures the fulfilment of the individual. And that happiness and fulfilment is not confined to the gratification of the body and its needs."

"Unrest and perpetual dissatisfaction is the very nature of being alive. You refuse to accept this truth. The driving force for progress is dissatisfaction. Man can never be fulfilled or satisfied."

"My philosophy says that the individual man can find satisfaction, peace and fulfilment. There have been instances of many individuals attaining that state."

"Then your philosophy works against human progress. Like religion it is an opiate. Revolution cannot brook it."

"The quest for the self can never be an opiate. "

PART VIII

A beautiful bird of ash-gray colour sits on the tree and sings melodiously. And then it is gone. I don't know wherefrom it comes. Its song has no meaning and does not relate. The song doesn't evoke any sentiments or arouse any buried memories. But the song makes me self-forgetful for a few moments. I don't know the species of the bird. I never studied the natural sciences. Mine is the ignorance of an educated urbanite. The villager knows all the names of birds and trees and plants. I know nothing. I don't know the bird that sings to me.

The bird comes and goes alone. Doesn't it have a mate? Would there be birds with no capacity to reproduce, individual birds so deprived congenitally or otherwise? And for this bird, is there no nest, no habitation to call its own?

Man is beset with worries, thoughts and hopes! A lot of dissatisfaction all round and all the time!

In the next street lives a lawyer friend, four years younger than me and junior to me professionally, who has built a spacious house. He held a reception and we went. He is engaged in business in addition to his law-practice. He had made a pile of money. He has two children.

Savitri comments : "The house is well-planned and very comfortable. The children are gems. What a good fortune!"

I react : "You are right, Savitri. You know the labourer Venkadu, who dug the well for us. He lives in a thatched hut at the end of this colony. He has four children, and his wife is a sickly woman. Recently he lost a ten-month old baby. He tells me that we are very fortunate because we have no children to bother us, and we live comfortably. Opinions about good fortune vary in this fashion. That way who is not fortunate?"

"There is neither head nor tail to your reasoning and philosophy. You said something like this during our visit to Mysore, do you remember?"

Yes, I remembered. We went round the magnificent palace and other imposing structures of the Raja of Mysore, and as a socialist and democrat, I remarked : "These things belong to the people. They are no longer the property of a single man." Savitri rejoined : "Imagine the feelings of the persons who have lost possession of them!" Then in a lighter vein I held forth : "Because of the sense of possession, differentiating between mine and yours, the grief of loss arises. Even that Maharaja of Mysore would have lived in a room in a corner of the palace, and he could not have lived in the huge palace all by himself. Who lived in the rest of the rooms? Perhaps his retinue and officers. And the gardens and the lawns? People like us, tourists and visitors go round now and derive a lot of pleasure, as did the retinue and the staff in the old days. It will always be like that! What is not ours in this wide world? The beautiful sunrise and sunset, the moonlit night, the trees and rivers, the hills and vallies all the things that give joy are ours! Nothing is everlasting and nobody can become possessive. When one realizes this truth, there will be no sense of loss, no grief and no envy whatsoever! The essence of socialism is to realize this!"

Whatever I said on that day is coming to me as a personal realization now. The ash-gray bird and its song, don't they belong to me?

My lawyer friend's house is new and therefore interesting. When one resides in it for a few months, familarity would make it as old and common as any other house!

When my thoughts take wing in this fashion, I feel free and joyous. "We enjoy the company of children, especially of Radha and Gopi, even though they are not ours. Even though they belong to Bhavanarayana, they give us as much happiness as they give their parents. Perhaps more. All trouble, worry and expense, their bringing up may involve, remains the parents' responsibility, and undiluted joy is shared by us! Shouldn't we congratulate ourselves on this good fortune? Think deeply, and indeed there is nothing special or profitable in the thought of possession or ownership. When that thought can be forgotten, we discover beauties and joys hitherto unknown and unperceived!"

Dressed in a beautiful sari of lemon yellow with a resplendent purple border, a woman was walking along our street.

"What a nice-looking sari! It is Conjeevaram silk. I don't have a single thing like that. You don't buy me silk saris at all!" said Savitri.

"What is nice and beautiful about it? It is the combination of two colours. And wherefrom comes our joy? From our seeing it. Even if you had purchased it, you would have got the same joy at its beauty and nothing more nor less. But you don't agree. Why don't you accept the experience of joy without demanding the possession of the object? Why turn that joy into jealous intolerance?"

"Well, in that case why purchase saris and wear them? One might as well wear the sky and the leaves of trees. Why wear them? One ought to be satisfied with the beauty of the colours. Go ahead and enjoy yourself," so saying Savitri made her exit.

I was dumbfounded. Was I becoming crazy, I reflected. I laughed at myself. The minimum necessities, food, clothing and a shelter cannot be dispensed with even by a philosopher! They are the limits of advaita!

But I was convinced in the correctness of my thinking. Progress and development for man consist not in the erection of huge mansions for residence, not in moving about in limousines, or flying in supersonic jet-planes. And those whose life-style involves all these things, what are their pleasures and recreations?

Drink, promiscuous sex and gambling — these are indicators of high civilization! In fact, the three ways of self-indulgence are common today in all social classes of men; a rickshaw-wallah, ryot, a clerk, a capitalist, a politician, whatever he may be, being a member of today's civilization, he gets them at the quality and price he can afford. Is that all what life means? The search for creative joy and the quest for beauty and goodness are dead. What worse poverty and misfortune could there be? There is increase in everything, in national income, in population, in money inflation, in the budget figures, but the happiness of man has dwindled into nothing! Whether economic equality in society will be achieved or not, the primary consideration must be the realization by man of the meaning and goal of life. When he fails to direct himself to that quest, no political ideology or revolution can save man!

I came to the conclusion that when the minimum physical necessities are available, a person can attain fulfilment and satisfaction. I need not have a mosaic-floor to walk upon, a mirrored, polished, ceramic bath-room to wash myself; I need not have the fertility to bring forth children. Why should I not have contentment? Comparison with others and craving for the same things they have, arouses dissatisfaction and anguish, totally unwarranted, and I was convinced of that. But could I convince Savitri too about it? In the matter of children, perhaps Savitri could never be convinced about my view. Well then, should I inform her about my disability? That was a moral issue. Personal morality or svadharma by definition is not governed by a universal or gneral code of conduct. It is a choice to be made by the person in the situation and the relationship in which he is placed. It is a choice for which the total responsibility rests with the person himself. I had to make that choice now. Should I tell Savitri right now that she could never hope to have a child by me and suddenly expose her to a mental crisis; or should I leave the matter alone, for time to work out its solution to the problem?

After a month's deliberation, I thought it wise to leave the matter alone and live in peace.

Before Hema's wedding with the doctor came off, there was a storm in the tea-cup!

Bhavanarayana came to know rather late in the day, through some source, that the doctor's late father had been a convert to Christianity. He married after he joined the army as a junior officer. He married a Christian girl, with whom he fell in love. He got married in a church after getting duly converted into his bride's religion. Dr. Veerabhadra Rao was born of that marriage. In his twelfth year Veerabhadra Rao lost his father. By that time Veerabhadra Rao's uncles had become reconciled to their brother and had good relationship with him. That became possible because the parents, who had objected to the marriage and the religious conversion died. And Veerabhadra Rao's father had never really given up the religion or customs in which he was born. He gave his son a traditional Hindu name, actually the name of his grandfather. The wife, Veerabhadra Rao's mother had never raised any objections, and had followed the husband's footsteps. She had adopted Hinduism quietly. That explained why Bhavanarayana and none of us could guess the fact or even suspect that the elderly lady had not been born a Hindu. The reason for the neglect of the doctor and his mother by the relatives, and perhaps the reason why Veerabhadra Rao did not perform the funeral rites for his mother according to the Hindu faith became evident in the light of this background now revealed.

Bhavanarayana was very much upset. The doctor's intimacy with me and Savitri, even after the wedding was settled, had not been to his liking, and his wife stopped visiting us. They tried to tell the doctor that he had killed the serpent and had incurred the burden of a sinful deed all for the sake of Savitri and myself, who were neither relatives nor friends of his. Perhaps his mother too had died because of the heinous sin. The doctor appeared to have brushed them aside, and perhaps spoke sternly. They definitely cooled off towards us. However, when the doctor's past became known, Bhavanarayana in his confusion resorted to me. He told me he did not know what to do now, at this late stage, when the wedding was only a week away, and all arrangements had been made.

"Did you ask the doctor about it?" I queried.

"Yes, he says it is all a fact. He says he has no religion. He too gave up Christianity long long back. His father became reconciled with his brothers and they used to visit him and receive him in the village reciprocally. But his mother and himself maintained a distance from them. Property matters, as in any other joint family, came in the way of a closer relationship. He says all these things now. Should he not have told us in the beginning? Was it not his moral responsibility?"

"Well, you never asked him! That he has no religion is true to his convictions. You introduced him to me as a progressive and a revolutionary. He never made a secret of it."

"I could never imagine that his being a progressive meant he was not a Hindu at all! It is too late for anything now. What do you advise me?"

"My dear Sir, we keep repeating that differences based on caste and religion must go, but when it comes to positive action, and presents itself as a personal problem, we flinch, we develop cold feet and try to run away. Why should we do that? Put it to your sister Hema, and let her take her own decision. Unless she objects personally, please go ahead with the wedding. This is her personal problem and not yours."

"Marriage, as the saying goes, is a hundred-year crop. Hema will have children, and they will have to get married. She should not face isolation."

"Just leave it to her. Hinduism is broad-minded, only individual Hindus are narrow-minded. The true Hinduism is spreading abroad, while it is being crushed here amidst the narrow walls of caste, custom and superstition. This is our misfortune."

"Since you have no problems, you can afford to think and talk in a liberal way."

"You can also be liberal. You never started as a self-proclaimed social reformer. But when an occasion presents itself to think and act liberally, why don't you do it? In any case, it should be Hema's decision. We should not come in her way."

Bhavanarayana went to Hema's work-place and had consultations with her. She was ready for the marriage. Bhavanarayana decided to go ahead, but his original enthusiasm for the match was gone. He had envisaged in the distant future marriages between his children and Hema's in the traditional way of thinking. Now that dream was gone. Accordingly the wedding was celebrated without much fanfare.

When the marriage was first settled, Bhavanarayana had promised to give Hema a sum of Rupees ten thousand, in accordance with the word he had given to his dead mother. Though the doctor did not make any demands, Bhavanarayana had mentioned it voluntarily in the presence of those assembled for the occasion. At the time of wedding he acted as though he had forgotten all about it. One of the two uncles from the doctor's village attended the wedding, and he too arrived just in time. There was nobody to act on behalf of the bridegroom except Savitri, who had assumed the responsibility herself, and who started making the customary demands on behalf of the bridegroom's party. This was specially resented by Bhavanarayana's family members. She reminded me and the doctor about the ten thousand rupees. I asked her to keep quiet. The doctor said to her, "Not now." But Savitri was not put off, and went on to talk about it with Lakshmi, Bhavanarayana's wife. Lakshmi appeared to have snubbed her. What the precise words were, Savitri refused to tell me. But she commented : "She has no control over her tongue. I never thought she would be so indecent in word and thought. They give no value to friendship and have no respect for persons!!" Savitri was offended, and as soon as the wedding rites were performed, we went home, without staying for the feast. "I don't want to see their faces again," said Savitri.

We were relatives to neither party, and yet the marriage brought about bad blood between us and the members of Bhavanarayana's family. Unpleasant exchanges among relatives will be forgotten sooner or later; but in our case that did not apply. And Savitri was firm. Though personally we had not exchanged any words, the relationship between me and Bhavanarayana too languished because of the womenfolk.

The doctor was leaving for Bangalore to spend his honeymoon. When he came to tell us, Savitri asked him : "What happened to the money?"

"They will give it after our return from honeymoon," he said laughing.

"I don't believe it. Because you have nobody on your side, they are taking advantage. They have no value for people. All they are interested in is money."

The doctor did not respond. He said : "Goodbye."

I did not like Savitri's behaviour. The right she assumed over the doctor and the concern she showed about his personal matter were not to my taste.

I was surprised why Hema did not come along with her husband to bid us farewell. True that we did not visit Bhavanarayana's place after the wedding. But we did expect that she would come with the doctor, and Savitri had kept ready a sari and blouse-piece to be presented to her. She disappointed us.

Standing in my verandah, I saw Hema getting into the car. I felt that beauty that had given me joy all these days was distancing itself from me permanently and there was a twinge in my heart. But it was meaningless. Indeed there is nothing in any object, its worth lies in the response the heart makes, I told myself. Instead of looking at the response and appraising it, we commit the blunder of identifying the object with the heart's response, and long to grab the object, to possess it, and this desire assumes greater prominence in the mind than anything else. In fact, in respect of woman, possession results in loss. It will be the end of the aesthetic response. That is why romantic love is all about the inaccessible beloved. The moment she is within grasp, physically, the romantic response is dead. Marriage relationship may bring about affection, understanding and intimacy, but marks the end of romantic love. Romantic love and marriage are incompatible, I reflected.

My response to Hema at the beginning of our association had not been romantic. My dream in which she appeared, her silence towards me, her distancing me and finally her marriage with the doctor aroused in me a romantic response. I became acutely conscious of it when I saw her getting into the car and leaving without a word or gesture. It was a subtle anguish of the heart, and there is no worldly panacea for it.

How do I relate to the ash-gray bird that sings to me, and how do I relate to Hema a girl of my dream-world and a source of my secret joy? They are of the same kind of experience!

The experience remained with me till it was evening. The sound of bells was heard by my inner ear. They continued to ring. I had visited Thanjavur, and when I heard the bells of the Brihadeeswara Temple there, my heart resounded and was filled with a profound emotion for the deity present there. I was not devotional by temperament, but that moment made me surrender to something, I knew not what, something beyond my mind and my ego. Now I remembered that event, and the sound of the bells gradually absorbed the anguish of my heart. In that rhythm of the bells, the anguish was gone, and peace reigned in my mind. Then a musical note, perhaps from a flute, filled the universe, and that certainly was my imagination! The mind has many mansions, and it is impossible to know where one wanders sometimes!

"I see that you are wiping your eyes. Is it because Hema left without a word to us?"

I was startled at Savitri's sharp perception!

"No, it's some particle in the eye...."

"Be truthful. I have been observing you since the morning. You are sad and you cannot hide it."

"Savitri, I can hide nothing, nor can I confess anything to you. The mind is fanciful. It takes me to the Brihadeeswara Temple in Thanjavur, and I keep hearing the bells of the Temple. And then the music of the flute fills the universe. My mind just floated and tears came to my eyes. That is it."

"Then it isn't because of Hema?"

"I cannot say with certainty, what is the cause and what is not. I am in such a state of confusion that I don't know what is real and what is fancy, what is thought and what is feeling, and what can be said and what cannot be said, because it won't make any sense to others. It is a peculiar state, shaking the very foundations of my ideas and opinions. I think it is a kind of escapism, I think it is turning away from the world and its values, I think it is a prelude to the advaitic experience. But I don't know. And I feel anguish because I don't know. I should not call it anguish really. The mind moves beyond its known limits, and it flinches at the freedom and joy it encounters in that movement. Doesn't matter. There is no danger of going mad." I laughed.

"I don't like the way you are. Please get up and get dressed. I came to you just to ask you whether you would accompany me to the Shiva Temple. And you anticipated me saying that bells are ringing in Shiva's Temple. So let us go. You will feel allright."

I was not in the habit of going to the Temple. Savitri always went with Bhavanarayana's family. She had no company now because of the estrangement. She wanted me to go with her. I welcomed it.

When I stood with folded hands before the deity, involuntarily I placed my problem before him silently. I prayed to Him to decide for me the moment of truth, when my disability should be made known to Savitri and how it should be made known. I placed my burden at His feet.

PART IX

In the month of July, my eldest brother fell ill again. Telegraphically both of us, Savitri and myself were asked to go and see him. We went.

He had a heart-attack. He was lying in a private nursing-home in Cuddapah. We were with him for two days and Savitri left for our village. I stayed on for another four days attending on my brother, whose condition was stable.

My brother brought up the issue of my adoping his third son. I tried to avoid the subject, but he was insistent. I could not help saying : "I agree. But you should first get discharged from the nursing-home."

"Did you discuss it with Savitri?" he asked.

"Not yet."

"Then go to the village tomorrow and bring her here. As soon as I am out of the hospital, we could do it."

That night, while serving food, my sister-in-law spoke to me :

"The boy is not a burden to us in any way. Your brother loves you dearly and thinks very high of you. He is proud of you because you have come up through education and you are a lawyer. He wants our little son to emulate you and study well and become a doctor or a lawyer. But he is in poor health and cannot supervise the boy's education. He wants to put him under your care. I totally agree with him. I look upon Savitri as my own dear sister. It is a fact that Padma (my second sister-in-law) and I do not see eye to eye in several matters. That is all because of her temperament. I am helpless and we cannot make it up. But I have no hesitation to put my boy in Savitri's hands. He is yours, bring him up.

"You see, he has been lying seriously ill for the last ten days, his brother came here to look him up, but Padma has not turned up. What crime have I committed that she refuses to visit us? Even if I happen to be the offender, she could have visited your brother in the hospital! I am sure he has not offended her. Is she so breathlessly busy? Her husband says she's busy and unable to come. He is a mouth-piece. She has him tied to the end of her sari and he cannot move freely. I don't know what stories she will tell you and Savitri when you go to her. I trust in God. We haven't done any bad turn to anybody. We don't want to grab others' property. How can brothers forget their bond of love!"

I finished my meal without speaking a word in comment or response.

She resumed her monologue :

"I asked Savitri to stay. She said she would be back again in a day or two. I didn't mention the boy to Savitri. How could I tell her? Is he a load on me? Because of the concern for his education, your brother has come up with this idea of adoption, and even now I don't very much like it. I cannot contradict him especially now, when even the slightest thing might upset him and bring on a crisis. I obey doctor's orders and see to it that every thing goes on according to his wishes. Well, his illness is like that!"

"My brother is in a hurry. But I feel it is unnecessary. Where can we go? All of us are here! If it is a matter of the boy's education, I can keep him with me and educate him. Where is the need for this ritual and process of formal adoption, tell me?"

"He will not find peace. It is all for his satisfaction we are doing it."

Well, in that case I should go through it, I reflected. When I had come to know for certain that I was not going to have children of my own, there was no point in delaying the adoption. I should inform Savitri and get her consent. That was the obvious next step. Without doubt, opposition would come from my second sister-in-law, Padma. She would offer her second son for my adoption. The issue would get complicated. Anticipating it, my first sister-in-law has already cautioned me : "I don't know what stories she will tell you and Savitri." I could take both the boys and keep them with me for some time. That would be one kind of solution. The question of adopting could be postponed and one of the two boys might be chosen at a later date.

With those thoughts running through my mind, I arrived in the village.

I sat talking to my second brother in the front room of his house. He asked me when the eldest brother would be discharged from the nursing-home. Answering his queries, I mentioned the matter of adoption too. My sister-in-law Padma who had arrived meanwhile said :

"Adoption? Don't worry. It won't be necessary. Please get up and have your bath, the water is getting cold." She was smiling.

As I went inside, she followed me.

"Where is Savitri?" I said.

"She is not well. She's resting."

"What's the matter?"

"You can ask her yourself. First have your bath."

When I sat down for lunch she told me.

"She has morning sickness. Giddiness and nausea. Signs of pregnancy."

"No question. Biliousness perhaps. What did she eat?"

"Believe me, it is real. That's why I say that mouths talking of adoption will now shut up. God is kind to you. He will not let you down."

The false symptoms had appeared once or twice some time in the past. There had been reason for hope then. Now I was certain for myself that it was impossible.

Savitri appeared weak with sunken eyes. I was struck by the change within a short span of four days.

"How are you? What is the matter?" I said.

"It must be true this time. Two months are gone. I feel the change in my body too."

A shiver went through my spine. My head reeled.

"How did it happen!" I exclaimed in dismay, sinking back in the chair.

"God's grace."

Women are up to anything! I reflected. She could say that quietly, most naturally, without batting an eyelid. Could anything be done for the sake of motherhood? I controlled myself, but could not make out what she was saying with an air of complacency.

"Let us go to a doctor and find out," I said finally.

I did not want to spend time there. I could not sleep that night. All things that had happened during the past year, our intimacy during the last six months especially her intimacy with the doctor, came up for review. She would never talk freely to men folk; that had been her temperament and training. But she developed an unusual concern for him, and became familiar and intimate though he was no relative. Why did she change in this manner? I had eyes but could not see!

When it had been scientifically established that I was infertile, what was the significance and meaning of Savitri's pregnancy? No need for an explicit comment! God's grace? Is she a second Mary, the virgin mother? Perhaps this unfortunate contingency could have been averted, if I had told her the result of my medical test immediately after it was known! But the story of her relationship dated still further back in time. Even prior to the doctor's sojourn in my house following the death of his mother, he had become a hero to Savitri, in my absence, when he shot the serpent dead, and had given her a brain-wash. A brain-wash indeed! The acquaintance and the attraction started with the injections, and opportunities one after another paved the way to forbidden intimacy! For once Savitri made bold and her overweening desire for motherhood must have swept aside all moral scruples!

They say that the husband is responsible for the conduct of his wife. If not hundred, at least ninety per cent of the responsibility rested with me!

Savitri, Oh, Savitri, is motherhood so important that it is the highest value? At least for taking the name of the legendary heroine, who fought with death for the life of her husband, you should have shown consideration for the feelings of your husband, and desisted!

The doctor was the real cobra, sneaking into my house, striking me, and totally destroying me! What is the way for me?

My eyes brimmed with tears, and I got furious with myself. I hated self-pity. I had to decide on my next step.

We returned to Cuddaph in the morning. I wanted to get Savitri checked by a doctor first, before assuming her guilty of transgression. These may be psychosomatic symptoms. They might mean nothing at all! Only the doctor could ascertain the truth. Hope did not desert me.

When I informed my first sister-in-law that I was taking Savitri to a doctor in view of her condition, there was a clear change in her, and her disappointment showed.

"Oh, yes, certainly. You should make sure. All sorts of false pregnancies occur. We cannot help it. What is written by fate must happen. No one can escape that."

Her words about fate and its inexorable nature meant different things to me. People's desires are born of selfishness, fate is the final arbiter!

The doctor came out after examining Savitri. Savitri tarried inside.

"What are your findings, doctor?"

"You are going to be a father. There is no doubt. Since it is the first time, and it has come a little late, you have to take good care of her."

That was a death sentence on me, and I froze. The future was a blank. An abyss of darkness.

The doctor gave some advice to Savitri and handed a slip of prescriptions to her. Savitri should have a regular check-up, she said.

I paid the doctor's fee and we came on the street.

A rickshaw was sighted. I felt reluctant to sit in it touching Savitri, by her side.

"There's a rickshaw, you may call it," she said.

"No, we'll take a jutka."

We got into a jutka (a horse-drawn light cart) and sat opposite each other with faces turned in opposite directions.

I conveyed the bad news to my first sister-in-law. It was 'bad' news for her too! "We'll go by the morning express," I announced. She raised no objections.

Fortunately my brother was discharged from the hospital that evening. He was not shocked by the news he heara. I thought I had an inkling into his mind. He appeared to have been in a hurry, as he thought I might adopt my second brother's son in view of my close relationship with him. He wanted to preempt such a development. He was apparently satisfied that Savitri was going to be a mother!

"Don't bother to take my boy for education now. Savitri in her present condition cannot manage the house and additionally look after him. I'll arrange for him to go to school here in Cuddapah. You have an eye on him and advise him. Send Savitri to her parents in the fifth month. She will need help." Those were my brother's parting words.

PART X

A week after my return.

My path was not clear. All my education and all my past thinking did not aid me to decide how I should act. The blow had stunned me. My ideal of non-attachment could not give me any reprieve from pain. I felt like a trapped animal.

I was finding it difficult to eat the food prepared by Savitri.

I could not concentrate on my court work. I got the cases adjourned.

Broad-mindedness and humanist liberalism are good to talk about and to preach, but when it concerns oneself, the difficulty and personal pain involved cannot be easily overcome. I kept invoking non-attachment as a mantra, but failed to assume it, not to speak of attaining it.

But I succeeded in overcoming my anger and hatred towards Savitri. The feeling of hurt was centred in my heart. There was no way to overcome that. I became indifferent towards Savitri and thought of her as a robot moving about in the house and doing the daily chores. She no longer related to me. I could not call her by her name. I felt great resistance to speak to her. There was no change in her. At least I was beyond perceiving any.

"Why are you so absent-minded?" she would say. I would not reply.

"You aren't eating. Is it because I am unable to eat? For my sake?" She would laugh. Her brazenness shocked me.

It was amazing that there wasn't the least trace of hesitation or shame, sense of guilt or contrition in her behaviour. Motherhood is not only an instinct, it is valued highly in our culture. But faithfulness to husband, isn't that too valued similarly in our tradition and culture? Didn't Savitri feel guilty at any time? I thought that a moral crisis had already come and gone! The upset and agitation she experienced after the serpent's intrusion, was misunderstood by me. Indeed she did overcome it with the help of her counsellor! I played my own part. She became used from that time onwards to having two men around her. She found she could manage both of us, one for love and the other for parenthood!

Bhavanarayana called on me after a long interval.

He told me that the doctor got a transfer to Kurnool at his own request so that he could be with Hema. There was no reaction from me. He changed the subject. "I have just heard the good news that you are going to be a father. I came to convey my congratulations."

I bent my head down in humiliation. He went on :

"Long ago you narrated to me your dream, a wonderfully significant dream it was, do you recall it? I think my interpretation and prognostication have come true. You said something and did not agree with me. But I have been proved right."

Yes, I remembered. I never suspected that the dream indicated my misfortune. I was proud of my intellectual abilities. I had been a self-conceited fool all along!

"That serpent I saw in the dream really intruded into my home. What do you say for that?" I gave vent to my misery suggestively.

"Oh, there could be a number of consequences relating to the dream, what of it? You were not hurt by the serpent! It rather chose its own death by entering your house." He made light of the matter now. He had raised a hue and cry over it and had roundly blamed us and the doctor.

"You can never guess how much mental agony it caused."

"Well, all that is past now. Only joy remains. How is her health? She must see the gynecologist regularly."

Savitri brought him a cup of coffee.

"You know Hema left without visiting us after the marriage. We had a sari and blouse to give her. They are lying there."

"Doesn't matter. She will be here for the holidays and will call on you. You know everything was in confusion about the time of the wedding. They went to Bangalore and toured several other places before they arrived in Kurnool. And the doctor got his requested posting when he completed the period of leave. That was indeed very lucky. I got the house vacated for him and arranged for the transportation of his things to Kurnool." Bhavanarayana was continuing in the same vein talking about his sister to Savitri. I couldn't stand it. I got up saying I had some work out in the town, and went for a long walk.

I sat in a secluded spot and started reviewing my position, right from the beginning, from that strange dream in which Hema emerged from the peepul tree.

The peepul tree was destroyed by fire. Dharma was dead. A snake entered my home. And the snake showed itself as Hema in the dream. I overcame my desire for Hema and stood by my dharma. This was the punishment that followed. What did Savitri say when she came to know about Hema and myself? Did she not say that she would have me marry Hema? Did she not express her disgust when I spoke about a combined or plural marriage? But she finally adopted the bizarre proposition! One husband for sex and another for progeny!! It might appear to be a rational arrangement, but the heart rejected it. How could I convince my heart? And how could I get the world to approve of it? I was not worried about the world! I wanted a solution to my personal misery. Pique, anger, revenge were absolutely alien to my nature. I could never hurt Savitri!

More than the marriage bond, it was the personal relationship between me and Savitri that had been destroyed. If she had had any love or consideration for me, she would have desisted from the step she had taken. She had felt no sense of responsibility towards me. She wanted to cheat on me! What responsibility could I have now towards her? I couldn't any longer continue a prisoner inside the four walls of that house. And I would have to define my relationship with the child to be born. It would be an unending role-playing and pretence I was not capable of.

Should I not forgive her, and accept her and her baby? Wouldn't that be the liberal, humanist view I had always advocated? Yes, but I had not attained to non-attachment of that level, and I could not assume it without being a hypocrite. If I could attain that level, that would be a different matter. If I could transcend the limits of my present ego, perhaps I would reach that level. I should go out seeking that goal, and return only when that goal was achieved. Till then I should struggle with my loneliness, struggle towards true non-attachment. I would be a traveller and a pilgrim, without an address.

My decision was made....

I prepared for my journey. Perhaps I would never return. I gathered just the few things I needed. Among them were my diary, the Bhagavadgita and a few books by Carl Jung. I drew two thousand cash from the bank and left five hundred in the shelf for Savitri. The bank cheque book would be with me.

"I am leaving for Hyderabad," I said.

"What will you get for me?"

I didn't expect that she would say that!

"What do you like to have?"

"Pearls."

"I'll get them if I can. If I fail, don't be sorry."

"They are definitely available. Only you have to make up your mind."

"Take good care of Raja."

"Do I take instructions from you daily about him?"

"He is your only companion. The doctor has left."

"Raja is a bigger philosopher than you. He won't eat his meal, but would sit meditating in front of the plate."

When I was seated in the train, those words : "Raja is a bigger philosopher" rankled in my mind. Wasn't it sarcasm? Raja was deprived of his masculinity. I was responsible for it. I remembered the day well enough. That was the day when the doctor shot a diseased dog, and Savitri praised him as a practical and courageous man. Raja did not drink milk because his wound hurt him badly. I pitied him. Does the creator feel any compassion for me for depriving me of fertility, I reflected!

Even to spend two days in Hyderabad was a difficult experience. I was all the time starting at my own shadow. I felt reluctant to meet any friend or acquaintance. In the book-shop I picked up a book by the philosopher J. Krishnamurti. I had read his books earlier. I went through this one to search for a solution to my problem. He wants you to observe the play of your mind. Well, I followed his suggestion, staring at my shadow. It brought my pain into sharp focus instead of relieving it. How should one take the quantum jump into non-attachment and peace from the observer's stand-point. He doesn't indicate. Observe and observe. Yea, but nothing happened! Can everyone see as he does? Try and try. How?

What is this "I"? Questioning the "I" is Ramana Maharshi's way. I had done the questioning many a time. Once I had a discussion with the doctor too. I thought I had some clarity then. I had noted it in my diary. I looked it up.

"The experience that the self is separate from the body, to the extent that it is a mental perception, is not the true self-knowledge. It is a certain state of the mind only!...I don't agree that in a state of unconsciousness, there is nothing beside the mind and the body. The soul exists. How does one know it? My body has been punished. My mind at the moment does not know the reason for the punishment. It is not in a position to know right now. But the soul knows it, and that knowledge in due course will be imparted to the mind too. The realm of chance not within the grasp of the mind truly belongs to the soul....When the mind is opened up to the soul and gets attuned to it, then the mind too will receive that knowledge....If you dismiss soul's existence, life will be fragmentary and meaningless."

These words became my guidelines. What chance had brought about, the pain caused by Savitri, had a meaning yet hidden from me! The soul knew and I had to find my soul. I had to attune my mind to its purpose. Then only I could hope for relief.

How should I go about in search of my soul?

I saw in a magazine a write-up about an ashram near Pune, which attracted a number of foreigners too, and the Guru appeared to be a modern thinker and experimenter well-versed in meditation and yoga. I remembered the Swamiji at Nallacheruvu and I remembered Narayana Reddi. I turned back the pages of my diary.

"I asked the Swamiji about the advaitic state of non-dualism, whether I could hope to attain to it in my life. In reply the Swamiji looked at me intently. A wave of joy swept my heart. I thought that was the answer to my question, an unspoken answer communicated directly." Perhaps I could meet a man like the Swamiji in the Guru at Pune!

"Your desire may get fulfilled but not in the way you expect it." That was another thing he had said. I should leave things to their own course. There could be no planning about it. "There is a divinity that shapes our ends, rought hew them how you will" I remembered Shakespeare's words. I decided to leave for Pune immediately.

I was sitting in the Public Gardens. I heard the song of the ash-gray bird. I saw the bird too. How did it come here? Did it follow me?

The same species must be here too! With the change of place and change of mental state, the same song that was a source of joy, brought tears to my eyes. I could no longer sit there!

That song had opened for me doors into a world of beauty and joy. All things beautiful in nature, the sun-sets and sun-rises, the moonlit nights and the trees and flowers had been God's special gifts to me. Today I was an outcast from that paradise. Nothing was mine, and I belonged to no one. I was alone, and pain was my consciousness. The bird's song intensified the sense of loneliness and pain and I wanted to run away from it, far far away from the song.

PART XI

The Guruji's Ashram near Pune was a modern set-up. It was like a Public School. The difference was that the students were all adults and elderly people in search of a meaning for life. Towards the living expenses, each had to contribute according to his economic status. The programme of activities included prayer, meditation, community singing, physical exercise, talks and question answer sessions. There was a wide variety to choose from. The basic principle was that each individual had to choose his own path. One could hold discussions with the Guru in an open session after his talk; or could seek private audience for resolving personal matters. He was not only well-read, but was also an excellent singer.

"What is the way to seek one's true self?" I asked like a novice.

"Get rid of your bonds," he said. Then he explained.

It's not running away from one's responsibilities. One has to free oneself from the artificial bonds created around the body and the mind. That would let the soul emerge in its self-effulgence. The body has many habits, all of them cultivated since childhood, and they imprison the soul. From the kind of food one eats to the manner of eating it, and from simple things like sitting, standing and lying down to the comforts and pleasures the body is accustomed to, one's identity gets involved and fixed. The dissociation of the identity is one way of starting one's journey of self-discovery. Then there are the entanglements of the mind, and the webs woven by one's intellect, which make one a machine or a robot. Mental crisis, grief, depression and things like that result because of identity with the mind-created bonds. Setting oneself free from them is another step, more arduous, gradual and slow. Work on both levels of the body and the mind can start at once and there could be no mechanical time-table or graduated procedure about it. The programme of activities in the Ashram would help, and each one has to choose for himself. The basic rule is that no one is permitted to criticize or find fault with another. No one can dictate to another or try to dominate by devious ways.

I sought private audience with the Guru. I explained my personal problem to him. He said : "This bond which you speak of and the resultant hurt that you feel are both of the mind. There is nothing specially sacred in the wife-husband relationship. All relationships are sacred; or none of them are so. It depends on your stance. You have built a prison round you and you are living in it. So it depends entirely on yourself to come out of it. There are human beings here with a variety of problems. Could you make peace with them and mix with them with all the innocence of childhood? You had it in you when you were a child, and I want you to regain it. When your soul becomes effulgent, free of mind's bonds, you will discover the joy in existence. Then your wife will be seen not as a villain, but a simple woman with a life of her own. And that child will appear as a gift of God. This grief will disappear. Life is a matter of joy. People make it a sorrowful affair."

In the light of what the Guruji said, I reviewed my problem. I did not grieve that the sacredness of marriage had been violated. Savitri destroyed our personal relationship and acted without any consideration for me. Personal relationship is based upon mutual confidence, trust and love. We have in our tradition polyandrous women like Draupadi and Kunti. They are revered. But they did not cheat on their husbands. Savitri could have told me even after the event. I was hurt because she isolated me and abandoned me.

I saw in the Ashram old people dancing, and men and women moving about half-naked or fully naked. There were Westerners as well as Indians. Some times I did feel embarrassed. But I had no right to find fault with anything or any body. I could not give up my loneliness. I could not make friends with anyone in particular. I could not be totally free with others with childhood innocence as the Guru wanted me to be. My contacts were limited to intellectual discussions. After some days I struck up some sort of friendship with an American called Allen. We discussed frequently Marxism and Existentialism.

Marxism could solve through social revolution and reordering of society general problems like distribution of wealth, but how could it solve personal and emotional problems like mine? Whatever might be the future set-up of society, the subjective grievances of the individual would continue to exist. Existentialism recognizes them. It wants man the individual to accept his loneliness. Being alone and being free are the same. Man has to create a meaning for life by living it. I discussed with Allen Sartre's view that Marxism could be married to existentialism.

Allen said : "When you look at the way of life in this community of the Ashram, you will find that Sartre's proposition is eminently practicable. We spend here according to individual means. To the extent we require additional resources for our needs, we are free to take up work and earn...in the community kitchen, in the Ashram office, in gardening, in agriculture and in a wide variety of fields. There is equality among us as individuals. We are able to enjoy individual freedom and lead a joyous existence forming our own personal relationships. There is nothing wanting here."

"The nucleus for this society is the Guru. Without him, would the community go on in the present fashion? What will happen to an individual when he goes out of this charmed circle into the wider arena outside? Will he be able to retain individual freedom and his present joy in simple existence? It is like an air-conditioned room. Till we get out of it, we feel all right. When we finally get out, we feel worse by contrast. Therefore my question is that the freedom and joy experienced here, to what extent are they the individual's permanent achievement and to what extent are they the result of environment."

"The experience of living here liberates the soul, and the individual will get so reoriented that he will be able to go out and face the world. In America, such experiments of group-living, living as new communities, are being carried out in select spots away from civilization. But they are in one way or another reactions to the ills of the machine civilization that has come up. They are sometimes merely reformative of the marriage institution, which has been the cause of a lot of problems with divorced parents and disrupted families, and the young ones adrift without protection or guidance. One may say that those experiments don't go far enough. The quest for freedom and the religious quest for the soul and God-experience have been brought together in the teachings and work of our Guru here," said Allen.

Allen arrived at the Ashram nearly a month after me. For a week he was only a tourist and a guest. Then he plunged into the Ashram life in right earnest. He was working as an assistant in the Library. I was in the Accounts section. I had a room with two cots, and as one fell vacant, it was offered to Allen. He became my roommate. We became personal friends. He listened to my story.

"Because of uxoriousness, the first man Adam fell into a morass and dragged us all into it. Woman doesn't deserve such a high value as to destroy a man. Is there no love, no friendship, no life without woman? What of it? You should turn your mind away from woman," Allen advised me.

One night before getting to sleep, we lay on our respective beds, and were discussing something. The light was off and it was pitch darkness.

"You are extremely intellectual in your approach to life. You are all the time busy processing your thoughts. You should turn to feeling and sensation to become an integrated person. Haven't you read D.H. Lawrence? What you need is sex," said Allen.

"I am fed up with sex," I said.

"Sex with woman, you mean? Sex relationship is the natural culmination of all friendship. Unless you allow yourself to go the whole hog, your cannot be rid of your blasted melancholy. You can never be free and joyous," said Allen. Suddenly jumping on to my bed, he hugged me.

It is a Western habit to strip naked before going to bed. Allen now and then stood before me without anything on. I didn't mind it; nor could I object to it. The Ashram respected individual freedom. But I could not stand Allen falling upon me and thrusting his nakedness on my person.

"I am not gay, please get back," I said and tried to disentangle myself from his grip.

"I know what is good for you, my dear fellow! Just a moment, I'll sure liberate you," Allen continued to struggle with me. I pushed him on the floor, got up and switched on the light.

"You're a damned egoist. You reject love! No salvation for you." Allen was breathing hard and went back to his couch.

My Superior muscle-power had given me the final say. It had been quite a wrestling match.

I met the Guruji next day. I informed him of the previous night's incident and requested him for separate accommodation for me.

"There is some truth in what Allen said. You should not hate him for that."

"I don't hate him. Let him be what he is. But I am not a homosexual, and would like to live separately."

"You understand you have no right to criticize him. You cannot discuss him with others. The question of being wrong never arises; you should get rid of it in your judgment of others."

"Certainly. Non-attachment has been always my attitude. I understand what you mean."

"With non-attachment as a guideline, you cannot achieve freedom and joy. You should not deny and shut yourself to the experience of life. You should change your attitude to positive response. Everything is natural. Invite life as it happens to you."

"I'll try."

I was allotted a small room. It had no attached bathroom. I had to share the common bathroom at the end of half-dozen rooms like mine. Among my neighbours were both men and women. Amrita, my next door neighbour was a Punjabi woman. Unlike the other Punjabi women, who usually wear pyjamas, she wore a sari. She had her three-year old son with her. She worked as a typist in my section. She told me she was there for good and will spend her entire life there. She was an M.A. and had earlier worked as lecturer in a College. She told me she was planning a book on the Guruji and his teachings from her personal experiences in the Ashram.

When she was a post-graduate student, Amrita fell in love with her lecturer Hardayal Singh. For one long year they exchanged endearments and letters filled with fanciful poetry and sweet promises. Their romantic love ended in marriage. Amrita found her dream gone. There was deep dissatisfaction in her sexual relationship with Hardayal. Physically their needs were incompatible. She was pregnant before the first year of the marriage was over. The birth of a son only widened the gulf between husband and wife. Amrita got employment as college lecturer, and made new friends. Anil Kumar, a colleague, became her lover. A fight ensued between her and her husband on one side and their families on another side. Amrita's family being tradition-bound blamed Amrita and asked her to obey her husband implicitly. She lost her job. She couldn't bear being a slave in her husband's house. Amrita's father was dead, but he had left some money and property in her name. She arrived in the Guruji's ashram to live an independent life.

I found Amrita fearless, straight forward and open-minded. She never appeared self-righteous when she spoke to me about her personal affairs, especially about her differences with her husband. I found her totally attached to her little son.

"To a woman her child is more important than her husband, is n't that true?" I queried.

"It is not like that," she replied, "Before marriage, I loved Hardayal absolutely. When the physical incompatibility came up between us, I expected him to have the courage to accept the reality and consider the problem honestly to arrive at a proper solution. He refused to do so. What happened to his professed love? Neither would he try to understand me, nor show me the least consideration as an individual with a right to exist. He was incredibly mean. Bereft of personal generosity, consideration and understanding, what do love and marriage mean? He called me a concupiscent devil incarnate! If only he had some pity for my weakness, what he characterized as my animality, I would have managed to stay on. I could perhaps have put a rein on my sensuality. Instead he provoked me, he broke my heart and made me hate him bitterly. I was his enemy and he drove me away."

"How did you find peace here? What have you gained?"

"Well, soon after my arrival, I found a friend and companion here. I had uninhibited sex. I enjoyed my freedom for full one year, doing or not doing, just as I willed. There is no criticism implicit or explicit in the Ashram. Now I have lost interest in sex. I have no special relationship with any individual here. Indeed as a human being I am related to one and all, but with no one in particular. There's a lot to be perceived, felt and understood in life and in nature, whose children we are. Sex is not the only meaning for life. By repressing it, institutionalizing it, society has given it undue importance and has made it attractive and fascinating. It is just an instinctive drive like others. And sex without love is transient and meaningless."

"Didn't you love that friend and companion, whom you found here on your arrival?"

"No. He lives with another woman now."

"And you don't feel jealous?"

Amrita laughed. She seemed to pity my ignorance.

"Why jealousy? No such problem arises, when one arrives at a true understanding of sex."

I could now grasp the basic principle on which the Ashram was run. The principle was freedom for the individual. Any traditional custom, practice and belief, which put pressure on the individual in society became inoperative, and hence there was no cope for mental distortions like jealousy, envy, possessiveness and acquisitiveness.

Reflecting on Amrita's past and her present, I could discover in myself mental attitudes and reactions, which were derived from the social set-up to which I belonged. When the wife is looked upon as a possession, her sexual affair outside marriage comes under theft of property, a shameful dispossession for the husband. When a sexual relationship is considered private and sacred, its loss of character brings on fear and the sense of sacrilege. It is mental suffering consequent on certain assumptions and beliefs. If the wife is looked upon as an individual, a person with freedom to judge and act, one has to respect her actions and give consideration to her feelings. If sex is accepted as a natural instinct without social and other taboos, jealousy and associated anguish disappear. If true love and not sex happens to be the basis for marriage, the husband and the wife will arrive at mutual understanding and respect. When there is trust between them, any problem can be solved. Absence of trust broke up Amrita's marriage. It is Savitri's dishonesty that has hurt me. If only Savitri could make a clean breast of the whole thing, I could have condoned her act. I think I loved her enough for that. But do I love her enough to accept the coming child? I can give no assurance to myself about that....

Amrita's son, Anand got used to me, and frequently gave me his company. I allowed him free access into my room. I started observing him in his activities, and gradually became a partner in his play. Early in the morning Amrita would go to the meditation hall and ask me to look after Anand when he woke up. Because he was entrusted to me, she wouldn't be in a hurry to return. I heat up the milk for him and I make my coffee. Then Anand fully engages me, till Amrita returns. Days slip by.

PART XII

Three months. I had written to Savitri and my brothers that I was on a tour of Northern India and I could have no definite address. I put in only three hours of work in the accounts section of the Ashram earning thereby two hundred rupees a month. That and another two hundred drawn from my bank sufficed for my maintenance at the Ashram.

I was bed-ridden for a week with 'flu. Amrita looked after me. She was constantly by my bed-side. Anand now attended the kindergarten school run by the Ashram.

One night after I had recovered from my illness, we sat and discussed things in general. Anand was asleep. Amrita said : "You are wilting for want of sex. If you want to get out of your depression and sluggishness, you need sex. There's no better tonic."

I laughed and said : "Even if I need it for health reasons, whom could I approach? That would be an endeavour. And I should be ready for a special relationship with someone. I don't want all that."

"Well, I arranged everything during your illness. I could offer this now. I like you. There is no special relationship between us, nothing binding. Sex will not alter that position. You should first give up your fear of bondage. You should think and live in freedom."

"Do you mean that I should act on impulse? Shouldn't there be no restraint?"

"Why restraint? When any natural tendency becomes a mechanical habit and deteriorates into a vice, then restraint is necessary. That kind of corruption of instinctive drives arises because of the repression society imposes. No restraint is necessary when one is spontaneous and natural in the act of living."

"What do you think is the distinction between man and animal?"

"Man doesn't know as well as an animal the way of living naturally. Man creates his own sorrows. That is unfortunate."

"Is there no other meaning or purpose for life except living according to instinctive drives?"

"No. To think otherwise and go on a wild-goose-chase is man's misfortune. That is a burden imposed on man by the civilization created by him in the past. To achieve harmonious group-living, the kind of which we find here in the Ashram, will be the wisest goal for humanity. When men get to that point there will be no problems. Man certainly is an animal. He should live according to his nature."

"I don't agree with you. True I have no problems here. But there is some dissatisfaction, some kind of a quest in me. I cannot spell it out, but it is there, I assure you."

"The suppression of your natural drives is at the root of your dissatisfaction. It is n't a casual observation I made that you need sex. Your refusal to recognize that need is the cause of your dissatisfaction."

"When I don't feel like it, why should I indulge in sex?"

There was no further discussion. Amrita did not behave like another Allen. She was not only unselfish, but also specially considerate and affectionate towards me. She was a charming friend. Just as she had served me food during my illness, she had now offered to serve me sex too for the sake of my health!

I gave repeated thought to one observation made by Amrita. How is man superior to the animal? Does his superiority lie in creating for himself problems and sufferings beyond those created by nature? He is clever enough to protect himself from natural ills and may have done better than the animal. He has separated his mental consciousness from his perception and is capable of conceptual thinking. The animal hasn't developed similarly. But man has converted his concepts into binding laws and has forfeited his freedom. All his misery is because of the self-created bonds, says Amrita. The Ashram asks men and women to overcome their mental bondage.

Nevertheless I did not succeed in forgetting myself and merging in the life of the Ashram, as Amrita was able to do. I felt no restraints. I had no reservations. I told myself I was free. But like a bird with a broken wing, I found myself unable to fly into the realm of happiness. Who would mend my wing, and enable me to fly?

I had recollections of 'happiness'. The happiness I once derived in the presence of Hema. The happiness I felt in the song of the ash-grey bird. The happiness that filled me when I heard the bells ringing in the Brihadeeswara Temple. That unpremeditated bliss, how could I get back? My quest was for that, my waiting was for that.

Meaning of life is not to be found in words, in philosophy or in specified values. It is bliss unrelated to the intellect. At the animal level one may live according to one's instinctive drives without any conceptual inhibitions, but such gratification of the instincts cannot be identified with the bliss I have been seeking. It is an awareness special to man, and its presence alone can elevate the pleasure of the senses to bliss. That awareness I had known and hence my quest for it. Its coming, like that of the ash-grey bird, I could neither will nor predict. I should become THAT.

I arrived at a theory. At the animal level the world and mind are one. At the human level they have become separate. Man's evolution lies towards separating the self from the mind. That self is bliss. That was my quest.

I mentioned this to Amrita one day.

"I don't worry about that. This life gives me satisfaction. I cannot imagine happiness or bliss beyond this. You might be indulging in fancy, aspiring for a non-existent thing and perpetuating your discontent, which may be intellectual in character," she said.

"Why do you go to the Meditation Hall every morning?"

"Meditation makes my mind calm and radiant. Its influence lasts through the day. It is analogous to physical exercise, I believe." After a pause she said : "There's another reason too. It happened some time ago, before you arrived in the Ashram. A woman lost her child. The child died of a sudden illness. She couldn't bear the grief. Then she left the Ashram. Since then I was besieged by the fear that a similar thing could befall me. I lost my peace of mind and sought the advice of Guruji. He asked me to meditate. When I said I didn't believe in God, he asked me to sit and meditate on whatever image or object I liked to contemplate. I meditate on Guruji himself."

"I think that the centre of your bliss is Anand."

"I prefer to say that my bliss is in living."

"If the centre is life, then Anand need not be so important as to arouse your feeling of insecurity. Your life has a centre and that is Anand. Without that beacon light, you will be lost in darkness...."

"I think you exaggerate. It is natural for a mother to love her child. If anything happens to the child, naturally the mother is unhappy. But I think life asserts itself and grief is overcome gradually."

"No, life will not be normal again. Not in your case. You thought that you loved your husband. But he failed to become the centre of your life. If he had become that, you could not have found peace here. Your son is the centre of your life and he is with you. Therefore you have discovered the joy in living. If he didn't have that central place in your existence, you wouldn't have been besieged by the fear of his loss."

"I dislike this kind of theorizing. I don't agree with you. And there's no need for theories to live."

"It is not idle theorizing. It is a part of my quest. I compare myself with you. I came here because I was disappointed in Savitri. Just like you. But I am not reconciled to life. As far as I know, consciously I have shed all my attachments. I have no reservations, and I consider myself free, but I am not able to merge totally in the experience of day to day living without asking questions or feeling inadequate inwardly. I attribute this to the importance Savitri has assumed in my life, all unknown to myself. There is no change in me even after four months."

"Your thoughts and theories bedevil you. Stop this intellectual activity."

Perhaps Amrita is right.

How could I stop thinking?

I first gave up reading books. After my work in the Accounts Section, I started spending the afternoons gardening. Then I entered the kitchen too to do odd jobs in the evening. I supplemented my earnings by a hundred rupees.

I gave up reading in the nights. Through the day I read only the newspaper.

I received a letter one day. It was from Nieland, a Dutchman, who had spent two weeks at the Ashram. He had discussed many things with me. He went to Calcutta. He wrote to say that he met a holy man by name Amiya Baba there. A householder with no Ashram. According to Nieland the Baba was a remarkable man and I should not miss seeing him. He wanted me to go there immediately while he, Nieland was still in Calcutta.

I wasn't enthused. Nieland talked of miracles the Baba could perform, but I was not interested in them as they did not relate to my problem. But Nieland also wrote : "He can fill you with happiness by a mere touch. I haven't found another like him in my extensive tour of India. Because of my discussions with you, I feel obliged to invite you here. Please do come."

One night Amrita suffered from a severe stomach-ache. She woke me up and asked me to call in the doctor. I brought a doctor who was a personal acquaintance in the Ashram. He declared that it was a case of appendicitis, and Amrita should be rushed to the hospital in town.

In another hour, Amrita was on her way to the hospital in the Ashram Van. She entrusted Anand to me, and asked me to get him to the hospital the next morning. The doctor who had examined her, and one Mr. Deshpande deputed by the Ashram Secretary accompanied Amrita.

At ten o'clock next morning, I went to the city hospital taking Anand with me to see this mother. The Ashram doctor met me and said : "I sent Mr. Despande at nine o'clock to give you the message. He didn't meet you?"

"What message?"

"Everything is over. Amrita is no more."

For a moment I was blinded with shock. I hugged Anand close to my heart. The doctor explained at length about complications, and about hemorrhage that could not be stopped, but my mind was fixed on Amrita's living image and the incredibility and enormity of her death.

The Ashram Secretary sent a telegram to her brother in Punjab. The Guruji arranged for the funeral at a spot close by and was present at the cremation. Amrita's mother and brother arrived by plane in time for the cremation.

The problem was Anand. He was with me. He could hardly recognize his grandmother or uncle. He refused to accompany them home, when they invited him. The Guruji showed them a document written by Amrita and addressed to the Ashram authorities. If anything were to happen to her, Anand should remain under the guardianship of the Guruji in the Ashram itself. That was her wish. When Amrita's mother and brother asked for the custody of the child, the Guruji suggested as a compromise that the boy should remain in the Ashram till he attained majority, and then he could decide to join his relatives.

Amrita's relatives left without taking Anand.

For the sake of Anand I decided to stay on indefinitely, giving up my proposed trip to Calcutta. Amrita had left a strange gift behind and had incidentally bound me to the Ashram.

Two weeks later, the Guruji received a lawyer-notice from Hardayal, Amrita's husband. He demanded the custody of his son, as he was legally entitled to it. He declared that Amrita had no right to give away Anand for adoption by the Ashram or the Guruji. As Amrita had never legally separated from her husband, the husband's claim was valid and had to be conceded.

A week later, when Hardayal arrived to take custody of the child, I tried to persuade him to leave the boy in the Ashram for some time and by frequent visits establish a relationship with the boy, before removing him from a place where he was happy and familiar. Hardayal rudely brushed me aside.

It was strange, I thought, that we were all helpless witnesses and could not ward off the attack by society, when Anand was wrenched away from us by his insensitive father.

PART XIII

Why did it happen?

Was there any meaning to Amrita's sudden demise? Why should the innocent child Anand suddenly be banished to a strange place to live among strangers who would have neither sympathy nor affection for him? Why should Hardayal behave heartlessly towards the child? These and other questions troubled me.

To Amrita's life and its abrupt end, which suddenly threw Anand into hell, there was no rationale, no meaningful justification of any kind, philosophical, ethical or artistic. As the existentialists say we live in an absurd world. The theories, meanings and justifications we arrive at from time to time cannot make us comprehend life. Meaning or purpose has to be sought in the realm of awareness which lies beyond the mind, and it is unconditioned bliss. I had come to this conclusion long ago. My stay in the Ashram had not been fruitful in attaining that goal.

I read Nieland's latter again. Nieland must have returned to his country by now. I had Amiya Baba's address. I decided to go to Calcutta.

I drew a thousand rupees from my reserves at home. After my Calcutta visit, whether I succeeded in my search or not, I firmly decided to go back home and face the situation. I compared myself with Hardayal and wondered whether I had not been stupid in running away from home! Association with Amrita and understanding of her personality and view-point, made me shed all sexual jealousy. But it did not automatically open up my heart to the bliss of living. I was a prisoner of melancholy. But observing the sorrow of humanity and the absurdities that made individual lives chaotic, I found my personal predicament a very small one. If sorrow is an inevitable concomitant to life, it is better I accept it without questioning. It is proper that I should go back to the allotted slot in life's set-up. If there is no escape from sorrow, better I go back and accept it living among my people and not away from them. Having arrived at that decision, I left for Calcutta as a last stop before returning home.

It was evening. Amiya Baba sat on a cot in his home in South Calcutta. The room was bare but for a carpet spread before the cot. About twenty men were seated on the carpet. There was no Bhajan or religious discussion or any talk by the Baba. He wore a loose, white shirt with sleeves upto the elbow. There was no religious or sectarian mark on his forehead. He was smoking a cigarette. It was a strange situation, contrary to my expectations. I entered and sat in a corner. As I entered, my eyes were met by Baba's. Obviously he gave me silent permission to enter.

After more than helf-an-hour, a middle-aged person approached me and spoke in a low tone : "Where do you come from?" I told him about Nieland's letter and told him I had arrived from Pune. He nodded in acknowledgment.

To some people Baba spoke privately for a few minutes. Some others simply bowed to him and left. He was touching the heads of some apparently blessing them, and touched the chins of some others in a gesture of affection, and to the rest he simply nodded and bid farewell.

After a while every one was gone. I stood alone in a corner. Baba beckoned to me. He took me into an inner room. He sat on a chair, and I sat at his feet. With half-closed eyes, he was meditative for a few minutes. Then he asked me to unbutton my shirt and he touched my chest near the heart. I shivered slightly. I felt an electric current vibrate through my spinal column. Removing his hand, he spoke to the middle aged man, Gopal, who had earlier greeted me in the hall. Baba asked him to fetch tea and biscuits for me.

Gradually a cool happiness spread over me and my mind was peaceful and receptive. I felt a new strength flowing in my nerves. As I sipped the tea, it was Gopal who engaged me in conversation, asking me about myself. I told him my address, my acquaintance with Neiland at the Pune Ashram, and how he had written me about Baba from Calcutta. Baba said something in the Bengali language to Gopal. And Gopal turned to me with a smile : "You have got what you wanted. Would you go back to your home now? Baba wants to know."

I was surprised.

I said : "Yes, you have put me in happiness. This bliss is your gift. Can I retain it as my own? What is the way for it? Till I know the way, I wouldn't like to return home."

Baba stood up. He asked me to see him the next day. Gopal added : "Eight o'clock in the morning."

I returned to my hotel-room. I didn't know how to spend time. The happy serenity that Baba's touch had imparted to me remained as a blessing. I sat at the window and became a passive observer of the city which lay before me with its buildings, streets and the afternoon din.

I looked into myself. I tried to understand the nature of the happiness Baba had bestowed upon me with a mere touch. There was nothing to think about. Bliss was rising in waves in my heart for no identifiable reason. I would discuss it with Baba. I had a sound sleep.

I was at Baba's place by eight in the morning.

The cot in the front room was vacant. Gopal greeted me and took me inside the house. Baba was wearing a silk dhoti. He was bare above the waist. There was no upper-cloth on his shoulders. He took me into the meditation room. He sat in the lotus-posture on a deer-skin and asked me to sit facing him in the same posture. I was asked to close my eyes. A few moments later, I heard him whisper close to my right ear one of the well-known names of God. I opened my eyes and found the Baba seated as before. He had not stirred, but I had felt his presence close to my ear, when he uttered the name of God. He asked me to repeat and silently meditate on the mantra, the God's name he had given me. I went into meditation and just forgot myself.

I was not aware how much time had passed, but when I opened my eyes again, it was at the gentle touch of Baba on my shoulder. When I emerged from the room into the hall, Gopal brought tea for me and Baba.

"You have to silently repeat and meditate on the mantra both in the morning and the evening. You may visit me in the morning. You needn't come in the evening," said Baba in Hindi.

I was eager to discuss with him my experience, and the nature of meditation and other usual things. He held up his hand asking me to stop all queries. There was a frown on his face.

"Don't analyze, don't question. There's nothing to understand with the intellect. Through meditation surrender yourself to the mantra and to the silence beyond. Don't try to hold the mind, and don't allow yourself to run after the thoughts that may arise. Be an observer and hold on to the mantra as the rallying point. The mantra is the path and the goal. The mantra is your true self. Your surrender is to the mantra and not to me. I am a brother to hold your hand till you are on your own. Everything will become known to you in its time. Don't be in a hurry to find out with the intellect, as the intellect cannot serve you in the least in this matter."

Visitors started coming in by nine o'clock. I sat in a corner. I saw Baba take the right hand of one old man into both his hands and close the old man's fingers into a fist, and then Baba said : "Give this ring to your son and ask him to wear it. He will be all right." It was about the illness of the old man's son. The ring just materialized in the empty fist closed by the Baba. The man bowed and touched Baba's feet in reverence and gratitude.

The flowers, fruits and other gifts brought in by the visitors were distributed in no time to the others, as they took leave and left.

I returned to my hotel-room by ten-thirty.

I didn't know how long I would be required to stay in Calcutta. I thought of finding a room or lodge for my stay in the vicinity of Baba's residence. Postponing that to the next day, I roamed the streets of the city aimlessly, becoming a simple observer abandoning all trends of thinking.

The crowds, the traffic noise and the scattered garbage – there was nothing to enthuse or delight about Calcutta. Many of the buildings dating back to the heyday of the Raj remained without paint or repair and gave the city the look of decay and old age. The places I walked round were all in that condition, but nothing I saw affected me. The unconditioned joy prevailed within me.

The next day I went to see the Baba punctually, sat with him and meditated as guided by him. Gopal said : "There is a personal friend of Baba's living in the next street. We have arranged for you to stay in a room in his house. You may take your food here at ten-thirty after your visit to Baba, and you make your own arrangements for the evening meal."

I expressed my grateful thanks for the arrangements made. Taking leave of Baba after that morning session, I said : "I don't know how I deserve all this kindness from you...." Immediately Baba touched me on my chin and said : "You are my son! But no questions" He said it in English.

Some days later Gopal said to me : "Baba treats each one according to his needs. He alone can perceive the samskaras of a person's previous births and his grace flows accordingly. He might initiate a man into meditation, but the privilege of sitting with Baba everyday for a period of time is a privilege rarely conferred. You are very fortunate."

When people congregate in the morning, sometimes Baba speaks on the Vedanta. The phenomenal world is not an illusion. It is play. Instead of renunciation Baba preaches love and aesthetic enjoyment. He preaches surrender to he unnamed Beyond, the One without a second. He dislikes institutionalizing man's religious quest. Individuals in real need arrive of their own accord at the right place at the right time. About these matters, Baba said that everything was predestined and predetermined. He did not conceive of any special mission in this regard.

After I took up residence in the next street, I spent most of my time in Baba's place. In the evenings I used to meditate in my own room. When I sat with Baba for meditation in the mornings, I was able to get into a state of mind, which was absolute peace, in which I forgot my identity. It might be called 'samadhi'. But Baba refused to discuss it or name it. In the evenings when I was on my own, my experience was different. I would become a keen observer of my mind. They were not thoughts, but memories of long ago : swimming in the village pond when I was twelve; getting fully drenched in rain while returning home from school; lying in the open on a moon-lit night and sailing with the clouds; fixing attention on a tree while travelling in a bus and observing the bird on its flight when it took off from the tree; many other things like that would flit before me, things that set my mind free even as a boy. Sometimes, adult memories of recent years also intervened. The vociferous arguments of my opposite pleader in the court; vivid scenes from stage-dramas enacted on the occasion of College Anniversaries; and the faces of old classmates or of certain beautiful women not acquainted with me but seen briefly and remembered for no reason at all. I stopped categorizing, questioning and analyzing, but allowed my mind to indulge freely in perceptive type of memories.

A month passed. Even during ordinary moments of my waking consciousness I was automatically rallying to the mantra and remembering it, in whatever business I might be engaged. This was a natural development and it helped me to treat the observed world as a mental picture or appearance on a screen. Actually for the great part of our waking moments, we don't need to think or speculate or enquire; in moments like travelling in a bus, or taking one's bath, or standing in a queue. But generally we do think, speculate on some problem, or worry about developments that would possibly come up at a future date; or regret some past happenings, beyond remedy. And this constant thinking and worrying saps mind's energies and increases life's burden many fold. I was never the worrying type. But I was fond of constructing theories about every blessed thing and I tended to probe the why and wherefore of every happening. Life doesn't require all this theorizing. When intellectual activity is put under restraint, feeling and sensation have a better play and life is experienced differently, in fact joyously. This wonder and joy presented by life, children have the capacity to experience, but adults lose it.

In the second month, I was able to attain the state of samadhi by myself in the evenings, which I earlier got only in the company of Baba. I espied a glow in my heart-centre, and later it become a circle of light around me, and I was in its centre as well as in its circumference, and then I would forget myself. It was absolute peace. The peaceful bliss thus became a steady ground for my mental consciousness.

Around this time, one day a young man called Kshitish Roy came to see Baba. Those were days when East Bengal went through a revolution to get rid of the yoke of Pakistan. Bangladesh was yet to be. Refugees in large numbers from East Bengal arrived in West Bengal and Calcutta was flooded with them. The Indian government was organizing camps to shelter and feed them.

"When people are getting killed, and atrocities mount, what is it you are doing? Preaching religion, meditation, love? You don't seem to belong to the present world; you are indifferent to the suffering around you. Don't you feel any responsibility to mankind, being a realized person?" Kshitish Roy put it straight to Baba.

"I see that," said Baba.

"What do you see? Newspapers? How can you understand or feel how bad things are? I am coming straight from there. In the situation, no man can sit with folded hands. I've come to Calcutta to wake up people like you," said Kshitish.

"Very good! Come here, you can see what I am seeing," said Baba and took Kshitish inside. We sat expectantly. Ten minutes later they returned to the hall.

Kshitish prostrated before Baba's feet.

"Tell them what you have seen," said Baba.

"Yes, I saw the refugee camp, which I left yesterday; I saw what's happening there at this very moment. Baba has shown me various other places too inside Bangladesh. There's nothing hidden to his eye. He has the power to see and to show it to others like me. Touching my eyes and my heart, he gave me the wonderful capacity to see. Baba so divinely endowed can do something for this suffering humanity. He can alleviate human suffering, if he wills. I pray to him to show mercy and love."

"I am an individual like you, Kshitish! What can I do, which you cannot do? Love, compassion, prayer to God, service, the man is capable of; but man cannot change or order the course of history. To think otherwise would be sheer arrogance and futile egotism. For the Bangla people all nights will not be nights of darkness. History will take a turn soon."

I had already observed Baba rejecting appellations like Bhagavan (God) and making it clear to his visitors that he was only an ordinary man but devoted to God. "When I live with this body and use this ego to live among men, how can I be called Bhagavan? God is there for all who want Him, who desire Him intensely and sincerely. I live to assure my fellow-men of that truth."

Turning to me and to a few others gathered there, Baba said : "Why don't you people go with Kshitish to alleviate the sufferings of those who need help? That is the purpose of his coming here. May be, something requires to be done by you, and that is His will."

Accordingly myself and four others volunteered to go and work in the refugee camps.

PART XIV

There was fear and despair in their eyes. They had run away from their homesteads leaving everything behind except the bare necessities they could gather in their hands, and their concern had been just to keep themselves alive. Humanity presented itself in a strange, unreal spectacle for me. I failed to respond emotionally. Neither grief, nor pity nor revulsion was there, and no reflective thought, political or social or historical. I had in me nothing but serene compassion for what I saw. This was certainly a change I discerned in myself.

The members of such families as had been victims of killings, kidnaps or rapes kept their sorrows to themselves and did not discuss them at length. The youngmen of those families had not run away as refugees; most of them remained to fight the war. A few boys had come as escorts to their aged or disabled parents. There might be a few cowards too, but it was difficult to locate them.

We the volunteers were engaged in the organization of the camp, and entrusted with distribution of food, maintenance of hygiene, distribution of medical aid and such other duties. There was enough work to do round the clock.

During moments of rest, mostly in the nights, I looked into myself and was surprised by the transformation within me. My mind was serene and alert, but no emotion or mood lingered there. This had never been so in my earlier life; I used to revel in some mood or other. Perhaps this should be called true detachment, not the kind of conscious striving for it, which used to be my second nature in the old days. And I did my routine work steadily unperturbed by minor irritants. I attributed the change in me to Baba's grace and guidance.

One night an idea came to me : I knew all about the refugees, but only intellectually, and I was not emotionally touched. But if I had been one of them, and had suffered as one of them, how would I have felt that experience? Didn't advaita mean identification with the experience of another living being? What would it mean to understand another human being through identification? I strongly willed to know what it would be like.

That night when I slipped into sleep, I had a dream. I saw Savitri lying on a cot. She was sick and emaciated. As I stood by her side, she opened her eyes as though aware of my presence, and looked steadily into my eyes. A feeling of weakness and insecurity entered me with that look of hers. Then there was no Savitri, she had disappeared. An infant looked into my eyes instead. My heart was overwhelmed with grief and I started crying unable to contain myself. Someone was telling me in gentle tones : "Savitri, don't cry, please don't...." I awoke full of grief and found myself enveloped in darkness lying on my back in my cot. For a few moments I did not know whether I was Savitri or my own self different from Savitri....

Savitri and the infant. That grief was undoubtedly Savitri's. I experienced it as my own. Then Savitri must be stricken with grief at the moment. She should have given birth to her child. Was she lying ill? It was long since I had left my home, and had not given thought to it for a good many days....

I went into meditation with my mantra. My mind became serene. I felt convinced that I had travelled bodiless to Savitri and had seen her and felt her. And the infant was a boy. A point of verifiable information.

The quality of advaitic realization is not entrance into another person's egoistic self. Serenity, detachment and freedom characterize that state, a state bestowed upon me by Baba. But it seemed possible that one could by an act of the will enter another person's mind and perceive its state. I had done that in the case of Savitri. I could now dimly surmise how it had been possible for Baba to bestow bliss upon me with a touch, and upon Kshitish the vision of suffering Bangladeshis.

A week later I was taken ill, as indicated in the dream. The dream experience evidently had a manifold meaning, whose complexity could not be interpreted or formulated at one level. That is where the intellect fails. The doctors declared it to be typhoid. I was shifted into a medical camp as an inpatient.

One night I woke up with enormous thirst. I couldn't get up by myself. I didn't know what to do. I could see other beds around, and it was not a dream state by any means. Then some one called me. I turned my eyes round. I saw Baba offering me a glass of gruel, holding it near my lips. No questions about his presence there at the moment arose in my head. I drank it and drifted into sleep. The next morning I remembered the event and wondered whether Baba had really visited me during the night. Those whom I asked said they had no knowledge.

The two experiences mentioned above could not be described as dreams. They gave me a deep insight into the nature of mind and consciousness. An individual is a moulded consciousness, moulded by the circumstances of birth, growth and environment, and these limits could be transcended. These limits constitute the ego, and the transcendence of the ego by releasing the consciousness from its trauma can widen the perceptions of the individual's mind. Perhaps that released consciousness is called the Self, or the Atman. The possibilities at the level of the Self, their nature and limits it was not easy to speculate. The glimpses I had by rising to that higher or wider level of consciousness, I attributed to Baba's grace.

The fever left me after that night of Baba's visit. Whether it was the result of medical treatment I had undergone or Baba's healing powers, it is futile to discuss. Both worked towards my recovery. Kshitish came to see me and arranged for my return to Calcutta.

"The gruel so kindly administered by you saved me," I said.

Baba smiled and said : "Would you not like to go back to your home? Your wife might be waiting for you."

"Well, by your grace I had been there and I saw her."

"It isn't enough that you saw her, should she not see you?"

"I don't think she considers it important to see me. Does she really need me?"

"Is that so? Do you really believe it?" Baba gave me a searching look.

I remembered my dream-visit to Savitri and I was again overcome with grief. Tears filled my eyes and I wept. Baba sat silent like a rock. Then I told him the story of my leaving home and the sense of betrayal that had kept me away from home. "If you ask me to go, I'll go," I said.

"Go" said he, and then after a moment's pause looked searchingly into my eyes and remarked : "Did you ever consider whether the fault was with her, or yourself, or with science or scientific testing or some circumstance or other? How are you certain that she is at fault?"

I bowed my head in humility. I said I would get myself tested again. I did so the next day in a Calcutta laboratory. It was great surprise. I was declared normal. I was after all fertile! Was this what is meant by God's play? The mercy of rain follows the appearance of the dark cloud. Without the cloud there could be no rain. And the cloud was His grace too!

I asked the Laboratory man the possible reason for a different result when I tested myself on the previous occasion. "There can be umpteen reasons for the test to yield wrong results. The test-sample may have been misplaced, or anything could happen in the process of testing, say owing to negligence."

I reported it to Baba. He said "Forget it. Never try to go into things long past. Live in the present."

The external world and the mind reflect one another. The observed and the observer are one. The ego intervenes. It is the ego that distorts the image of the world. A man's life reflects his own mind, and he is totally responsible. Responsible even for events which are apparently not in his control.

Advaita once experienced would continue to afford glimpses of truth, and under its influence, the ego becomes a mere curtain to be pushed aside at one's will to be face to face with reality.

I had been friendly with my neighbour Dr. Veerabhadra Rao. I was attracted to him because he was intellectually stimulating. Then I consulted him professionally. I was jealous of him as a friend of the family. A seed of falsehood grew into a tree and it broke through the walls of my ego-house, levelled my home, and in the process liberated my consciousness into the freedom of advaita. All this was divine play and divine grace. Whatever might have been the agony and the grief caused to me, there was a driving force from the beginning, the divinity that showed light at the end of the tunnel. I bowed to Baba as an incarnate divinity and took leave of him to return home.

The baby smiles. At me. At the world.

Savitri is happy. I brought her pearls on my way back.

Gopi comes with a white poodle.

"Uncle, would you care to adopt it?"

"Why do you ask?"

"After your experience with Raja, I thought you wouldn't. Now that you have a baby too."

Raja died when I was away. Memories of Raja and the pariah dog, which was shot dead under the peepul tree rush back.

"Where is this poodle from?"

"A friend of father's sent him two. We offer you one."

"Go and ask your auntie."

Gopi goes inside.

The peepul tree has flourished. Sometime ago, a few branches were cut by vandals. The tree has put forth new ones.

Savitri comes out with the poodle, and says :

"Gopi says that Hema and Veerabhadra Rao are expected here for the New Year's Day."

"What is special about it?"

"You know they never visited these people after the marriage. Recently the promised money has been paid and the old scores have been settled, says Gopi."

"So the revolutionary after all extracted his marriage dues!"

"Would you have given them up?"

"I would have gone to court."

"Well, he is only a doctor. He showed his displeasure by refusing to visit them."

"That is something. He didn't shoot them down, as he did the pariah dog."

"Your sense of humour doesn't amuse me."

Well, it is like old times!

Veerabhadra Rao arrives and duly calls on us. He appears to have gained weight since I last saw him.

"What happened to the revolution? Are you still preparing for it?"

"Internationally the opportunity was lost. When India interfered in the Bangladesh affair, China should have come to the aid of Pakistan. And Pakistan failed miserably to fill the bill. Not only was an opportunity lost, but the leftists here received a big blow."

"Leave alone international politics. I thought you spoke to me in those days about the individual's preparation for revolution. I want to hear about that."

Veerabhadra Rao laughs. "Yeah, that is the only thing left now. I am writing a book. It is entitled : *The Frontiers of Human Experience*. You will find in it some of the ideas discussed with you further developed and explained. Materialists so called are not true materialists, because they take matter as an intellectual concept and go along with science and scientific reasoning applying the same methodology to human relationships. And where has science ended? In uncertainty principle? I take sensation as basic experience, and showing feeling and thought as its modifications, and analysing sex to sadism as belonging to the spectrum ranging from pleasure to pain, establish human identity materialistically for the reconstruction or revolution one may envisage in the society to come."

"Why do you take sensation or touch as the base of human experience?"

"Because that is true materialism. Matter is not absolute and science has already gone beyond that concept. Matter can be absolute only in man's experience as sensation, and fulfilment for man is possible only in sensation. Not in feeling or thought, which excludes the object. In human relationship there is no absoluteness, nor any final fulfilment. There is always tension in human relationship, whether it be love or competition. When thought and feeling are submerged in sensation, as it happens in orgasm, man or woman finds the absolute. Because of the overriding importance given to the will, which is manipulated by thought (as concept, memory or desire) man is alienated from the absolute fulfillment, which he can attain through surrender to sensation. Sex experience now is looked upon only as a sort of tickling or a thought-event. Its nature of being absolute sensation is not realized by modern man. Similarly man rejects and avoids physical exertion, working with the body, or putting the body to work. The primitive man enjoyed his physical exertions, and never despised them. Work was not alienated from play. Only when man accepts sensation as the primary human experience, that will lead him to fulfilment, and he will be on the path of discovering the meaning of life. Man like other living creatures can live in contentment and peace when he knows this."

This is Veerabhadra Rao's quest for the centre of experience in man, or main's materialistic soul. I could discern something of Amrita's philosophy in this, though she did not arrive at this kind of formulation.

"But the absoluteness of sensation, when thought and feeling are merged in it, can be of only a short duration. Take orgasm."

"Well, eternal bliss is possible only in death. As you say sex orgasm may be limited to a few moments. With the training of the mind...its thought processes and the will...it should be possible to find absoluteness in all physical exertion, and orgasm could be prolonged indefinitely, converting the sex into an absolute."

"This sounds like tantric sadhana! Is this the future basis of evolution or revolution?"

"I don't like your pigeon-holing every new thing into some tradition or other. When a workers' society is established, and all privileges are done away with, I already discussed with you how competition and comparison would lead to tension between individuals, and that tension would require release. Sex in the first instance provides that release. But in society as a whole, power and exploitation must cease. Then recognition of sensation as the primary value will come into its own, and will lead to man's fulfilment. Then ego would lose its hold on man."

"Why think of this materialism as you call it? Why should we not try to establish brotherhood, love and co-operation between individuals, and among men?"

"That is old hat. That is an impossible dream, a product of idealist thought."

It is futile to argue with him further.

After he leaves, I speculate on certain trends clearly manifest in modern society.

For achieving fulfilment or absoluteness in sensation, one need not have to wait till the coming of the New Society envisaged by Veerabhadra Rao. Drugs like pethidine, alcohol, and varieties of sex-experience sought by the young, all seem to point in that direction. They are, however, life-destroying. Guruji's experiments in the Pune Ashram and Veerabhadra Rao's quest are sophisticated variations of the same thrust of modern life. In which direction humanity is headed, it is impossible to predict. The attempts of civilized man to transcend the mind and reach the absolute are apparent in both directions.

It is interesting to think that Veerabhadra Rao should have attracted me and played such an important role in my life to send me on my quest, when our thinking lay in the opposite directions. He entered my world as a serpent, became the cloud overcast, rained advaita on me, cleansed me, and merged within me. As an advaitin I see him as a vital part of myself. I sit in silence for a long while. The silence becomes vibrant with the song of the ash-gray bird.

SHORT STORIES

The Fish-Eyed Goddess

The South beckons to me; the temple-town of Madurai, which means "delicious," and its goddess Meenakshi, the "fish-eyed one." Twenty years ago, I had a classmate in Madras. He hailed from Madurai. His ambition was to converse with me in chaste Telugu. His ancestors having migrated to the Tamil country, he spoke a corrupt form of Telugu. He loved to hear me speak the language and wanted to reply like one born to the manner. We used to meet frequently, apparently on account of linguistic affinity. But I am not sure what motives really brought us together. Perhaps we just liked each other. We corresponded for a while after leaving college and then forgot each other. After the linguistic division of Indian states, we live within the bounds of our separate spheres and seldom meet. Now this call from the Tamilian South, I wonder whether it has anything to do with my college friend Gurumurti! Yea, that was his name. But I don't think so....

People from all over India go on pilgrimage to Madurai. I am not religious enough to think of pilgrimages. I want to go, perhaps just for the sake of going : to get away from the everyday faces and their worn-out phrases, both of which I have lately come to feel as a constraint and an unmitigated burden. A bid for freedom. Going places where nobody knows me....

With my wife dead and my three children at school, during the last two years, I've relished my loneliness, which perhaps has brought about in me some imperceptible change, I have not cared to identify or analyse. I keep busy round the clock. I make money. I have no time to think of my loneliness. Occasionally a certain absent-mindedness seizes upon me. Then I forget my surroundings. I am gone. Unknown to myself. After a while I come back with a start and don't remember anything in particular about the experience, if it can at all be called an experience. One evening at a *Bharatanatya* recital, it happened. From nowhere it came, a mood of melancholy, and emptiness, and then forgetfulness. I was nowhere, I lost my moorings. When I got back, I felt I was none the worse for it! Another time I had to get up abruptly from bridge, unable to concentrate as the mood seized upon me. Excusing myself I went into the toilet, delayed there, and returning, sat at a window looking blankly at the sky, my mind bereft of all thought. It was something I couldn't talk about to others. There is indeed nothing to talk about. The "seizure" has been something queer, but nevertheless pleasurable. I haven't thought of avoiding it. And now this impulse to travel South, I suspect, is a seizure too. I want to go... Should I go?... Yea, for a few days.... Somewhere into the Southern country? ... No, to Madurai, the delicious city of the fish-eyed goddess!

Once, I boarded the train, I told myself, the questioning would cease, the insistent questioning in the mind. But the mind doesn't want to relinquish its responsibility. Why am I going to Madurai? What is this meaningless excursion? Would any sane person undertake a journey like this? What is happening to me? Why am I going at all?... The mind keeps on and on. Granted Madurai is delicious in meaning, in sound and in imagination too, nevertheless in actuality, it is only a city, like any other city, and what would you do there in that city? Of course, I am not at all sure. Before entraining, I had a vague idea, or the mind had it, that there would be all the time in the world to think, formulate and plan. Now that I am in the train the mind is unable to make any headway. I say to it in answer, "Well, then I will go and have a look at the city of Madurai, visit the temple of goddess Meenakshi go round the palace of Tirumala Naik, the Telugu king who ruled the city long ago; and after that return home with the satisfaction of being a tourist." "You would have enjoyed it better in the company of friends" counters the mind. Friends? Ah, there is the rub! It is friends I want to avoid, it is my language I don't want to hear, it is my life I want to forget; and forgetting enter freedom, the freedom of Being. I say this firmly to silence the mind. But there is a lurking doubt whether I am not being foolish!... Be that as it may, well, why should I not search for my lost friend Gurumurti? I dig up his memory again; but the mind says laughingly, "You don't have even his old address; where do you start your expedition?" Well, I give up....

Tired of its questioning, I ask the mind to watch the outside world for a change. The men and women and things around me. I am surprised at what I see. Being always busy with our own affairs, we look at people with labels across their faces, labels of status, relationship, etc., and within a framework of preconceived notions and ideas. Such a procedure is inevitable and necessary too to get on in the world. But when you have all the time and the freedom of being purposeless, you see people differently and a wholly new vision of human beings unfolds! Look at man, for instance, as a machine or a marionette, or a strange animal, oh, you observe a lot of fascinating things, things that make you laugh and weep.... There is a family seated on the opposite berth — husband, wife and their six-year-old daughter. The relationship is so obvious that I decide to ignore it and look at them individually as separate entities. What do I see? Each one is alone, each one is an island, desperately trying to get across; making a lot of sounds and gestures, which all the time fail to build bridges. What is communicated among them, what is supposed to the known to one another, is superficial and unreal merely creating an illusion, an endless deceit! Of course it works, the make-believe world, till something happens. Not a catastrophe, not even a quarrel, some little thing will do to show up the nature of this surface world.... The husband goes into the bathroom. His absence in a few moments brings an electric change in the wife, a change in her face, movements and gestures. She glances at me, then gives me a frank look, inquiringly, curiously and searchingly; fidgets looking for something — does she really want anything? — meddles with the newspaper, the napkin and the thermos flask; and says something in her language to her daughter, who is indifferent, lost in her own world of fancy, looking out of the window. The woman certainly tries to communicate something as a human being to me, which I shall never understand with my intellect. This is the gap of civilization. The husband returns and she lapses into her wifehood. She ignores my existence. The presence of her husband is a restraint on her being. What she is, what she wants to be, he can never know! Being a husband ! No simulation on her part; and no imposition on his part; they look a normally adjusted couple. And yet there is this gulf between them. In all relationships, perhaps, this is so. One Mr. Rama Rao is a gentle person with infinite patience, as far as I am concerned. He is deep, silent, uncommunicative and hence untrustworthy in the eyes of my colleague. The truth of Rama Rao neither of us knows; nobody ever knows.

No end to this way of thinking, if this can be called thinking at all! These are questions of a different kind, for which there can be no sure answers.... I tell the mind let the questions be! Don't try to find answers.

It is six a.m. at Madurai. I leave it to the jutkawallah to take me to a good hotel. Raya Lodge is evidently named after the Telugu King Krishna Deva Raya, whose viceroy Tirumal Naik had been at Madurai. I am pleased to fancy that I am to be the paying guest of the great Raya himself! As breakfast is served, I inquire of the bearer about the time appropriate to visit the temple. From the window I see the temple-towers of goddess Meenakshi. The morning worship concludes at 8 a.m., I am informed. So I decide to visit the Naik's palace instead. It is a little away from my lodge, at the other end of the town. I am shocked to find Government offices housed in the historical monument. I can't go in. Desolate I climb up the stairs and walk on the terrace. A bird's eye-view of the city reveals nothing to me. The Mahal no doubt is sturdily built, but that is neither here nor there! No sign of the ghost of Tirumal Naik! The Government clerks and their clientele have driven him out! Is it for this you came to Madurai! The question again comes up. Avoiding it, I hastily return to have my lunch and a midday nap.

When I get up it is 5 p.m. After a cup of nice South Indian coffee, I walk straight to the temple. At the entrance, I buy the "worship material" by way of good manners. As I walk in, the melody of *Shahnai* greets my ears. There is a pleasant lake inside, beautiful and serene. The sculptures are exquisite. It is a different world. An American couple is admiring the sculptured figures. A fourteen-year-old boy, their guide, talks to them rapidly in English. I proceed to the abode of the deity. There is a painted board : "Hindus only" non-Hindus are not permitted to go beyond the lake and the sculptures. Further on there is yet another limit. If I intend going into the presence of the deity, I have to remove my clothing at that point. I find many visitors have only an upper-cloth on them, which they twist round the waist as a sort of belt and proceed with naked torsos. The rule doesn't apply to women. My shirt is my problem and I stop at the limit to gaze at the deity from that distance.

The worship proceeds with the recital of Sanskrit hymns. I fail to get a satisfactory view of the goddess. I like the atmosphere and the solemnity. In the abode I get an extraordinary sensation of frozen time. I seem to plummet deep into timelessness and get lost. It is like receding in the corridors of history to an obscure point of no return. It is awesome and yet blissful.

The worship over, walking back to the temple entrance, impulsively I look behind. I see a woman and our eyes meet for a fleeting moment. I walk on and after a few steps deliberately slow down. I expect her to pass me by. She doesn't. She too must have slowed down; or stopped! I look. The distance is maintained. I pause at the temple entrance to reutrn the bamboo-container of the worship material to the shopkeeper, pay him and retrieve my footwear left in his custody. I turn to look at the woman as she approaches and encounter a straight, inquisitive look from her. She is gone and I keep wondering whether she smiled to greet me, or is it my imagination! In a few moments I hurry into the street and look for her. The stretch of road in both directions bears no trace of her. She is gone. I walk up and I down, looking into the open doors of houses in a vain attempt to find her. The feeling gains strength that she greeted me. I desire to meet her. As the urge to see her grows, I regret bitterly my delaying at the shop for the sake of a pair of shoes! What wrong priorities! I feel disgusted at my scale of values. I am miserable at having let go something precious.

The mood continues into the night. I keep visualizing her with that Mona Lisa smile of hers. Was she really interested in me? Why did she follow me and keep looking at me? Where did she vanish suddenly?

Next morning I am in the presence of the deity with a naked torso. There is good attendance of both men and women. They join the priest in chanting the hymns, not usually done at other times. I listen raptly absorbed. The worship over, people disperse rapidly. They rush back to their forenoon chores. The temple itself is the place of daily worship for these families. Meenakshi is obviously a living goddess to the people here. The woman of the previous evening is not in the morning's congregation.

Returning to the lodge, I don my business dress and walk to the shopping area. I want a new spectacles' frame for my reading lenses. I enter an optician's shop. The shopman is busy with a woman customer bent over some frames strewn on the table. I sit in a chair on the right side of the shopman. As she looks up, I realize that she is the same person I have been searching for! She appears most non-committal now.

I immediately gather that she is not only English-educated, but also has a job. Her choice now wavers between two frames, which she examines repeatedly. The shopman is unhelpful as he recommends both in the same breath and she is unable to decide. Impulsively I intervene and recommend one. She accepts without so much as a nod or a glance at me and asks the shopman to fix the glasses at once.

"At least two hours' time is required. My assistant will be coming in now," says the shopman.

"I want them in an hour please. You see, I have to attend college."

She gets up to leave. As the shopman turns to me, I hurriedly tell him : "I'll be back in a short while. If you don't mind, kindly select a suitable frame for these glasses." I leave my glasses with the broken frame on the table and follow the woman out of the shop.

After we walk a short distance, she enters a shop and buys a couple of pencils. I go along and buy a packet of blades, in the same place. As we come out of the shop together, she says :

"You don't belong here!"

"I don't. I am from Nellore."

"What brings you here?"

"Oh, just nothing! I mean...I came without any specific purpose. I am here all alone...really, I don't know why...."

"Why do you follow me?"

"I saw you in the temple yesderday."

"Does it matter?"

"I wanted to talk to you even yesterday."

She walks on silently.

"Are you a college lecturer?"

There is no reply.

"Please, if you don't mind, come and have a cup of coffee with me in the restaurant there. That is, if you would excuse my intrusion." So saying I walk in the direction of the restaurant, and I am glad to find that she follows me.

We sit at a table facing each other and I order coffee. She looks straight placidly at me. No smile, no word, no expectation.

I look in vain for some sign of reaction from her. Her serenity strikes me as strange, almost solemn, before which I feel humble. I am at a loss for words. Coffee arrives. "When coffee is over she will leave me" I tell myself. I should say something. I shouldn't miss this opportunity. What shall I say?

Her eyes turn from me to the coffee cup. I realize that it is the extraordinary serenity in her face and manner that has struck me dumb. I have known women. I am forty. Till now I never felt diffident with women. After my wife's death, I haven't given thought to women. This woman's presence and its impact upon me is something special.

"What do you teach in college?" I ask her.

"Philosophy."

"I wonder whether you have a philosophy of life of your own! What do you believe in really? Materialism, Dialectical Materialism, Existentialism, Vedanta or what? Do you care for any of these you teach, really?" I ask light-heartedly.

"Advaita."

"I too graduated in philosophy. Twenty years ago. A long time now I haven't bothered about anything philosophical. But I came here like a philosopher. To forget my everday interests, to be absolutely lonely. Isn't it queer that I should remember philosophy and since you happen to teach it, perhaps it is something to talk about. I have no beliefs, and Vedanta means nothing to me."

There is no reply. She has finished her coffee, while I talked. She takes a look at her watch. I empty my cup with a sense of utter defeat. I pay the bill and we come out.

"Thanks" she says and gets into a rickshaw.

"May not I know your name?" I ask desperately.

"Meenakshi." She is gone.

Is that a joke, or is it her real name? I don't give up. I must meet her again. I walk back to the optician's shop.

Indicating my choice of a frame, I tell the shopman that I would wait there till he gets the spectacles ready, as I have nothing better to do that morning. My thoughts centre round Meenakshi. She will come, won't she, to pick up the spectacles she ordered!

In less than an hour my spectacles are ready. The time is eleven o'clock. And there is no sign of Meenakshi.

"What about the lecturer's glasses? Are they ready?" I inquire of the shopman.

"Of course, half-an-hour ago, they were ready. She said it was urgent and I gave priority. You see, Sir, she hasn't turned up. It is just like women..."

I drag myself to the lodge totally depressed.

In the evening I am drawn to the temple. I stand with folded hands in the deity's presence. The goddess is exquisitely beautiful. She stands with a graceful bend in her lithesome figure, a benevolent smile, and a parrot perched on her left forehand. Such captivating grace of femininity is rare in temple idols, though there may be found other qualities. Madurai Meenakshi is femininity idolized. As people press to come in, I am forced out of the presence. I choose the lake to contemplate upon for the rest of the evening.

As I gaze at the shadows in the placid waters, I become aware of someone coming and sitting a little distance away to my right. I turn to look, and, lo and behold! It is Meenakshi wearing her new pair of spectacles! Serene and contemplative, she doesn't appear to notice my presence at all. Excited at my extraordinary good luck, I approach her and quietly sit by her side. She glances at me and now she gives me a smile of welcome. I am overjoyed.

"What do you think of the temple?" She takes the initiative and asks.

"Excellent and marvellous. This lake too. It is wonderfully clean and beautiful...."

"The lake is important to the temple as the heart to a human being."

"Do you consider the heart more important than the intellect? Feeling more important than reason?"

I long to make some conversation with the beautiful woman and overcome the barrier between us.

"Yes, of course; otherwise why should one come here at all?" she says.

Her seriousness sets me thinking. In the morning she said she is an Advaitin. She is not only formally educated, but discriminatingly intellectual. She has poise and dignity. She gladdens my heart as never before any human being did in my entire life. To meet a woman like this, is a rare chance!

"In *Advaita,* logic appears to be more prominent than feeling. At least that is my impression. Jnana or knowledge takes priority over devotion and surrender. Am I right?" I plunge into the discussion.

She replies : "No it is not so...What do you think of Meenakshi?"

"Which Meenakshi?" I venture to say jocularly trying to cross the barrier of seriousness in our discussion.

"Doesn't matter. You know both are one."

The implication of it, and the perfectly, serious manner in which she says it, shocks me, and yet delights me. From the Advaitic point of view, of course, her reply is perfect.

"Are you surprised?" she asks me. "Form and concept go together, and the name too. What the name and the form convey to you, their impact upon you is what really matters, and, therefore, Meenakshi is one and not two."

"I don't see it clearly. That is an idol and here is a living person. Even granting the impact of beauty is similar in art and life, I do prefer a living person to a mere idol."

"What causes such preference is the essence of illusion, *Maya,* The two are not two but one. When you see two and prefer one to the other, it is ignorance. To be without such preferences, and to see the truth steadily as one is *Advaita.* It doesn't mean one cannot or should not distinguish between what is beautiful and what is not, but at least, in beauty itself one must be able to see oneness so that the apparent many in creation is known to be an illusion."

"Creation is illusion, they say; and then emotions and sentiments and other reactions caused by the sentient world must necessarily be illusion too. If the attempt to go beyond such things is called self-realization or *Advaita*, is it not in effect a rejection of the world as we know it?"

"Names and forms and their impact on oneself, the emotions and sentiments, as you call them — these do not exist as so many entities. They are all one and that oneness is the truth. The multiplicity and separateness is illusion. The statement, 'the world is illusion' does not mean that the world does not exist. Creation which is called Nature or Prakriti has neither a beginning nor an end. It is infinite and eternal, and yet every single thing in Nature has a beginning and an end; is subject to birth and death. Nature itself has no beginning and no end. Creation is flux but Creation is not unreal. To go beyond the flux is to attain to oneness. That is *Advaita* and not renunciation of the world."

"Then what about renunciation? Isn't that a prerequisite for Advaitic experience?"

"No, Renunciation truly means, as I have said, to have no preferences. Renunciation is *sama drishti.*"

"Then I have no *sama drishti,* for I happen to prefer the beautiful lady to the beautiful idol," I assert and add the comment : "Isn't it better to have dams and projects than to build temples like these? We are modern. Nehru says our irrigation projects are our temples. I agree with him."

"I see no difference even then. In the old days, the idol and man were one. Today man and the machine are one. Just a change in the concept of man. Even today the old habit of idolizing is not dead. Why do they erect statues to Gandhi and Nehru? Why not spend that money on projects? And why do you come to Madurai?"

I don't answer. I admire the directness of her thought and wish I could see her point. I am wholly charmed by her presence.

Yes, why have I come to Madurai? The question comes up again and there is no rational explanation.

"I come to Madurai to meet *you*!" I say this with a dash, but in all earnestness.

"May be so!" comes her reply!

The solemnity of it, because there is no accompanying smile, no breaking of barriers, as I expected, baffles me for a moment. She is certainly extraordinary and plays it cool!

A woman of sixty comes along, Meenakshi gets up, joins her and starts walking away. Just like that! Her sudden departure without so much as a gesture of farewell hurts me to the quick. Swallowing my pride, I too get up and walk behind the two ladies. My idea is to locate her residence. Realizing that at the entrance I might again be delayed retrieving my footwear, I decide to go ahead of them and wait there.

As she steps into the street in the company of the old lady, Meenakshi gives me, what seems to me a smile of approval, and a slight nod presumably an invitation to go with her. I follow.

We walk into the next street and stop before a small house. The old lady takes out a bunch of keys and opens the front door. After the verandah enclosed with iron railings, there is on the right side a flight of steps leading to the first floor. While the old lady walks to the door of the ground floor, Meenakshi and I climb up the steps. Meenakshi opens the apartment with her key.

There is a bookshelf, a table, a few chairs and a sofa. As I recline on the sofa, she sits in a chair nearby.

"You didn't introduce your companion to me," I say this a little pricked at her manners.

"Jnanamba. I am her tenant. I call her auntie."

"You live here like a parrot in her cage? O God, how many locks!"

"Like the soul in the body! Only three locks you know. She opened two and I opened the one upstairs. In Vedanta, *triputi* means the sight, the seer and the act of seeing. And finally they are one."

"I no longer relish this dry discussion on Vedanta. Having arrived here, all that seems to me utterly irrelevant. Something profound, passionate and powerful has caught me. I am in a wonderful dream. It is your presence."

She smiles.

I pause and ask : "Is there no one else?"

"Each one to oneself. To think there is someone else is nothing but illusion."

And she goes inside, leaving me alone!

Moments pass. I feel uneasy. I don't know what to do with myself. I look at the objects around, scrutinizing them one after another. A small photo of Sri Ramana Maharshi in a corner of the table attracts my attention. I go near and peer close at Ramana's face. I encounter his affectionate look. I continue to look into his eyes and feel reassured. I feel at home.

She has brought me coffee. She has changed into a white sari. There are jasmines in her coiffure. She is a goodess, magnificently beautiful.

The coffee is like *amrita.* There is none to beat the Southerners in preparing delicious coffee.

"What made you come to Madurai?" she asks sitting beside me on the settee.

I talk about myself in an introspective mood. I tell her finally, that a certain longing for freedom and peace has drawn me here and I know no specific reason whatsoever.

"Your wife?" she asks.

"She died two years ago."

"As a person she may be dead, but what she represents in you is not dead?"

"I can't say. I am not sure. I haven't had any desire for woman these two years. Something has changed in me. I haven't ever mourned her death. Just feel tired of life, which is but a repetition of one day after another. Nothing interests me. You alone are different. You are a dream come true. I worship you. That's why I followed you. You are beautiful."

"What is beauty?"

"It is just a liking, I suppose. Supreme liking."

"And what is 'liking,' if you can go further?"

I do indeed search for the source of liking and come back with : "Well, it is ME! The liking and me are identical."

"In *triputi,* the seer alone remains finally. Your conclusion is that you came to Madurai for your own sake! Is that right?"

"No, not for me. For Meenakshi." I tell her pointedly.

"Is there any difference?"

"No. Really no!"

"Is that the final truth?"

I simply nod assent.

She invites me inside.

* * *

Whatever happened to me after that, I can't say in words, for words there are none; and I didn't know whether I, my ego, existed or not. I was lost in something which may be called bliss.

When I hear a knock on the door and come back to myself, I realize I am lying in my own bed in the lodge. I cannot recall when and how I came back. I open the door and the bearer inquires :

"May I get you your dinner, Sir?"

"What is the time?" I ask.

"You have a watch, Sir," he says.

Surprised at my own absent-mindedness, I look at may watch and find that it is just nearing nine p.m. I tell the bearer I have no appetite.

I sink into a profound sleep.

The next morning too there is an inner satiation and a profound peace that envelopes my being, which makes me absolutely inactive. I bestir myself to have a bath and drink a cup of coffee. I look at the newspaper vaguely and lay it aside.

Then slowly the questioning starts and the mind is asking : Who is she? Is it possible that sex could ever be so deep and blissful? Who is she? I have very little information about her.

She is a college lecturer. Alone and perhaps unmarried too. The wonder is I never asked her. Do I love her? Ordinary passion did not enter this relationship. Ethics and society, the past and the future did not figure. It was a coming together. She bestowed upon me bliss I had never before known in my life. Who is she? What sort of woman? Remembering the previous night brings tears to my eyes; a profound richness of feeling suffuses my heart.

As the day wears on, thought and plans take shape; thoughts of marriage, of living with her, sharing the rest of my life with her, and making her my own for ever and ever....

I decide to settle the entire matter that evening itself.

After a light lunch, I get into bed and daydream. After a while I am in a different state of consciousness....

I am dead, my body lies motionless with several people crowding round it. I hover above and witness the whole scene. My little daughter seven-year-old Girija is weeping and I try to persuade her that I am not really dead. It has no effect on her, for she cannot see me, nor hear me. She persists in looking at my body and not the real me beside her. There is an unbridgeable gap. What shall I do now? I move from her much worried and then wake up....

At 5-30 p.m. I search for Meenakshi in the temple. Then I walk directly to her house. The door of the front verandah is open. The apartment upstairs is locked. Is she not back from college ? Has she gone somewhere else? I climb down and stand at the open door of the ground floor apartment. A boy comes up.

"Jnanamba." I ask for the lady of the house.

He goes in and fetches her. The lady is mournful and deeply engrossed in some recent loss. She looks at me inquiringly.

"I have come for lecturer Meenakshi."

She simply waves her hand despairingly and cannot find words as tears roll down her cheeks.

"Gone...she is gone..." says Jnanamba in a choking voice and covers her face with the end of her sari.

I stand uncomprehending.

The boy explains to me in broken English.

The previous night at about nine p.m., Meenakshi lit the stove for boiling milk and the loose end of her sari caught fire. She had widespread burns on her body and died in the hospital round about midnight.

"No...No...No..."

The boy proceeds unable to hear my protests....

Her lifeless body was taken away by her brother and mother who arrived in the morning from her native town....

Now the old lady's curiosity prevails and she asks me who I am. I mutter something about my daughter being Meenakshi's student. I inquire : "What about her husband and children?"

"The husband went to the States four years ago. She has no children. She didn't join her husband in the States."

The next day I go round all the colleges in the town. Finally, I succeed in locating her place of work and obtain from the department a group photo in which she, the philosophy lecturer, sits third from the right in the company of her colleagues and students. I go to a photographer and ask him to enlarge for me the little image of Meenakshi in that photo into a portrait. The result is not satisfactory. The portrait bears no connection to the living person I knew.

While I can recollect her important words about *Advaita,* how can I ever recall the presence and the bliss! How can I ever account for it all with the details I have gathered!

What she gave me was absolute fulfilment, with Beauty, Bliss and Me fused into an eternal moment.

The tragedy has seared me as much as the fire did her body.

Day after day, I stand before Goddess Meenakshi in the sanctum sanctorum of the temple. The parrot poised on her left hand may wing its way into the beyond at any moment. Meanwhile, she the symbol of Beauty, Grace and Bliss, smiles at me gently, compassionately.

Thy Will Be Done

It is drizzling. Duty. One cannot shirk one's duty. 'Cheemacha! don't get wet. You will catch cold.' Mother used to caution me. Always indifferent to her words. Paper boats. Getting soaked in the rain. Cold and then fever. Yet mother never got angry. Never complained to father. He would have flayed me alive if she had.

This dripping umbrella. Garudayya would have the consideration, I thought, to wait for me at the door. But where is the fellow! The doors are wide open, the reading-room is empty and he goes into hiding somewhere among the book shelves. Or on some fool's errand.

Huh...Huh... I cannot help this shivering. 'Cheemacha! Put on your sweater, my son.' Mother again. What a long time ago it was! Never remembered it all these years. But now, why now? No fear of catching cold or fever now. When you have someone worrying over you, all kinds of ailments visit you. Now e ven ailments leave you alone. When one has stepped into old age....

Old age? Of course. No flesh, the flesh has dissolved. Only the bones remain. This teak-wood chair daily reminds me. Eight years since retirement. Eight plus fifty-five is sixty-three and not a day less. I am an old man Shashtipurti Sixty. Only no celebration marked the event.

Never wanted to return to the place of my birth and childhood. Dreamt of something else. The Lord of Seven Hills has willed otherwise. It is by His Grace, I am Library assistant in this College. Had to beg the Devasthanam's Trust for the job to keep me alive. I don't complain. That's again His Will, the manner of bringing me here. O Lord, let Thy Will be done!

No, this is no longer a means of livelihood. This is my place ordained by Him, Who leads me on the path of Dharma. One has to go on with one's duty. One has to go it alone. He is nevertheless kind and merciful to me. He has spared me the worst humiliation of going to Bombay...to that son, who is no longer a son of mine. That contingency will never come! My son died fifteen years ago. So I told him, and so I declared to the world....

He lost his dharma, his caste, his religion, his parents....A diseased limb of mine. Operation painful, but successful. His mother dying before the event, was spared the ordeal. She was lucky. And the ungrateful wretch of a son would not attend his mother's funeral. Why did he ever return to India? He should have spent the rest of his beggarly life in the States. The lap-dog of a white woman!

'Kichoo has passed in the first class.... Kichoo is off to the States, you know. Tatas have offered him a salary of six thousand rupees. Arrived in Bombay and joined duty.... He will be here tomorrow.' These proud announcements and eager expectations of a loving father...what happened to them? Did he ever think of me, or his mother, or his family? I was made a fool all right. The ungrateful outcaste arrives with a white woman, whom he calls his wife, lodges in a hotel and starts negotiations with me! Most disgusting! Let him go, go away, never to show me his face. As long as there is life in me, there shall be no need to see him again!

Venkatesa, O Lord, be merciful! Thou hast removed all earthly bonds one after another, and I always have said : 'Let Thy Will be done!'

"Garudayya! Garudayya!!"

"Swami?"

"Where were you?"

"Arranging yesterday's books, Swami."

"Didn't you notice my arrival?"

"No, Swami."

He is lying.

"Today's newspapers, where are they?"

"I put them in their places."

"Get me *The Hindu*."

'India accepts Colombo proposals'...shameless compromise.... 'Johnson's Baby Powder'...Kichoo's children. Anglo-Indian brats. Hare Ram! What does he call them? Tom, Dick, and Harry? Not Hari but Harry. He lacks assertion, male assertion and individuality. A white woman, if it had to be, then why could he not get her into the fold through Arya Samaj or some Samaj, which would have been a lot better than this abject surrender to an alien person and an alien culture....

"Good morning, Sir." Oh! the postman. Why doesn't he leave the post on the table? He waits every day, to deliver it into my hands. Courtesy, no doubt, but very tiresome. Postman Hussain is old-fashioned, but a good man. Oh, yes, a good man.

Three book-lists and one magazine. Shall I rip open the wrapper? Tear the veil off the purdah woman! Get at the nakedness of the sleek foreign magazine! LIFE, Hi Life!

Then I was only ten. Looking out from an upstairs window. In the neighbouring house, a woman was changing her dress. A naked woman, a full-blown woman. It was the beginning of 'life'. Life to Americans is a never-ending adolescence.

Letters. Letters. Nobody writes to me. Touching them is a pleasure, though. Looking into the addresses is a harmless habit. May be a waste of time, but no harm, no harm....

To Chi. Prabhavati, First B.Sc. Class. That is her father. Writes a document-writer's old hand.

A pink envelope. To Kumari Janaki, Second B.Sc. Class. Why should she be getting any letters to the college address? Her parents are here and she lives with them. Address typed. May be from a book-seller. The post-mark?...Oh, it's perfumed! From New Delhi! Definitely not from a book-seller. Its delicate scent gives it away...mm....

Janaki is herself a delicate flower, a parijata. A pure, delicate, white blossom of a beauty. She says nothing. Her presence is a silent greeting, sometimes her smile is. Oh, she comes like a princess, with the gait of a swan, never alone, but in the company of her maids-in-waiting. Half-hidden by them. Waiting till I ask her, she silently returns a book or two. The titles she wants to borrow, she seldom says them, but slips me a paper on which they are listed. Those exquisite lips often conceal themselves behind the shoulder of a friend and do not speak. Only her eyes speak....

And this scented message is for her, for that noble goddess! No doubt, some infatuated young fellow. It is for her, but is she for it?

"Ting"

Nine-thirty.

"Swami, shall I take the students' letters to the letter-board?"

"Oh, yes."

The pink envelope falls into the table drawer.

Slowly the students come in.

All the time, all the time, undisclosed secrets burn. Who is he? What does he want? How dare he?

A false note destroys music. Adharma reduces a flowerlike existence to nothingness. Can't purity and beauty be saved? Is it an impossible wish in this world?

My life's dream was destroyed by Kichoo. A fine green tree ruthlessly cut down at the roots. Kamalakshi, Kichoo's sister burnt the dead trunk into black charcoal. Who could expect a well-brought-up girl like her to end her life as she did? Autopsy and abiding shame. Ashes. Nothing but ashes.

"Ting...Ting...Ting..." Ten O'Clock. All are gone now. The room is desolate. What is left now? Dharma. O Lord, Thy Will be done! Surrender and peace. *Saranagati.* Surrender.

"Garudayya!"

"Swami?"

"Remove these books, will you?"

Garudayya goes inside with the books. For the next half-hour he is safe.

Alone, alone with the envelope. Yes, the young *devadasi** of Srirangam full of sweet fragrance. Helpless. Pitifully exposed. Inviting.

Torn. The rose of an envelope is torn open. Maidenhead broken. The little secret is out. The blue-bell of a letter, the exquisite blue paper is out...oh!

'Darling Janee! It is like beckoning to one's pet bitch!

Darling Janee,

How can you accuse me of forgetting you? You know the reason for my not writing to you. Do you recall that day and that moment before our final parting when you whispered into my ear, being so close to each other, as indeed we were at the moment, that our hearts would always beat in unison, and our secret should be kept, that I should not think of writing to you till we met again? It was an order, wasn't it? It is hardly two months, and I get this letter charging me with forgetfulness!

Unless you tell me specifically what you were told by a distant relation of mine, which evidently provoked you to write this letter, how can I explain and clear your doubt?

'The last sentence of your letter perturbs me.' Why have you developed a sudden revulsion to life? You give me fifteen days for a reply. And why should you say, 'We'll never meet again if the reply fails to reach me within that time!' All this sounds very

---

* A dancing girl attached to a temple.

strange and ominous. In a month's time I'll be there with you to dismiss all doubts, I promise. Love and XXX.

Yours
Raman

So she whispered into his ears...being close together...with the hearts beating in unison...and what else? The little hussy! It's the same story again and again. Kamalakshi I never suspected. And here is Janaki again, my little parijata flower. Going into dust! Oh God!

II

There was nothing, nothing shameful about Janaki's suicide! That is what the autopsy report said. Then was it only a temperamental aberration? Not an ethical one? Why did she do it then? It doesn't make sense.

That letter is still in the table drawer!

You give me fifteen days time for a reply and why should you say : We'll never meet again if the reply fails to reach me within that time?' She couldn't answer that. Because, because the letter was not delivered to her! and then she killed herself. Just as she had threatened. Oh, my God!

She died for the man at Delhi, died because he didn't reply, or so she thought. The reply, the reply that could have saved her was all the time lying here, here in the table drawer! The terrible responsibility of it! Oh, my Lord!

Did I kill her?

Can you escape the responsibility? It *was* murder!

Why did I do that? I didn't mean to. I only stopped the letter. To save her from the fate of Kamalakshi.

You killed Kamalakshi too!

No, no. She was punished for her adharma, for her sinfulness. Janaki's death is an accident. Those born are destined to die sooner or later. I am no more responsible than if it were a traffic accident.

No more responsible? A growing plant, a fragrant creeper is callously clipped and destroyed. You have read about love, but this is the first time you are confronted with its truth and power.

But love is only another name for lack of restraint, self-indulgence, isn't it? I understand its power, its corrupting power only too well, because of Kamalakshi, hence my attempt to save Janaki.

What appears to be indulgence to you, might have been to Janaki and Kamalakshi the glory and essence of life. Otherwise would those girls die for it willingly?

They died because they were wanton and irresponsible.

Was Kamalakshi really wanton? Did she not come to you for permission to marry, and did you not refuse to give it? Wasn't that what really led to her suicide?

But the man she wanted to marry was not a brahmin! How could I approve? Did it mean that she should carry on with him a clandestine affair without shame or fear of consequences?

Well, take a look at your past. What do you think is the final outcome? Under your shadow, under your authority, nothing came to bloom or fruition. Nothing has survived. Why should it be so? Try and see the evil within yourself. Then you will own to your responsibility.

By birth, tradition and upbringing, a pious Vaishnava Brahmin that I am, always devoted to Dharma and striving for moral purity; and in the evening of my life...a *saranagata* to my Lord Venkatesa, how can I be evil, how have I become evil? It must be some fear or cowardice, some weakness for the dead girl Janaki, that speaks to me with a false voice thus, and accuses me of crimes I have not committed.

Well, well, well. Go back, go back, into the remote past, and look.

My father was a *bhakta,* being a priest in Rama's temple.

Yes, and did he not seduce the milk-maid Veeramma?

That was only a rumour, an unfounded scandal, wasn't it?

What about you, his son, who pined as a boy for Veeramma's little daughter, Malli?

That was hardly sex, was it? I was only seven. That girl was eight or nine and used to fetch parijata flowers for father's worship....

Yes, and then you used to cling to her, eager to kiss her but not bold enough to do so.

Sometimes we used to play like other children. All play at that age was innocent. I loved to boss over her. She was from a low caste and then only a girl; so I teased.

You didn't go further, because you were afraid of your father's wrath. He didn't like to see you playing with Veeramma's daughter. Can you guess the reason?

No, no. Not so. Even if it were to be true, I couldn't be responsible for my father. In all my life I have dreaded adharma and I have no regrets. Let the Lord be my judge. Why should I hold this debate with myself? An exercise in futility. Let His Will be done!

"Garudayya, let us go up-hill and see the Lord."

"Shall I get the bus tickets, Swami?"

"Not on the bus. Let us go on foot."

"Too difficult, Swami, at your age."

"Age has nothing to do with the power of the soul, Garudayya."

"But it is the body which will be put to strain."

"Is the soul greater, or body?"

"I have no knowledge of these things, Swami."

"Will you accompany me, or not?"

"Nowadays the bus is the thing, Swami. I prefer the bus. But I shall certainly go with you and we can rest on the way. Let us start in the evening."

"Then this Saturday. Don't forget."

*　　　*　　　*

Cripples...Lepers...The blind...The orphans..Families who have made begging their profession.... All on the steps leading to the Lord.

Steps...Steps...Steps...

Oh, what an effort!

Ups and downs...Stones...Rocks...Bushes...Trees...

And the Sky.... The sky and the clouds....

Darkness falls.

"Garudayya, what is the time?"

He has a radium-dialled watch.

"Eight fifteen, Swami. We've almost arrived."

*　　　*　　　*

Drizzling...This drizzling will be the death of me. Oh, how cold! It's slippery. The feet find it difficult. What a terrible weakness! Garudayya hasn't turned up as instructed. He must be fast asleep somewhere. But the time is up. I must make it alone to the presence of the Lord. Go and see Him. How is that there is no one to help me at this hour! Just a little help would have done....

Why do you ask for the help of others? It must be His help, His mercy. If it is there, everything will be there. Without it, there can be nothing....

Oh, oh, my God!....

*　　　*　　　*

Where, where am I? What is this bed ? Where is the temple? Where is my Lord?

Oh, I fell, I fell down...on my way to the temple....

My right leg. Broken perhaps. I didn't go in I couldn't go in to my Lord.

"Please drink this milk."

Who is she? so considerate!

"Mother, who are you? Are you the doctor or nurse here?"

"Doctor, yes. But not of this hospital."

"Where are you from?"

"Bombay. We found you near the temple. You had lost consciousness. We saw you slip and fall. We brought you down hill in my car. The right leg is fractured. Why do you cry, Sir? Is it very painful?"

"You had the darshan of the Lord?"

"No. We were about to go in. Then we found you. How could we go leaving you there? We may go now."

"In Bombay there was the High Court Judge run over by a car, but no one took care of him!"

"You expect everyone from Bombay to be irresponsible, do you?"

She is laughing. Pure laughter. Real laughter. A good woman.

"What is your name, mother?"

"Prema. Prema Nanchari."

"Nanchari?"

"That is my full name. The god Balaji is my family God. It is His consort's name."

"Nanchari. It's my mother's name too. Are you a brahmin?"

"No."

"What caste?"

She smiles hesitantly. "I'm a Harijan. Do you mind it?"

Hare Ram! Sriyahpathe! I'm still alive! Is this my punishment?

"You are weak. Please rest for a while."

"Appa...Appa..."

"Mm...Mm..."

"Appa, I'm Kichoo. Do you hear me?"

"Kichoo...Kichoo.... How did you come, my son?"

"Ramanujachari sent a message to me."

"Why?"

"Because you had an accident."

"Kichoo...Yes, Kichoo...I am finished."

"Why, father? Does it hurt very much? You will be O.K. As soon as you pick up a little strength, we'll go to Bombay."

"No, no. This body is useless hereafter. The Lord asked me to come up the Hill to see Him and I failed. Well, I failed Him Kichoo. My boy, please set fire to this useless body and burn it of all sins. Do it, my boy. That is your Dharma. You shall do your Dharma. Let His Will be done."

The Burden of Ash

Anandarao lit a cigarette. He tried to gather the quicksilver of his mind into the cup of concentration. The office-file lay waiting with its flap-arms inviting his attention. But he had lost interest in it. In the stillness of thought which smoking invariably provided him, he scanned the image of his own mind. The cigarette's burning end now covered by its heavy burden of ash was almost scorching his fingers. But he desisted from discarding it, waiting for the ash to drop of its own accord. It was a fascinating moment.

"So you have started it again! Like a delinquent child, doing it on the sly!" Kamala startled him. Automatically he flung away the butt into the darkness outside.

"Wanted to slip in quietly and leave your cup of milk. But...what *is* this weakness? Tell me, don't you have any will power? You *know* what is the matter with your health."

Taking the milk from her, Anandarao failed to bring up the smile he wanted to, and quickly hid himself behind the cup. Kamala watched him. When he handed the cup back, she demanded : "Now, give me the packet also." Anandarao did not move.

"I could not understand your cough last night. Now I know. It is not as though you can take it. You are allergic. It brings you the cough. And still you go to it again and again. Well, it beats me. Shall I suggest a way out, if you can't stop it by yourself? Just promise me with your hand in mine that you will not touch a cigarette again without my permission. I am not merely nagging; I promise not to make it too rigid. You can have a cigarette after telling me, you know. Only, it takes away the burden of responsibility from you."

"I'll consider that."

"The cigarettes please."

"Oh!"

Anandarao handed the cigarettes to his wife.

"Now for the pledge. Won't you take my hand?"

"Not now, please. I said I'll think it over."

"Everything has already been thrashed out. No more thinking. Your hand, please."

"No."

Anandarao got up and went towards the window. Kamala pursed her lips and went out.

It was true that there was nothing to think over. His responsibility towards himself and towards his family demanded that he give up smoking, once and for all. But knowing what was one's duty did not make it easier to practise. What was this urge to smoke in spite of all the arguments against it? What was it that weakened his will and made him shamefacedly give in again and again? Was it a neurosis or what?

Anandarao looked at the darkness and at the lonely stars, bright but lonely....

He was then nine years old. He suddenly woke up from sleep sometime during the dead of night. In the darkness he saw, like a danger signal, a bright red spot. It was like a rose-bud, secretly born. It glowed off and on like a strange insect breathing. It moved sometimes. There was an aroma too, mildly exciting. Something caught his heart, which he wanted to express but could not. At the moment he never realized that it was his father smoking in bed in the darkness. Though this happened more than once, he could not bring himself to associate the dream-like experience with the trifling white thing called a cigarette, when he saw it in broad daylight.

Father was very strict with his children. He forced them to do many things and gave them advice which he himself never followed. He had not got through his school-final examination. But he insisted on Anandarao doing well in his studies and getting an M.A. He had amassed wealth, which Anandarao with all his education could never hope to earn. The number of cigarettes father used to smoke in twenty-four hours, Anandarao could not hope to smoke even in a week. There was a vast gulf between his father and himself. The only link was perhaps the urge to smoke. Even that he seemed to have inherited against his father's wishes.

When he was in the tenth class, one day he went to the cinema with a friend. More interesting than the cinema was the way his friend was smoking cigarettes one after another. He was sending out a straight jet of smoke by narrowly rounding his lips and creating a tiny parallel to the beam of light overhead that connected the projector-hole and the screen. The cigarette smoke curled up and merged in patterns in the beam of light above. The whole thing was excitingly new. Anandarao also wanted to do it. That attempt at smoking, though not very satisfactory, was delightfully funny.

As soon as he returned home, his father asked : "How was the picture?"

"I liked it though I could not follow the Hindi."

He got a slap on the face. He was taken aback, and wondered why his father should get angry at his inability to follow the Hindi dialogue. His father said : "What is that smell from your mouth? Started picking up bidi-butts on the sly, have you?"

"No, it was a cigarette."

"Where did you get the money for it?"

"My friend offered me one."

"Who is that friend? Better give up these bidi-cigarette friendships"! After that for many days he didn't touch a cigarette.

When he was doing B.A. in the city, the occasion came again in a cinema theatre. Smoking in theatres was not then prohibited*. Anandarao was among his friends, who were all of them smoking. Some of them were blowing their smoke deliberately towards the girls in the front row, and passing remarks intended for them, but apparently as a sort of running commentary on the picture. It was in this mood that Anandarao also lit a cigarette. The girl in front of him started giggling at a remark he made. Then she went on throwing an occasional glance at him and became quite responsive. Thus Anandarao discovered an intrinsic connection between manhood and cigarette-smoking.

The second World-War was over. The air-force people arranged a celebration at the military aerodrome to which they invited some citizens and representatives of institutions, including students. The guests were paired off for a twenty-minute demonstration flight in small training crafts, for an aerial view of the city. Anandarao was paired with a thirty-year old married woman, lecturer at the women's college. They became acquainted during the flight and sat together at the tea-party afterwards. After tea, he lit a cigarette, also offered at the party.

"I never thought you smoked."

"I am sorry, I hope you don't mind."

"No, not at all. In fact my husband smokes. What I mean to say is that you are very young, and I didn't imagine you smoking. It's alright. Of course, but you should have first asked me, shouldn't you? But really, I don't mind. Since we are friends."

It pleased him, her calling him a friend.

"Of course, you should have asked me about my objection before, and not after," said Kamala when he kissed her before they got married.

It was not that Kamala had an aversion to cigarette smoke. Her objection was purely on health grounds, and she was justified

---

* In 1940.

in her stand. A woman had to be concerned about her husband's health! Who else?

Anandrao turned back from the window. He found a good deal of dissatisfaction and a certain emptiness within him. Education, marriage, career, children — when all these steps had been climbed one after another, quite successfully, what else remained in life? Was it only one's concern about status, money and health? Even those values could not be strictly described as concern for one's own self. Because they were more for the sake of wife and children, for the family's security and its future. It appeared to him that, after forty, a man had no 'self' left. He did not live for himself but only for his family. That was the truth! Therefore if he were to leave the matter to Kamala as she had suggested, he might be able to conquer the enemy, the cigarette. But there was a great reluctance in him to do so. Perhaps if he thought again, he might overcome the reluctance....

Two nights later, Anandrao was sleepless with intermittent cough and Kamala said : "You can't give up smoking by will and you won't agree to my suggestion. Then what is to be done? I don't understand your attitude"!

"Well, perhaps I can do neither just yet. Why don't you let me be for a few days? Your nagging every day really drives me mad." He replied.

"Look, I am only saying that something must be done about it. For your own sake. And I only wanted to share your burden. Why don't you leave it to me?"

Anandrao was silent for a while and then said with a laugh, "where is the guarantee that I will keep my pledge? If I have the strength to keep my pledge, I might have given up smoking by myself!"

There was no reply from Kamala.

The next evening, when Anandrao returned from his club, he found his bed shifted into his study. "I thought you won't mind sleeping here till your cough is better," said Kamala.

It was just like Kamala. She would not give up fighting. Who could say that she was not fighting for a right cause this time?

That night, alone in bed, he was looking into the darkness and thinking. The cigarette issue was really a storm in the tea-cup. But Kamala had taken it seriously. The result was this enforced loneliness, meant to be a punishment!

Was it a punishment? Nobody liked loneliness. Loneliness had no meaning. But then, did life have any meaning? Life derived its meaning from values like duty, love, authority, responsibilities, status, money, health, etc. All these were against the loneliness of man. They defined in different ways, man's relationships and man's community with other men. But loneliness, by definition, was a state of unrelatedness with others. Every relationship and so, every value touched a man's self only upto a limit. Even Kamala the nearest to his self, was still outside the bounds set by his loneliness with himself! It was impossible for her or for anybody else to obliterate this loneliness. It was an interesting thought. But was loneliness, on that account, absolutely meaningless? Why had the Yogins and Rishis sought loneliness? They had embarked on a search for the self. Why? Did it not make loneliness also a value? It was not a social value, but could it be rejected just for that reason? Was it a value of life or not?

Anandrao could not give a positive answer. He found his mind unsettled. He got up and lit a cigarette.

As the cigarette drew to its end, Anandrao thought that he had found the answer. On grounds of health, and from a rational point of view, it was clearly his duty to give up smoking, but he could not do it; he had an urge for it. An urge that could not be rationally explained. Because...this burning end, this bright spot, glowing with his life-breath in the midst of darkness was the very symbol of loneliness which he had always sought. He wanted, of all things, to be alone with himself!

The burning end had shed its burden of ash.

Hotline To God

Surya Rao anxiously waited outside the *puja-room*. His wife Suvarchala had been inside for over two hours now. Through the window he could see the car-driver wiping the front screen for the third time finding nothing else to do, while he waited. It was getting on his nerves. By temperament Surya Rao was intolerant of delays. He won't allow any gap in conversation with visitors, and would conclude all transactions as quickly as possible. He hated to see servants idling; and would send them on some errand or other. This waiting for Suvarchala's emergence from her prayers was something of an ordeal for him. But he couldn't go on his present mission unless she gave him the green signal. It was already approaching twelve noon. He had an appointment with the auditor at the 'Dwaraka' hotel at half past eleven. If he further delayed, his mission might fail.

Before it struck twelve, the door opened, and Suvarchala came out as Surya Rao rose from his seat to know the result. Wiping the perspiration on her brow and neck with the end of her sari, a tired Suvarchala sank into the sofa, and turned towards her husband with a genial smile... "It was not an easy thing, you know. I prayed hard and He finally granted the favour on condition that we would go to the Hills and performed the Lord's marriage within six months from now. Now you may go with confidence. It is all His grace!" "I'm late by half an hour. I hope it won't matter. You have a cup of ovaltine and take rest. I won't be in for lunch." Surya Rao left with his zip-bag secure under his left arm-pit.

Suvarchala did not trust servants. She did her own cooking. She made a cup of ovaltine and refreshed herself. In matters of diet and health, she implicitly followed the advice of her husband. And her husband always acted on her counsel in all matters concerning his business transactions. This rapport between the two was anathema to her in-laws. She perceived it very early in her married life. Her father-in-law would not agree to any division of property. The major part of the income from the fields, the rice-mill and sundry business, which was concealed from taxes in the second account was being diverted to the two daughters of the family. Suvarchala decided to stop it. Surya Rao was an engineer in metallurgy, and had worked in Calcutta before his marriage. He had a number of blue-prints to start his own industry, but he lacked courage and decision. After the marriage, his father asked him to remain at home and manage the rice-mill. For any new enterprise, he refused to advance the required capital. If Surya Rao did not like it at home, he was welcome to seek employment elsewhere. Suvarchala stepped in, advanced the fifty thousand she had got from her parents and asked her husband to go ahead with his plans. The couple arrived in Hyderabad. They initiated the execution of their plans. And simultaneously gave notice to the father that unless he complied with their request for family money, they would inform the Income-tax people and have the mill raided, besides filing a civil case for division of property. The father abused his daughter-in-law roundly and parted with a lakh of rupees and bought peace.

From childhood, Suvarchala had great faith in God. Lord Venkateswara was her favourite, and she was convinced she had a rapport with Him. Surya Rao had not taken it seriously and had even made fun of her. But during the last twelve years, he had acted upon her advice and solved many a problem he had to face. He gradually developed an implicit faith in her spiritual capacities. As her prayers grew longer than ever before, and her fasting denying herself all nourishment became a frequent affair, he couldn't say no to them; but worried about her health, and consulted a doctor as a routine to keep her nourished and strong. Suvarchala's marital happiness and domestic happiness lay in the personal care her husband bestowed on her. She had an eleven-year old son, Venkatewara Rao, who was studying in a Public School in the Nilgiris. She had not asked the Lord for another child, and He had not given her one.

Sometimes she did feel lonely. But her son's stay at home during the vacation and other holidays, also created problems for her. He seldom obeyed her. Further he made fun of her prayers and piety. He was not only irreverant, but advised his father to take her to a psychiatrist. She came to realize a little too late that it had been her fault to put him to school in an English medium, culturally un-Indian institution. But she had to do it to remove him from the influence of her in-laws, and because it was a matter of status and prestige. Her son having turned into an inveterate critic, whom she only tolerated, she dreaded to have another child.

After drinking ovaltine, she went into the rear garden. There was a sun-flower blossom brightly smiling at the sun. She had a special liking for it, as her name Suvarchala meant a sun-flower. The servant-boy was at work, watering the plants. "Is this the proper time to water the plants?" she asked him. "I went shopping. Then I had to clean the rooms and make the beds...I happen to be the only one to do all these things. Where is the time?" "No lunch today. Master has gone out. I'll give you two rupees. Go out and eat something."

When the servant-boy left, she bolted the front door and lay upon her bed. Her childhood came back to her. Her elder brother had been a competitor and a rival always. Whenever her parents were found to be partial to him, he being a male and the first-born, she would quietly meditate and pray to her God. Her sitting in a corner and refusing to eat was taken for sulking by her parents. She never demanded any justice from them; nor did she beg them. She merely registered her protest, and silently prayed to her God. After a time the parents came round and recognized her ways. They treated her as her brother's equal, and would consult her wishes. Her brother stood first in his studies. He was a hard worker as a student. She despised him for wasting his mental energies in reading and learning by rote. If only he would devote the same effort to prayer and meditation, he could obtain the grace and favour of God. The brother passed the entrance test and joined the Medical College, the same year she failed in her school-final examination. After that she refused to take the examination again. Her parents tried to persuade her. It was then that she placed a personal issue before the Lord for the first time and he directed her not to take the examination. The direction was received through the fall of a flower from the feet of the Lord.

The method of petitioning the Lord continued over the years and had given guidance and assurance on several occasions. She had been blessed with success. Her husband had become totally her man. She had been able to rescue him from the grip of her in-laws, and establish an industrial unit at Hyderabad all because of the grace of the Lord. The present Income-tax problem too would certainly be solved by his grace.

Suvarchala's brother had left for the United States and as a doctor he was reported to be earning a lot of money. She felt that she too was doing well and was in no way behind her brother. The only snag was that she and her husband had to adopt secret ways of safeguarding their wealth from a government bent upon grabbing it all through high taxes.

It was just 2 p.m., when the car arrived. It was Surya Rao.

"We did it, darling. He wanted five thousand. His usual percentage. The old statement filed earlier was returned, and the new one safely put in its place. The auditor said that his personal fee was one thousand for his trouble. I paid him."

Suvarchala could not follow all the details. She asked : "Where did we go wrong?" It seems I shouldn't have shown the car in my personal account. It should have been put in your account.... "We are husband and wife. Does it make a difference?" "In the government's view it does make a lot of difference." "Can we utilize the money in the puja-room?" "May be. We better start the construction of our new house. That would absorb a lot of cash." "Did you have your lunch?" "Of course. What about you?" "I had a cup of ovaltine. I want to have some sleep."

* * *

Surya Rao's aunt, Yasoda, widowed some ten years ago and living with her only son in a remote village wrote to him requesting him to take her son Ramana under his wing and show him some employment at Hyderabad. The boy had completed his B.Com. and was languishing in the village. Surya Rao consulted his wife.

Suvarchala recollected having met Yasoda at the time of her own marriage and again on two other similar occasions. She had also seen the little, dark complexioned boy, who had accompanied the elderly lady then. The fellow must have passed B.Com now.

"Would you like to give him a job?" she asked.

"We do require a trustworthy fellow, preferably one from our own people, at the factory. The people here are unreliable. They are here today, but gone tomorrow. They come to know confidential matters and even resort to black-mail. I've already had experience of one or two cases. I am for employing this Ramana."

"Well then let him come. But we cannot feed him in the house here. See that he has his lodging and food both at the factory.

"Of course, you are right. He is not our guest. We'll treat him as an employee only. We are business-people."

Surya Rao wrote to Yasoda, and accordingly, one morning Ramana arrived. Black and plump, like one of the stone-images found in temples, Ramana with his white teeth and frequent grin, struck Suvarchala as a strange figure. She was both apprehensive and condescending, and became studiedly indifferent after a while. Ramana had his lunch in the house on the day of his arrival. Suvarchala was amazed at the quantity of rice he consumed. "If there are ten boarders like your cousin, the hotel-fellow will either put up the rate or go bankrupt in no time!" she said to Surya Rao. "You say that! It's a villager's habit, you know. It only shows that even after going to college in a town, he has not taken to the refined ways of the town. I prefer that." "Did you notice him wearing a red *namam* on the forehead soon after his bath? It looks queer for his black complexion!" Suvarchala said with suppressed laughter. "Well, it is something. He did not add white ones on either side of the red *namam.* That would make him Lord Venkateswara! I think he will get over these things after a few days in the city."

Even after four months, there was no change in Ramana. He did learn quickly all his daily chores in the factory He was assigned bank-work and was asked to deliver messages and receive cheques from customers. He was paid Rupees two hundred fifty for his personal expenditure, and no salary was yet fixed by Surya Rao. Yasoda wrote to Surya Rao to send some money from the earnings of Ramana. Then the question of fixing a salary came up, and Suvarchala was consulted.

"Shall we pay him four hundred a month?"

"You seem to have a soft corner for your cousin! In these days employment itself is a favour and a gift. You may make a start with three hundred. After one year, we may give him a rise. If you pay him four hundred now, they will any way ask for a further rise next year. What would you do then?"

Surya Rao agreed with her. He informed Ramana that three hundred was the monthly salary, and the balance due for four months, a hundred rupees was being sent to his mother on her request.

Ramana required some clothes. He asked for an advance of two hundred rupees, and Surya Rao obliged.

When Ramana appeared in his terene shirt and trousers, said Suvarchala : "Why this extravagance? You could have gone in for cottons." "These are economical, sister... They don't get soiled quickly, and I can wash them myself." "Look here, Ramana, this is not a village to address people as brother or sister. You should address me as madam and your cousin as sir. Remember, this is the way of the city, and now you have a proper job." Suvarchala thought that she had made his position very clear to him. The usual grin on Ramana's face disappeared for a while. But he didn't mind what she had said.

Then Surya Rao added : "Well, Ramana, you have to do one thing for us. You see the servant-boy here is not only irregular, but cheats us every morning when he goes to buy vegetables. Daily you are anyway coming here at ten in the morning to see me. Why don't you come an hour earlier to fetch us vegetables and groceries? After all, it is our own work in the house."

Ramana did not raise any objections.

Towards the end of the financial year, the accounts had to be rewritten for reducing the tax burden. An expert accountant did this work for Surya Rao for a sizable amount as special fee. Ramana was despatched with the books to the accountant. Surya Rao said to Ramana : "You should learn this work of rewriting from the accountant, whether he is willing to teach you or not. Put him questions and find out. Next year we are not going to waste money on the fellow for this work. Better you become an expert in it."

There was no reaction from Ramana.

As soon as the Income-tax returns were filed, the couple went on pilgrimage to Tirupati. They had a vow to fulfil. The previous year, Suvarchala had obtained the Lord's grace to solve the Income-tax difficulty by her vow to perform the Lord's marriage. Already it was overdue by a few months. There was no problem, if she would pay a fine to the Lord for not adhering to the time limit. She had to deposit it in the Hundi. Ramana was suitably instructed to keep watch both at the house and the factory. They would be back in a week.

The required fee was paid to the temple authorities, who

conducted the ritual of the Lord's marriage, witnessed by a large number of couples, who had also paid for it. After that was over, Suvarchala got her husband tonsured, offering his hair to the Lord. They put a hundred rupees each as a voluntary offering.

When they returned home, the servant-boy had absconded. In spite of their telegram, Ramana was not there to greet them. Surya Rao phoned to the factory. He was told that the servant-boy left the very next day after their departure. Ramana was down with high fever and was lying in his room at the factory. The chowkidar was the only person who attended on him and provided some sustenance. Surya Rao felt depressed. When he went into the backyard, he found Suvarchala in tears. All her plants including the sun-flower were ruined.

After a bath and some rest, Suvarchala sat in the puja-room for two hours meditating on the Lord. Then she came out and told Surya Rao to send an urgent telegram to his aunt Yasoda to go over to Hyderabad to attend on her son.

Yasoda arrived and Ramana was admitted in a hospital for treatment. Yasoda was given charge of the kitchen to prepare food, serve the inmates and then take the requirements of Ramana to the hospital. She would keep him company in the nights at the hospital. After ten days, Ramana was discharged.

Yasoda discussed Ramana's future plans with Suvarchala. There was a marriage-offer for Ramana. He would get twenty thousand rupees towards dowry from the girl's parents. The big offer was made in view of Ramana's present position in Hyderabad. The people who made the offer wanted to visit Hyderabad and ascertain things for themselves. If only Suvarchala and Surya Rao would put in a kind word, and conduct the talks giving an assurance about Ramana's future, his marriage would be settled, and he would continue to serve them as their own man. Yasoda proposed to take Ramana home for a week to give him rest and nourishment and send him back. It would be easy to pick up health in the village, she said.

"I'll inform my husband," said Suvarchala without committing herself to anything.

What roused the resistance of Suvarchala to entertain Ramana any further in service, was Yasoda's hint that Ramana might be taken as a junior partner by receiving his twenty thousand dowry from the marriage party. The couple discussed the matter and ruled out any such arrangement. They informed Yasoda not to be in a hurry to send Ramana back and asked her to wait till they sent a call for him.

A fortnight later, two persons approached Surya Rao to discuss Ramana and his future with him. Surya Rao could easily see that Ramana's position in the factory had been misrepresented to them. Surya Rao had half a mind to maintain the lie, and help Ramana to get married. But he wanted to consult his wife. While the visitors were there in the drawing room, he went inside to talk to Suvarchala. An enraged Suvarchala said : "Absolute nonsense! Please tell them without mincing words that he is nothing but a coolie here. What kind of joke is this! Partnership we refused even to your father and sisters. This fellow is not indispensable. We could get a dozen fellows like this one." "Being non-committal for the present, we would help him to get married, and then things will take their own course. Why bother?" Suvarchala was emphatic. "That will not only break up the marriage, but will turn both the parties into our enemies blaming and abusing us to eternity. Unpleasantness now is preferable to all that odium later on. Why should we get into it in the first instance?"

Surya Rao would not cross his wife. He told the visitors that he had no intention to take Ramana as a partner in his enterprise. They left making it clear that they were withdrawing the marriage-offer. A few days later Ramana wrote to say that he was prepared to go back to Hyderabad. It was evident that Ramana and his mother had not been informed about the withdrawal of the marriage offer.

The couple thought that there was no harm in asking him to come back to do his old job. "I knew all along that he would return. What else can he do? His mother will gradually realize her place. If she brings up any such matter before me again, I'll teach her a proper lesson. No more face-saving politeness!"

That night, Suvarchala lying asleep by Surya Rao's side, suddenly started kicking her feet and throwing her hands about, crying and restlessly moving her head. Surya Rao switched on the light and shook her out of her nightmare. As soon as she saw him, she clutched him in embrance, shivering and hard-breathing, till his assuring words restored her to calmness. Surya Rao had been worried about the state of her nerves recently, when she showed signs of hysterical laughter and fickle moods, and he was thinking of consulting a neurologist. He couldn't decide, as he attributed everything to travel-tiredness and the Ramana affair that followed their trip to Tirupati. He concluded that this must be a fit.

After a while, Suvarchala told him, "You know that fellow, that Ramana, he's a dare-devil...It was he, who actually sat on my chest and strangled me!..All because we spoiled his prospects, his marriage. Nothing but vengeance.... Tell him not to come back!"

"What happened? Was it a dream? What did Ramana say, what did he do?"

"What worse can he do?" Suvarchala broke down into tears, and hid her face in her husband's bosom.

Surya Rao didn't question her further. She got up at the break of dawn and switched on the electric geyser. While she was bathing, she slowly recollected everything exactly as it happened in the nightmare. That must have been the so-called 'rape!' She was in bed for her afternoon siesta. Ramana with his *namam* and usual hand-bag came and stood grinning. "You like a *dasari* in your get-up, a pucca vaishnava mendicant during Sankranti," she remarked jestingly. He suddenly jumped on her, pinned her hands down, sat on her thighs and entered her. Shocked and helpless, she was kicking her feet and struggling to free her hands, but couldn't, till her husband woke her up. Though what had happened was only a dream, somehow she felt she had been violated and lost her integrity as a person. She had lost something. It was an irreparable loss. There was a sense of utter void.

At breakfast Surya Rao asked her again about the nightmare. She couldn't tell him the whole thing. "He tried to strangle me, to rob us of our money and wealth. You know, he looks dumb, but I have always had an apprehension, not very clear to me myself. Whenever I had to be alone with him, when he came on some errand in your absence, I experienced some sort of fear, but I used to brush it aside considering who he was. Now that I had this nightmare, I feel he should not come back. We cannot have him."

"I'll see to that. But you must consult a neurologist. You should take some tonics, and stop your fasts for a period."

"There's nothing wrong with my health, except some tiredness."

For some reason, she did not enter the *puja*-room that day.

Two weeks later, there was a raid by the Income-tax people on Surya Rao's residence and the factory office. They went straight to the *puja*-room and discovered the secret place. The gold biscuits and the currency fell into their hands, as unaccounted money.

Suvarchala had a fit. She was admitted into a nursing home first, and later taken to a psychiatrist. The treatment continued, but she never again became her former self. Surya Rao put up the factory for sale and joined his father back at home.

The Dream

The intermittent rickshaw-bell. The lone wail of a bitch.

In dim light of a zero-bulb, Pankajam lay moaning. Her eyes were tightly closed and there was expression of pain on her face. Lokamma shook her to wake her up. She touched Pankajam under the chin and declared : Fever is gone! You were talking in sleep you know! dreaming?"

"Water...water," said Pankajam.

"You are drenched in sweat. No water, drink some gruel."

"I hate it. It makes me sick."

"You have to take something, you know; something to keep you going. I left a glassful here a long while ago. I thought you would need it as soon as you woke up. You continued to sleep. Let me see....Oh, it's gone cold."

Lokamma handed the glass to Pankajam. Sitting up and taking the glass Pankajam inquired : "What might be the time now?"

"About half-past ten."

Pankajam drank two gulps with an effort of the will and returned the glass to Lokamma.

"You didn't have any clients tonight?" Pankajam asked.

"Oh yes, some college boy. New and nervous. Got rid of him, quick and easy." Lokamma said with a laugh.

"Sit here." Pankajam invited her to sit by her side on the bed. Lokamma had been standing all the while.

"A terrible dream I was going through," said Pankajam, "If you hadn't come and called me back to this world, I don't know how long I'd have been hanging, you know, hanging just like that.... You see I dreamt I was dead and taken to Yama Loka."

"Silly girl! Would this fever kill you? What nonsense! Take my word, you will be fit and ready in just three days' time."

"That isn't it, Loka! I really wish for death sometimes. I'm not afraid to die. But then I'll have to face Yama's torture. Considering that perhaps it is better I manage somehow here."

"What is your complaint now? There is no Yama and no Yama Loka. Stop worrying."

"How do you say that? Didn't you see him, lorry-driver Venkayya, who brought me here? Yama with the same blood-shot eyes, was no worse. Thick black whiskers; a shining burning *gada* in his right hand; and on his head a gold coronet. I shiver to think of his eye fixed on me. He asked me, 'Why did you keep sinning, woman, why?' "

Lokamma started laughing. "Sin and merit? You mean you were watching the old movie 'Savitri' again in your dream! That wonderful Yama Loka scene, you know!"

"Maybe it is cinema, maybe it's real. I was shivering with fright. That was for real. All the time my brain kept working, working on a plan to escape, to run away. I kept arguing with Yama as best as I could : 'I'm not to be blamed, Lord. My mother married me to an old fogey. Couldn't afford a proper dowry to get me a young husband. The old fellow took the life out of me and treated me like a slave. I ran away, had to, with lorry-driver Venkayya, who made promises, made me believe in him, but only to betray me. What about punishing him? Throw him in Hell! As for me, I had no other way to live. Would Waheeda Begum feed me for nothing? I have to earn and live. And there are so many others too in the profession — six of us in my place, and daily there are clients! You must punish all, the rickshaw-wallahs, the taxi-drivers, Waheeda Begum, Hussain,

Rangayya — all of them depend on our earnings. After deductions, and payment for food, what do we get? A meagre rupee per client, and a rupee more when we dance. Why blame me, what is my fault in all this?' I was making out a full case, you see...."

"Let that be, said Lokamma with a yawn. I want to ask you a favour. How much money have you in your account?"

"Not much. Last month's earnings went towards the cost of the new saris. This month out of the sixteen rupees I earned, ten are already spent for the doctor's bill. The balance is there. Why, what happened to your money? You ask me!"

"I have ten rupees in my account. I've managed to make two rupees tonight. I need just three rupees more to buy me a new sari, just like the one you have. It's nice."

"All right. You may draw it from Waheeda from my account."

"Thank you. I knew you wouldn't say no to me." Lokamma took Pankajam's hand in hers and pressed it gently.

"After that, you know what Yama said in reply?"

"Oh yes, the dream."

"What you have told me doesn't help you. Every sinner gets his or her punishment. 'None shall escape the law.' And no sooner did he say that, one of his men was already dragging me away. 'Ah, wait a bit' I said, 'my knee is giving me awful pain.' I fell in a heap refusing to move. 'I have seen lots of folks like you,' he said and lifted me on to his shoulder and started moving at great speed. I thought it was not altogether a bad thing and clung round his neck, pressing myself against him. I even gave him a kiss on the cheek hoping he might soften towards me. But no use, he carried me to an open well of boiling oil and tried to drop me into it. I tightened my grip round his neck and would not come off. He started shouting, 'Give up, give up'. I didn't and waa hanging on desperately.... How long? How long?...But then you came and woke me up and saved me in time.... I never gave up, you know!"

Lokamma laughed.

Pankajam didn't laugh. She closed her eyes feeling exhausted after her long narration.

"You feel sleepy. That's right. Sleep now, I'm going." Lokamma stood up.

"No, no...please stay. If I sleep, I may dream again. I'm afraid to sleep now. Please stay for a while, won't you?"

Lokamma sat down. A few minutes passed. Pankajam opened her eyes, and inquired : "Are you feeding my bitch regularly?"

"Sure. Would she leave me, if I didn't? She waits there till eternity. You have made it quite a regular thing. I can't imagine where she disappears in the day-time, but in the evening, she is very punctual for the meal. A stree-bitch, what in the use of feeding her every day? Will she keep watch, or be of any other use?"

"That is the only good act I am doing. In my childhood my mother used to tell me a story of the Pandavas. They were on their last journey towards heaven, and all fell to the ground except Dharmaraj the eldest, wh alone deserved to go on the heavenly chariot with his earthly body. And with him was left a black dog. If I go to Yam Loka, I think I'll have my street-bitch following me."

"What sort of silly fear is this, Pankajam, all because of a few days' fever! If we are to think of this profession as sin, what else do we do for a living? We have to go on with this till we have our chance to go into the cinema, and once we get that chance, we start earning enough to get married, and then gather religious merit too."

"I don't believe it! Lorry-driver Venkayya brought me here just on that hope. But where are the film-people? Did he really know any of them? Deceit, deceit, nothing else! He got a big price from Waheeda. He sold me to her. She said she would train me as a dancer, and on that pretext, put me in the trade. I had no other go but to yield. It is already three years since I came here. Do you still think that some film-people will really come for you or me? No, no, this is our only life and must go on till death comes."

"They will come! We had three men the other day, you remember, they were from a film-company."

Pankajam made a sound with her lips indicating her disbelief. "That rascal Venkayya didn't feel as much as my street-bitch feels for me. Six months ago, he came here fully drunk and beat me... for nothing! What cause did I give? None. And the blow I got on my knee, it still troubles; while I walk, suddenly the pain appears. I have seen the last of that fellow. I have begged of Waheeda not to allow him to meet me any more. The hope of films, I know, it is no hope, it is empty nothing." Pankajam burst into tears.

"What is wrong with your life now? Who on earth is not sinful? All those respectable people, the money'd ones, are they not coming here to be with us? If one is clever enough, one must catch and hold a money-bag. Then one would move from this place. And live comfortably and happily ever after..." said Lokamma.

Pankajam remembered suddenly. There was just a ray of hope, a silver lining in the cloud. But one couldn't be sure. She wondered whether it would be wise to share her secret with Lokamma. Lokamma might become an obstacle. But she needed Lokamma's advice badly. She wanted her opinion about it. Perhaps the matter could be safely put as a general proposition, as a possibility.

"Catching and hoding a money-bag? You mean marriage? queried Pankajam.

"Maybe. Or some safe legal settlement."

"I suppose that can come only later. How is one to know the right man, who can be trusted?"

"No question of trusting. First settlement and then the next step into the future."

"Suppose property settlement is not forthcoming, but he will keep you as his own. He is not a money-bag, but an officer, already married or something like that."

"That is no good at all. They want pleasure without payment. Each visit here costs a minimum of fifteen rupees. If he takes you out of this place, it works out cheaper over a period till he gets tired of you. One should never trust that type."

Pankajam fell silent. She closed her eyes. Lokamma yawned. She said : "I am sleepy. I'll go now. Thank you for the loan. Goodnight!"

Pankajam didn't get to sleep immediately. With eyes closed she was recalling something that happened six weeks ago. The whole scene. Tall and handsome, the young man had something special about him. As four of them, including herself, stood before him, he didn't even take a good look. Impulsively, as though it mattered in the least, he nodded towards Lokamma first, but suddenly changed his mind and said : "Not you...You," pointing to Pankajam, who stood next to Lokamma. The choice was made and the other three went away. She could judge from his manner that this was his first visit to a place like this. She felt bored and indifferent. He asked something and she replied not even caring to understand his question. She asked him straightaway without hesitation : "Won't you give me some present please!" She didn't want to lose the opportunity an inexperienced visitor presented. He handed his purse to her! There was fifty in all. How much could she take safely? For, if she took more than he would be pleased to part with, the matter would go to Waheeda, who frowned on such things. It was against the house rules. "It is for you to make a present" she told him. He took out a fiver. She regretted that she didn't take at least twenty chips, when the purse had been in her hand.

He held her face in both his palms and bent over her looking deeply into her eyes. His fingers moved gently along her cheeks.

She felt strange at this tenderness and avoided his looks. His lips closed against her right cheek. His deep breathing caused a queer sensation. "What is all this acting!" she asked herself. Is he from the film-folk? A director?"

"Do you belong to the film-world?" she asked.

"Why do you think so?"

"Just a guess."

There was a pause.

"I'm an officer," he said.

"Police officer?"

But a police officer won't come like this. He would order the girls to go to his place!

He smiled and said : "An engineer in charge of construction."

No matter who he was, she had certainly lost an opportunity of making some more money. 'But why is he so slow, why doesn't he get on with his business?' she kept wondering, while the insects gyrated round the electric bulb. She was totally indifferent.

"Why are you so quiet? Why don't you say something?...Shall I go away?" he said suddenly. That struck her as funny, his threat that he would go away! Let him go. Who cared as long as he paid up. She didn't reply. It might be impertinence, and Waheeda advised silence to all kinds of queries from visitors. Putting forth a smile with effort, she said : "What is your pleasure? You are free to command me Sir!"

"Tell me about yourself. Why and how did you come to be in this place?"

What a nuisance, what a bore!

"I've always been here, Sir. I don't come from anywhere in particular."

"Look, there are tears gleaming in your eyes. You're not answering me. All right, you needn't tell me...."

There were no tears though. The mention of tears had a strange effect on her. She remembered her dead mother suddenly; remembered her difficulties in the last five years. But nothing could make her shed tears, no, she had a stone for heart; her courage and fortitude were great. She was proud, and what did the stranger know about her!

For all his strange approach, the man did not fail to prove his manhood, and he did share his pleasure with her. While doing so he succeeded in drawing tears from her, grateful tears for an experience she had seldom had. She melted and found herself telling him her story, every little detail of it. The angel of a man, she wondered, why was he frequenting filthy streets and sinful houses!

"Haven't you got a wife?" she asked him.

"Yes and no. She has gone away, left me for another man."

"Why? What for? Is the other man more handsome or rich?"

He nodded in reply. He might have meant that was so, or he might not have relished the question. She didn't press for an answer.

"Then why don't you marry again?"

He smiled, and took her hand in his and pressed it.

"Are you healthy?" he asked.

What a question to ask after every thing was over!

"Once a week the doctor comes here. That is Waheeda's arrangement. No doubts on that account."

He laughed and said : "What will your Begum charge, if I choose to visit daily?"

"You have to ask her. But would you?"

"No, I won't. But will you come away with me?"

"Impossible."

He tried to persuade her. "I'll make you happy in every way, short of formal marriage."

She couldn't trust him.

"I'll be back here in two months. Take your time to decide and let me known then."

He asked her name while leaving.

Pankajam didn't mention this to anyone. If Lokamma heard it, she would be sure to inform Waheeda. There was nobody she could trust or confide in. Each one to herself. Lokamma might be a friend. But it was impossible to know when she would change and do some thing adverse. What did she do in the matter of this street-bitch? It was she, Lokamma, who informed Waheeda that a street-bitch was being fed regularly, and Waheeda started charging five rupees extra on Pankajam's mess-bill. Of course, Lokamma might not have thought of the consequences. Anyway all information went to Waheeda without fail. Would Waheeda consent to her leaving the place with the officer? No, never. Why should she? Waheeda had paid a hundred rupees to Venkayya, and unless Pankajam paid up that amount, she had no right to leave that place. Would the gentleman be willing to pay the money, when he, indeed had a mind to keep his word and return? He was in a sad, peculiar mood on that night. It might have been just an impulse. If he ever wanted to marry again, why, he, an officer without any imaginable defect could get a nice bride from his own caste. Why should he return here for the sake of a prostitute? But his wife having run out on him was a stigma, a factor to reckon with and the man could not think of another formal marriage and a wife.... He would certainly come back. That was her hope. Her hope made his return a certainty; and if he returned, she would go with him without hesitation. That would be an unshakeable decision. How long could she continue in this place and suffer this Yama Loka? Nothing worse could befall her hereafter. Even if the gentleman were to prove unworthy of her trust, and she were to find herself again on the street, she would find some way to live....

* * *

Four days later when Pankajam got up from her sick bed, she conceived the idea of domesticating her street-bitch by chaining it in the house for a few days.

Pankajam's friendship with the street-bitch had a curious beginning. Of the six girls maintained by Waheeda Begum, three were habituated to drink being senior members of the establishment. The three juniors Pankajam, Lokamma and Ayesha being new-comers were learning to drink, for it was the considered opinion of Waheeda that drink would help the girls in their profession, and would come to their rescue in some difficult situations. Ayesha had learnt it, but Pankajam found it beyond her to overcome her aversion to drink. One day she managed to gulp some liquor, but it upset her stomatch. She had to run fearing to be sick in the kitchen-cum-dining room. And by the time she went to the rear door opening into the gully, she vomitted and was retching frightfully. A street-bitch came up suddenly and started lapping up the vomit, which contained undigested food, and in no time the door-step was cleaned up. Pankajam felt grateful to the animal. She felt drawn towards the bitch. The bitch did not go away, but was looking at Pankajam expectantly asking for more. Pankajam rushed into the kitchen and brought some food for the bitch. After that the animal became a regular visitor at the rear door, arriving punctually at he hour of the evening meal. Pankajam fed the bitch without fail. She gave her the leavings and some rice and bones on her own behalf every day. When this came to the notice of Waheeda, she started charging Pankajam for it. Pankajam didn't mind and looked upon the bitch as her own. When she was ill, she had asked Lokamma to feed her pet. Now she wanted to domesticate the bitch.

The bitch responded to Pankajam's call briskly waving the tail and approaching her with a dance-movement of her behind. Pankajam fed her as usual and after that put around the animal's neck a yellow leather-belt, hooked it with a chain and fixed the chain to the neem tree in the back-yard. She had got the belt and the chain from the bazar through Rangayya, the watchman.

Pankajam petted and played with the bitch for a while; and at last, when she turned to go inside, the bitch stood looking into her face with mute understanding. Pankajam stopped and watched her from a distance. The bitch turned round and round, scratched the ground a little with her fore-legs and then settled down meekly. Pankajam returned late in the night again, just before going to bed, and found the bitch asleep in the same spot.

The next morning Pankajam got up very late. She went into the back-yard to greet the bitch. But she was not there! The chain remained fixed to the tree. The bitch was gone with the belt around her neck. Pankajam opened the rear door and looked out in vain. She found Akhtar, Waheeda's brother washing himself. Akhtar an indispensable male-support for the establishment was maintained by Waheeda. On seeing him Pankajam grew suspicious that he might have let off the bitch as a sort of practical joke. She asked him about the animal. He said : 'Go and find it in your small room.' The small room was used by the women when they were in menses. Pankajam thought that some one had transferred her bitch to that room and went there. The room was empty, and then she understood the indecent insult implied in Akhtar's remark.

She went to Waheeda. Waheeda was very sympathetic. "I don't know, daughter! Why, where might have the creature gone!" Pankajam asked Lokamma. She said : "She might have been barking and pulling at the chain, and somebody must have taken pity on her. Sure to be back in the evening, your precious friend. Watch out till then."

"I wanted to have her with me during the day-time. So that she might get used to me," said Pankajam very much disappointed.

Lokamma laughed almost derisively."Playing with a street-bitch! A street-bitch can never become a house-pet. What a foolish fancy!"

"Why not? Isn't she coming daily?"

"That's different. She comes because she is hungry. Not for your nice company! Waheeda may not approve of allowing her inside the house."

Pankajam now suspected Lokamma. Waheeda was generally indifferent to such small matters. Indeed she had been sympathetic a little while ago. It must be Lokamma, who unchained the bitch. Well, she, Pankajam must be patient. The bitch would any way come back in the evening. She was now her own thing, wearing her yellow-belt.

The bitch did not turn up that evening. Pankajam waited for her the next evening, and successively for five evenings. On the sixth evening, as Pankajam opened the door, she found the bitch lying on the door-step. Pankajam called her inside. She noticed that the bitch had several wounds on her body. She placed the food at the usual spot. As the bitch limped towards the food, Pankajam noticed that she was badly hurt and one hind leg was held up. She had been severely beaten by some one, mauled by dogs and perhaps stoned by urchins. Pankajam was sorry for her, and as she ate the food, she stood watching with affection and pity. Pankajam was figuring it out. The bitch had been removed from her usual haunts to a distant corner of the city, and got beaten and bitten by dogs heartlessly.

As soon as the poor creature finished its meal, Pankajam tried to hold her in her hands and wipe the dirt and blood off her body. But the bitch growled at her and warned her off. She showed her teeth with a raised upper-lip, and didn't permit Pankajam to touch her. She appeared to be apprehensive of the pain Pankajam might cause her. She was reluctant to be chained again. She had lost her trust in the goodness of human beings.

Pankajam was heart-broken. The bitch turned back into the street.

* * *

A week passed. Pankajam felt emotionally bound to her street-bitch. She gave up the idea of domesticating her, whose wounds were healing. But the bitch would not allow Pankajam to touch her any more. She was, however, a punctual guest, arriving with a wave of the tail, greeting Pankajam and departing promptly at the end of the meal.

Pankajam ceased looking upon Lokamma as a friend any more. While Pankajam was bed-ridden, Lokamma had been able to earn more. Her credit with Waheeda went up. Lokamma was now behaving condescendingly towards the other girls. Financially Pankajam was at the bottom. Her account was over-drawn, though she was ready for the trade, she didn't have more than two clients for the whole of that week. One afternoon, Waheeda sent for Pankajam. She spoke in her mixed dialect of Urdu-Telugu. The gist of her long-winding talk was : a new police Inspector had taken charge, a widower with a wild fancy for girls. He had sent word that morning and wanted a nice companion. Pankajam was aware that in all such instances Waheeda would send the girl least in demand at the moment. Listening to Waheeda, her heart sank. Waheeda came out with a new explanation. She said that this Inspector was different and had to be treated with special respect, for he was a connoisseur, and was sure to take offence, if someone in the ordinary run were to be sent to him. Pankajam had been selected after careful thought. Pankajam was alone found to be worthy to please the sahib and bring credit to the reputed name of Waheeda. Pankajam was not taken in by her mollifying words, but she could do nothing to save herself. She had become a back-number in the estimation of Waheeda. As an incentive, Waheeda added, that she would make a present of that fifteen rupees, which Pankajam had yet to earn, if she willingly went and returned with the compliments of the officer. This was Waheeda's generosity!

Pankajam sallied forth with full makeup that night.

The Inspector was a man on the wrong side of fifty, pot-bellied and huge like a dark he-buffalo. Pankajam was not daunted by his appearance. Her problem was drink. He insisted on sharing his drinks with her, and she had to comply, or pretend compliance. She did her best evading and pretending. Her difficulties began after the drinking bout was over. It was nothing but punishment, the punishment she had dreaded was waiting for her in Hell. The dream, she thought, had come true. For, the man was not a human being. He was pinching, biting and causing her pain in all sorts of ways in all sorts of places on her body. He used her body as his wild fancy led him. He was being unimaginably nasty and filthy. Finally he lay like a log and snored.

Pankajam's pride, her will, her self-confidence were crushed. She had thought that tears were foreign to her. But on that hellish night she wept and wept till she had no more tears to shed.

The Inspector did not think of sending her back to the establishment the next morning. He decided to take her with him on camp. He sent a message to Waheeda that he was very much delighted, and the lady would be back two days later. When he announced it to Pankajam, she was terrified. She fell on his feet and begged him to take pity on her; that she was very weak and had not yet recovered from her recent illness; that she would be grateful to him in all births to come, if he would kindly send her back. But her pleading was in vain. He said he wouldn't so much as touch her. He just wanted her delightful company. He would take her to a doctor and buy her medicines and tonics. He imagined he was being nice and gentle to her, and saying so he pinched her cheek affectionately! It brought tears into her eyes.

Two days later, returning to her place, Pankajam wondered whether she was Pankajam or someone else! She had been to the other world, to Hell. With wounds all over her body, sadly limping, dusty and dirty, her bitch had so returned, after five days of desolation and hell; returned to her, Pankajam only for the sake of that meal. Hunger indeed was a great urge, and now, she, Pankajam was in the same plight! Could she expect pity from Waheeda? Sympathy from Lokamma? Doubtful! Whoever would bother to think of her!

She heated her own bath-water and had her own fomentation. She pitied herself; wiped her own tears; and loved herself. For two days she didn't speak to anyone. And none spoke to her! They were quite indifferent. She did not think of going and complaining to Waheeda, or narrating her tale of woe to Lokamma.

Lokamma did not give her so much as a glance. Pankajam waited every evening for her bitch, waited for her only friend, but she did not turn up. Pankajam knew at last what to think of it. During her absence, none had fed the bitch. They might have driven her away with blows and insults. Maybe she would never again see her friend.

It was a Sunday and Lokamma invited Pankajam to go with her to the matinee show. Pankajam excused herself saying she had a headache. Lokamma would not listen and went on pressing her. Finally she said : "If you go with me, I'll tell you a secret something that is in your own interest, will you go or not?" Pankajam was curious and tempted. She accompanied Lokamma to the show. Lokamma did not easily tell the secret. She made her promise to keep it to herself, and told her when they were returning to the house in a rickshaw.

The next day after Pankajam had left to keep company with the Inspector, a gentleman had called and asked for Pankajam mentioning her by name. Waheeda said to him : "There's nobody with that name here." "She was here two months ago. Where has she gone?" he inquired. "Don't know. We don't keep old stuff. There's fresh stuff coming in, always, otherwise who would step into this house, Maharaj?" was Waheeda's reply. The gentleman turned down the other girls and left the place. Waheeda was furious and had squarely abused Pankajam for having violated the rules of the house. She gave a long lecture about the risks involved in divulging names and identities. She advised the girls not to converse at length with the visitors. Finally she had asked the girls to keep the episode a secret from Pankajam....

Pankajam understood that he was *that* gentleman, her man, keeping his word. He had come for her, but her bad luck, she had not been present precisely at that moment! She was then in the other place, Hell! Was it her fault? How could it be?

The rickshaw entered their street. There was a small group of urchins blocking the way. The rickshaw-wallah rang his bell and shouted : "Make way, make way." A few boys looked back and made way. As the rickshaw passed the group, Lokamma inquired : "What is it?"

"A dog....crushed by a lorry...dead." Pankajam jumped down and hurried to have a look. The yellow-belt was there. Her street-bitch was dead!

The Old Man and the Snake

My grandfather, who brought me up from childhood is dead. He died of cobra-bite. In all these years I could never really learn to love him. During the last three months we had not spoken a word to each other, till, this morning, he suddenly burst upon me with anger and spoke unprintable words, and asked me to get out of his house, snapping all ties between us. I had nothing to regret, and I was preparing to leave. Then came the news that my grandfather himself had quit, quit this world, leaving me to myself. I suddenly felt like weeping, as the past seemed to divide from me and leave me in peace at last.

My grandfather hated snakes. He had a passion for killing them and had developed considerable skill in dealing with the dangerous ones like the cobra. It was almost a vow with the old man that he would never see a snake without killing it. And he must have seen quite a good number in his life-time. Well, he ended his life with cobra-bite. The long-suffering snake had overcome him at last!

My mother was his only daughter. Three of his sons had died in infancy. People said it was due to a curse from the previous birth; and even related it to his present propensity to kill snakes, especially the cobra, regarded as a sacred thing. My grandfather brushed aside such notions with contempt. He was a Brahmo, a rationalist and a reformer. My grandmother was a believer and though she felt anxious about her husband's welfare, she kept her counsel. For, she admired his courage and daring and was awed by it; not merely silenced by his overbearing ways.

My grandmother rejoinced at my birth and looked upon me as an answer to her prayers and her propitiation of the Cobra-god, Nageswara. My grandfather was glad because there was an heir. I began to live with my grandparents quite early in my childhood. My earliest memories are of my brief visits to my parents, who lived in a town some distance away, where my father had a government job. My grandmother and I used to travel by train. The forward journey was a joyous one full of eager expectation, while the return journey was invariably gloomy. My mother was a goddess and my parents' house was heaven itself. On the return journey, the separation from my mother used to darken my mind, and as I sat looking out of the moving train, I imagined all good things were running away from me bidding me a quick farewell. It was an endless farewell. The sense of loss remained for two or three days.

"Whatever is the matter with you?" my grandmother would say looking at me anxiously.

"Nothing." I didn't know how to explain.

"It is the change of water, my poor dear, the town-water doesn't agree with your health, and a week's stay has already made you pale and sick," would be her comment.

On one occasion my parents came to see me. By then I had two sisters. We had a very happy time together. I taught my sisters some village games and introduced them to a number of tricks unknown to them in town. They asked me imploringly to return with them so that we might be together always. I made up my mind to go. I approached my grandmother and requested her to permit me to go with my sisters and parents to town. I didn't tell her that I had no idea of coming back. She went to grandfather.

"Who will bring him back?" he said.

"You may have to go a few days later."

"You think I have nothing more important to do? I can't understand this readiness to dance to his tune. He has met his mother and father here. Why does he want to go with them? Let him attend to his studies. Enough of holidaying."

So my people left that afternoon without me. I made one more attempt by petitioning my mother. But grandfather's will was final.

My defeat and surrender were unbearable. Angry and helpless, I was overcome with self-pity. That night, my grandmother, by whose side I lay whimpering, did her best in hushed tones to console me. Suddenly my grandfather pounced upon me and dragged me by the arm to the front door of the house. He pushed me out saying : "Go, go to your parents, we are not holding you here." The door closed on me with a bang and I heard it locked on the other side.

It was cold and dark outside. I wanted to go, but how could I? The railway station, the train I had to take, the ticket, everything was uncertain and impossible. More formidable was the thought that my father and mother might send me back again. They had already given me away to my grandparents. This brought fresh tears to my eyes. I was squatting, embracing my knees with my arms and pressing my face down on them, whem the door opened and my grandmother stepped out to lift me up into her arms.

As I lay again by her side, in silent humiliation, I discovered after a while, by the wetness on my head, that she was silently shedding tears for me! I wondered why she should weep. Then a feeling of warmth and love welled up in me for her, and I decided that thereafter, I would live with her for her sake and would not care for the company of my sisters and parents.

One day I saw my grandfather chase a cobra in the front yard of the house. I saw the snake rising on its tail with a hiss as the blow aimed to finish it off failed to do so. My grandfather's agility saved him. The snake disappeared into a pile of stones lying along the compound-wall. The pile of stones was instantly cleared and all suspicious-looking holes were plugged securely. A new brick-wall replaced the old earthen compound-wall. But all the time there was no trace of the cobra dead or alive. My grandmother continued to apprehend danger from the cobra, for cobras are believed to be vindictive and to have long memories.

I had very few playmates in my childhood. My grandfather forbade my mixing with the children of the village. He had nothing but contempt for the other brahmin families in the village. My grandfather had been a reformist in his youth having joined the Brahmo Samaj. He had constructed a prayer-hall as a rival to the village temple and had led the Brahmo movement in his time. He was also the wealthiest land-owner of the village. These things alienated him from the others, and he had his prestige. He looked upon me as the heir to his prestige.

Hanumanthu was our chief-cultivator. He was a *kapu* by caste. Sometimes he took me to his house and his son would present me jambo fruit. Hanumanthu's wife always gave me a tumblerful of butter-milk to drink. These were the only permissible things a non-brahmin could offer a brahmin. In Hanumanthu's household, I was most drawn to his daughter Subbulu, three years junior to me. From the beginning she bound me to herself by her attractive ways. She would tickle me or do something provocative and run away, drawing me into a race after her. She would suddenly throw her arms round me and give me kisses. We used to take long walks. Subbulu and myself, along the canal bund. Then she would whisper to me : "I am your wife."

After finishing school in the village, I was allowed to spend four years in town for my college education. I spent my vacations with my parents. During this period my grandfather was ill for some time and stayed with my parents for treatment. I expected my grandfather to die. It was almost a hope. But he recovered from his illness and forbade me from going up for LL.B. after I had finished my B.A. He did not want me to become a lawyer but wanted me to settle down in the village. My parents refused to intervene on my behalf, and very reluctantly I returned to the village after my graduation.

I met Subbulu again. In the four years I had been away, she had changed remarkably. She was now like a brown cobra with the freshness of having just cast off her skin. The sparkle in her eyes, and the grace of her movements, her teasing words and her challenging manner fascinated me. I had arrived in the village in a mood of despair.

Subbulu's family had done well during those years. Hanumanthu had purchased some land and was no longer an employee of our family. His son had got a government job and had left the village. Subbulu had just finished school.

Subbulu came to my house and was with me for quite a while in my room upstairs. When she was about to leave the house, my grandmother called her and said : "What were you doing all this while my girl?"

"He was showing me some books."

"But you have finished school, haven't you?"

"No, I haven't. I want to be trained as a teacher."

"So you will be employed like a man and earn! Isn't it about time that you should think of marriage? Let me talk to your father. I don't like girls of your age going about idly. I'll tell him."

"Please ask *him* about it. I don't know."

With a swift turn of her face, she ran away. When she said, "him", the jerk of her chin actually indicated me even though her words apparently referred to her father. I was amused. It was just like her. Then my grandmother spoke to me. "Suryam, I don't like your being alone with her.... Please, my dear boy, don't do these improper things. It does our family no credit. No, my boy, you have read books and — you should know better. If your grandfather comes to know about this, imagine the consequences ." She touched my chin with the tips of her fingers affectionately and begged of me not to provoke grandfather.

"Oh, grandfather is a social reformer, ma. Don't you worry. If he orders me to mary her, I might as well! In any case what else do you want me to do in this miserable hole of a village? Do you expect me to sit in meditation? Subbulu is my friend since childhood. She is not a stranger and she is a very lively girl." I spoke in a lighter vein, but I made my intentions also quite clear. My grandmother was shocked but silently kept her counsel.

After that, Subbulu refused to visit my house, and I suspected that grandmother had something to do with the refusal. Then I started visiting Subbulu. This brought me into frequent contact with Hanumanthu, who had recently joined the communist party. Hanumanthu found me in favour of radicalism in politics and introduced me to his party members.

I was glad of the opportunity to align myself with a political party, which was, in the nature of things, a sworn enemy of my grandfather and people like him. I became very critical of my grandfather and his views of social reform. He would never admit the Marxist theory of class-conflict. He was for reform through education and enlightenment. He believed in the improvement of the individual as a basis for the improvement of society. When I pointed out to him that what he called culture or enlightenment was itself an off-shoot of a man's economic status, he would not accept the idea. In his view enlightenment and an aspiration for it was a human value, while money, its possession or non-possession might be a social value, but not a human value. When I told him that culture was a mirage, and what was real and substantial was money and its power, he dismissed the whole matter as gross materialism. After one or two such discussions, he refused to enter into any more discussions with me.

But one day he called me and said : "Even granting your materialistic view of society, I wonder whether you have understood your own position in it. As a rich man, you cannot rub shoulders with the communists."

"Well, grandfather, is money more important than culture? Justice and fairplay are part of culture or enlightenment, aren't they? A feeling of human brotherhood and a striving for its attainment in society are not anti-cultural. I am in pursuit of true culture." I wanted to pay him back in his own coin.

"But, my boy, your striving must follow an ethical code. There must be fair-play in give-and-take. Opportunism, aggressiveness, violence and hatred cannot be the right means to attain the goal of human brotherhood."

"This is the plea of the privileged class, Sir. Any ethical code is valid only to the members of one class whose interests are common. There can be no ethical code between two classes, whose interests are diametrically opposite. I feel genuinely concerned for my fellowmen oppressed by an unjust social system, and, therefore, I am on their side."

My grandfather did not pursue the argument further. But he went and settled a bride for me, without so much as giving me an inkling about it. In fact, he made it appear that it was a match chosen by my parents and not by him. At that time I was taken in. My mother pleaded that it was my duty as the first-born to get married and facilitate the marriages of my sisters. I could not say 'no' to her.

White-complexioned Shanta was like a doll made of flour, so fragile she was. I found her inadequate for my sensuality. If I had vaguely hoped for a change in the taste of life after my marriage, I found that hope was belied. I turned to politics and to party activities in full measure. This must have disappointed my grand-father too, who expected me to give up politics for my wife.

Suddenly my grandfather started encouraging me in my political activities even as a member of the Communist Party. He advanced me money liberally and approved of my candidature for election to the Assembly on the party ticket. He financed it as much as the Party itself. But I lost the election.

Then I grew tired of politics. My grandfather fell ill and entrusted me with the management of his affairs. I discovered a new interest in spending money and in earning it by devious means. Hoarding of food-grains, smuggling them outside the state, black-marketing, and bribing government officials — in all this variety of the business-life, I discovered the true variety of life's business. For, races, drink and damsels too preoccupied me and made me forget myself.

It was at this point, Subbulu re-entered my life. Her return gave me the chance to pull myself out of a situation, which was fast becoming untenable. I was spending far more than I earned, and finding it impossible to exercise any self-control. Shanta had gone to her parents for her first confinement, six years after our marriage. My grandfather was away from the village, having his treatment in the city-hospital. Subbulu had become a school-teacher and after working in different places, she got herself transferred to our village. Thus our old friendship was revived.

In about three months she enabled me to steady myself. I began to stay at home and conduct my affairs effectively. My relationship with Subbulu was no longer a secret. My grandmother too came to know of it, but did not interfere. Hanumanthu indeed made some noise about it, but Subbulu took up residence in a separate house, as she was no longer dependent on her father.

Shanta's child was still-born, or died immediately after birth, some such thing happened and I was not greatly concerned about it. I did not visit her. A messenger came from Shanta's parents. My affair with Subbulu had reached their ears also. When the messenger arrived, my grandmother demanded that I should visit Shanta at once and make it up with her.

"Alright, alright, I will go," I said.

"You must bring Shanta back with you," she said.

"Yes, if she wants to come," I said in a somewhat petulant tone.

"Then what have you decided about. Subbulu?" She brought it out at last.

"There is no question of my letting her down."

"I warn you I cannot allow her to enter this house any more, no, not even for a casual visit. If you don't listen to me, my boy, I will find my grave in a well."

"No, ma, if you insist on these conditions, I will myself quit this house."

"What an impossible rascal you are! What do you expect Shanta to do then?" She whined and whimpered.

"I don't know."

"At least, at least, can't you meet that hussy somewhere else and not here? Shanta would not know about it."

I smiled and said : "I will try."

"On my life, my darling boy, please listen to me, wont you? Shanta is such a good girl, an angel, I wont have you hurt her. No, not for anything..." she pleaded, and broke down in tears.

I too wept. I took her hand in mine and said impulsively : "No, ma, I will not hurt Shanta."

While I was away on my visit to Shanta, my grandfather returned to the village and took immediate charge of the affairs at home. He even took the trouble, during that brief week of my absence, to go and see the authorities and get them transfer Subbulu to another village. So on my return with Shanta, I found everything was in my grandfather's control and I was expected to submit to him.

In despair, I went to see Subbulu, who was in a state of fury and revolt because of her transfer.

"Don't I have any rights at all? What does your grandfather think of me? What do *you* think of me? You talk of a hundred obstacles in the way of our marriage. I didn't mind. But when I am not allowed to stay in my own village, it is really too much for anyone to bear. Now please tell me, whether you will marry me immediately or not. This must be settled here and now."

"Alright," I said without giving the matter any thought.

"It is not just nodding your head that will satisfy me. I am serious. You should go and ask for a divorce from your wife on the grounds that for six years she has not borne you a child, and her being an invalid makes her unfit for married life. You must see a lawyer immediately."

I silently nodded my head.

It was true that Shanta was not doing well. She was sent to the T.B. sanatorium at Madanapalle. When I was taking leave of Shanta, she brought up the subject of Subbulu. "My health is none too good. I have no objection, if you decide to marry her. None, really." She said it quietly, without any trace of emotion in her tone or in her face. I was taken aback, for the thought had just crossed my mind, when she gave precise expression to it as though she read my mind and was not willing to stand in my way. Her words had a strange effect upon me; they destroyed that very thought in me. I was moved. An upsurge of feeling of desire and passion for Shanta overwhelmed me. I took her hand in mine and said : "No, don't say that. It is unthinkable. I have wronged you, but I will try to change my ways. If I fail to change, please, please forgive me and accept me as I am, an unworthy husband. You will always be my wife." I don't know quite why I said those words. It was done unexpectedly. I had lost all control over myself.

The course of my life had zig-zagged like the trail of a serpent. It had never been straight. I wasn't bound either by morality or idealism or love. But I had also failed to get free from whatever it was that bound me. Like the legendary serpent-bond, something made me a prisoner, and all my writhings had been in vain.

I had promised Subbulu to get a divorce and marry her. I had also promised Shanta to try and change my ways. Which promise was I going to fulfil? I didn't know, I didn't want to know. The will was utterly lacking in me. I allowed days to drift. Meanwhile, Subbulu pressed me every time I met her; and Shanta wrote to me regularly.

A year went by. I succeeded in getting Subbulu reposted to my village. Yesterday she made a triumphant entry into my house unmindful, nay, in defiance of my grandfather's presence. She stayed for the night, and through the night she gave me hell repeating :

"The divorce....the marriage..." *ad nauseam.*

In the morning, when Subbulu left, grandfather came up to me. He had not spoken to me for the last three months. He burst out in anger, the like of which I had not witnessed in recent years. "You have neither morality nor decency. You don't belong here. No, you don't! The bond is broken. Get out. Get out of my house, will you?" He shouted at the top of his voice. "I want you to get out immediately," he added in a cold tone and left.

He left for his morning walk with staff in hand, towards the fields, as I watched his old man's gait quickened by his recent emotional outburst.

I wonder whether it was the same cobra, which long ago received a blow but escaped unkilled, that finally confronted him this morning and revenged itself against him after so many years! Nobody knows what the life-span of a cobra is. May be revenge prolongs its life indefinitely. However, it may be, my grandfather died in confrontation with a snake, killing it and killed by it.

Well I remain!

* * *

Three months after grandfatéer's death, Shanta returned, her health restored.

Subbulu broke away from me. "You have no morality, no loyalty, you have ruined my life," she told me.

But is it at all possible that one can ruin another's life?

One Who Did Not Die

The jasmine is in full blossom. The flowers may wilt and die, but the hair which wears them retains the perfume long after their death. In life's book another chapter commences. When desires get fulfilled, zest for life is on the wane. But the love for jasmines, despite long association with them never declines. Prasuna's thoughts hovered round the flowers as she prepared a garland. It was something she did with relish after all these years.

Her thoughts went back to twenty years....

Before she got married, she had imagined an idyl : a husband with the status of a civilian officer, a car, ornaments and dresses of her choice, and plenty of leisure. All of them she was able to get, the dream was realized, and people said she was a lucky woman. Three years went by, and she became aware of an inadequacy, which she had scrupulously ignored, though mentioned by a few close relations on both sides. She had yet to become a mother! Even in that matter, she was being assured by doctors and astrologers that she had only to wait for the golden moment. And yet she was dissatisfied. She could not identify the cause. "I am bored," she would say, and her husband would suggest that she had too much leisure. Her father-in-law suggested religion and philosophy, which she ought to study to find a meaning for life. And the Collector's wife advised her to take further interest in women-welfare activities. She did not act upon any of these suggestions. The problem for her was that she did not look out for anything, not even for the expected motherhood.

Her husband arrived. "You haven't gone to the club yet" he said. Prasuna held up the English novel she had been reading. "I want to finish this." "Well, instead of reading, you have been counting the jasmines on the creeper." "The story started dragging along, so I took my mind off for a while." "Just like real life?" Prasuna wanted a change of topic. She queried : "Why are you back so early from the club today?" "I received a telegram, Venu is arriving. By the evening train. I wanted to tell you and then go to the railway station to receive him." "There has been no letter from him for a long while." "It is just like him. He is appearing for the civil services examination, you know. It is a fortnight away. He wants to relax, he says, A peculiar fellow!" "Shall I get you a cup of coffee?" "Welcome" Prasuna hurried indoors.

*　　　*　　　*

The rain was unexpected. Venu had gone for a late evening walk. Prasuna thought he would have got drenched. Venu loved solitude. In that he was unlike his brother, who couldn't do without company. After his arrival, Venu had spent the first two evenings playing chess with his sister-in-law. She thought he would follow the routine today also; she sat ready with the chess-board and chess-men. Venu came on the front verandah dressed to go out, and from there briefly announced to her that he was going out for a walk and left : Venu give the impression of a well-informed person with good manners, but his less than courteous behaviour leaving her to fend for herself, left Prasuna very much displeased.

Perhaps because Venu happened to be the youngest of her three sons, Prasuna's mother-in-law petted him and always spoke in praise of him. She gave an account of Venu's likes and dislikes, and set forth his opinions on every blessed thing, irrespective of the listener's interest. Therefore her mother-in-law's visits had brought the invisible presence of Venu also into the house long ago, though this was Venu's first visit to his brother after the marriage. And it was Prasuna's first meeting with him. Prasuna had been keenly observing Venu searching for all the special qualities his mother had attributed to him. Whatever might be special about him, he was a loner. He was not very communicative, and preferred one-word answers. Prasuna thought it might be reckoned as egotism, if not self-conceit. It was not shyness or reserve, because he looked straight into her eyes, and always spoke with certitude and conviction. He was of a different species from his brother, her husband.

Prasuna was aware of Venu's delicate constitution, about which she had been cautioned by his mother, and felt worried that he was getting drenched in the non-stop rain. She could not send an umbrella as the attender had already left. A dripping Venu finally arrived and went straight into his room from the verandah. Prasuna waited in the drawing room. After a while Venu entered and sat in the sofa opposite. Prasuna absorbed in the book she was reading, pretended not to notice him.

"Got fully drenched," said Venu.

In reply Prasuna gave him a look. Freshly washed perhaps, his face was noticeably bright and his eyes sparked. Venu struck her as a handsome person.

"It was a sudden down-pour. A shower bath for me."

"You suddenly decided to go for a walk, didn't you? The rain too must have thought of greeting you suddenly."

"I thought you would go to the club for a change."

"Did I tell you so? Are you an expert in reading others' thoughts?"

"Well, I am not. My desire to go for a walk and be alone, and your inclination to go to the club, I thought would coincide."

"You have a manner of explaining yourself. You are a philosopher, aren't you?"

Prasuna's husband arrived, and the colloquy ended.

* * *

Venu was down with fever. The doctor treated him for malaria. The civil services examination was only ten days away. Prasuna's husband was anxious for Venu's quick recovery. Venu in his sick bed was a different object of interest for Prasuna. Venu was something of a child. He was even ridiculous sometimes. She was very much drawn to him and changed her attitude towards him. Whatever she said to him by way of ideas or opinions acquired a fresh value, as he gave them serious consideration and would start expanding and expounding them as if they were his own ideas. She recalled her days as a University student and recaptured something of that enthusiasm for ideas. She asked him :

"Why does one lose one's zest for life?"

"Desires get fulfilled."

"What is to be done to recover it?"

"There must be new desires."

"Well, they say desires are the root of all sorrow. From the state of desirelessness one should journey towards peace or nirvana. You are advocating the opposite."

"Physical desires explore all possibilities for fulfilment but when they are restrained either by circumstances or deliberately by the will, they do get sublimated to another level, you may call it the spiritual level, and finally bestow peace and bliss, called nirvana. The desireless state of which you have spoken is sheer ennui or boredom; it is no way for nirvana. It is not spiritual sadhana to repress or kill desires. The cause of repression is fear. Fear is not the same thing as self-control. Fear leads to death. Self-control, which means a steady contemplation, a detached contemplation of desire, will ultimately lead to peace and immortality. Life means desires; and hence fresh desires must be born to give fresh zest for life."

"Well, all this is beyond my comprehension, Venu. This appears to be your personal interpretation to an established tradition."

One day the subject of Venu's marriage came up.

"Venu, since you are sure of your job, your mother and I wish to know what kind of bride you'd like to wed. If I have the details, I can be on the look out for a suitable bride."

"Some girl. It doesn't matter."

"You speak like a true philosopher," laughed Prasuna. "But you keep saying that one should entertain desires. You needn't feel shy. Let me have your idea of a future wife."

"Well, she must be like you!"

"Stop flattering, and let me know."

"I can't think of anything else. Kindly change the topic."

Prasuna stopped all personal talk for two days, though she attended to all his needs. Venu recovered, and though somewhat enfeebled, he was ready to go to Delhi for the examination. His brother made all arrangements and wanted him to stay with a friend's family and not in a hotel.

After Venu's departure, Prasuna was back with her old problem of meaninglessness. Venu's presence and his illness had helped her to forget it for a while. Her husband had no interest in metaphysics. To go deeply questioning into obvious things was a futile and ridiculous exercise in his view. What you see before you is the world, and what goes on is life, and your daily actions and reactions are sufficient to engage you. Why indulge in imaginary problems? Venu was absolutely different. He delves deep into every single thing. He seeks links and meanings. He has a quest, and a mere government job may not mean much to him. That was Prasuna's estimation of Venu. It was interesting to listen to the two brothers discussing certain matters. The elder brother is a rationalist, and refuses to go beyond. Venu avers that reason must be transcended to reach truth. How? Venu says there is no charted path for it. He cannot convince his brother and needn't till his brother would see the necessity for it. Desire and a conscious resistance of desire, the struggle, the tapsya that mould result out of it would pave a way through the heart. Venu was a seeker of truth on that path. He had confided this to Prasuna, who was a patient and indulgent listener, when he was bed-ridden with fever. When Prasuna reported this to her husband, he dismissed it as craziness, which marriage would finally cure.

Venu was asked to come back to his brother after the examination. But Venu replied that he was going to Madras and from there was planning a tour of the South in the company of a friend. He wrote no letters after that. From Madras his mother informed Prasuna that Venu had visited the Aurobindo Ashram at Pondicherry and later the Ramanashram at Tirvannamalai. But he had not yet returned to Madras. Meanwhile, Prasuna's husband was transferred and posted at Bellary. Without waiting for the civil services examination results, Venu joined up as a lecturer in a Madras college. To the invitation from his brother to visit Bellary, Venue replied that he would go there in the vacation, and in the meanwhile he wanted his sister-in-law to be on the look out for a bride for him, as she had earlier promised him. The letter reassured Prasuna and her husband that Pondicherry and Ramanashram had not very much affected Venu. Prasuna seriously considered a few girls known to her for Venu's prospective bride. "She must be like you." Remembering Venu's words, she felt a warmth of affection pass through her.

* * *

In December Venu arrived in Bellary in the company of his mother. He had to attend the viva voce of the civil services examination in another ten days. "You always come with some examination or other imminent and not as a free man to spend sometime with us," complained Prasuna. "I fear I might develop a fever again!" said Venu. "Well, this time you have brought your mother to attend upon you." "Mother wants to go round the Vijayanagar ruins at Hampi. We could all go together," said Venu. Prasuna agreed that would be a nice trip for all of them.

By the time they got ready for the journey to Hampi, Prasuna's husband had to stay back in view of certain urgent matters that had come up in his office. Therefore only the three of them could go in a Chauffeur driven car to Hampi.

When they were inside the Virupaksha temple, Venu said : "Though this is the first time I am visiting this place, somehow every thing looks familiar." "You must have seen pictures of all these structures and carvings; and then read a few historical novels on the Vijayanagar period. It is a matter of imagination." He brushed aside Prasuna's observation and expressed himself forcibly : "It is not imagination. Suppose you have lived in a place; the streets through which you walk daily, the temple you visit and the festivals and other celebrations associated with the temple round the year, they do become a part of yourself so much, that even after an absence of many years, when you return, they would affect not merely as memories of a dead past, but as immediate living experience. Even so do I feel going about this place. This Hampi bazar, these several temples, they are today empty and deserted, but in my mind's eye they are full of people, full of crowds, festivities and activities. You might call this my illusion or imagination, but as an experience it is valid. In fact I feel that I lived here in my previous birth, most probably as a *sardar* in the Raya's militia."

"That is wonderful! You are then the right person to write a novel describing the life of the period.... Mother, did you hear him? It appears he was a *sardar* here in his previous birth. In Krishna Raya's time probably."

Venu's mother supported her son : "Why *sardar*? He would have been a commander. We should not mock at these memories of a previous birth. When I was a small girl, on one occasion a sannyasin visited our house...." Prasuna stopped listening to her. Whatever Venu might say, that would be strongly corroborated by his mother!

They walked along the Hampi bazaar towards the Kodanda Ramaswami temple, Venu was a few feet ahead. He suddenly stopped to allow the women to catch up and said to Prasuna, pointing to the Tungabhadra river : "My memories become even stronger than before on this spot. I must have stood here talking to some one for long spells quite frequently."

"Well, you could resume your conversation later when we return from the Vittala temple! Now we have to proceed quickly."

After visiting the Vittala temple, they returned to the guest-house at Hospet that day.

The next day they were looking at the Ramayana carvings in the Hazara Ramaswami temple. Noticing that Venu stood still at a particular scene from the Ramayana, Prasuna became inquisitive. Sita standing in front of the cottage, was pointing to the golden deer evidently expressing her desire to have it. The next picture depicted Rama shooting an arrow at the deer. "How exquisite is the deer!" exclaimed Prasuna. Venu moved on without a word. Prasuna said : "But for that fatal temptation, Sita would have avoided the disaster." Venu took a different view. "Both Rama and Sita were born for a specific purpose. They couldn't have avoided the sequence of events, whatever was their awareness at the moment.... We, who know the story can detach ourselves from that time-sequence and looking at the whole thing should evaluate good and bad differently."

"Your philosophizing beats me!" she said.

As they proceeded towards the Elephant-stables, Venu said : "Shall I tell you the story of the *sardar*?" "What *sardar*?" "You forgot him? The story of my previous birth here." "Oh yes, please do. Have you recollected it fully?"

"The *sardar* fell in love with a flower-vendor, a beautiful girl. He first saw her near the Virupaksha temple. Then he used to meet her in the Hampi bazaar and on the banks of the Tungabhadra. The bond of his love for her became an obsession. It was a serpentine embrace. On one rainy night, when his mother lay critically ill, ignoring her he ran in haste to his beloved flower-girl. Though he spent the night in her company, the struggle in his heart between his mother and his sweet-heart made him restless, and the death of his mother the same night made him a changed man. Then the king's military expedition took him away from Hampi for about a year. When he returned, the flower-girl was not there. He learnt that she had married a foreign trader and had left Hampi for good. He was in great despair. He had nothing to live for."

"Then what happened?"

"I don't know."

"It is a romantic story all right. Shall I tell you the proper ending? He got married to a nice girl and fathered ten children. Later he was promoted to the rank of a commander."

Venu's mother, who had not heard the full story asked Prasuna about it. When she recounted it, the mother remarked : "That perhaps is the reason why he asks me to be by his side always. This time he wants me to accompany him to Delhi."

"So you are planning to go to Delhi! Well, well."

"Why don't you join us, Prasuna? We could go to Kasi and Prayaga. The merit of visiting holy places will soon bestow a son on you."

They came to the underground temple. The guide said that there was nothing worth seeing there. Venu wanted to go and Prasuna followed him. The legend was that in the Raya's time there existed an underground tunnel from the Raya's chamber to this temple. There was stagnant water in the temple and the sanctum was inaccessible. Venu went as far as he could. There was just darkness beyond that point. Prasuna was behind him. When he was about to turn back, she screamed; "My god, cobra!" Fear choked her and she caught hold of Venu, and holding on to him tightly she shut her face against his back. Venu remained perfectly still, and turning his head round saw a cobra moving away slowly after withdrawing its raised hood.

Venu said in gentle tones : "Sister, the cobra is gone."

It took some minutes for Prasuna to become her normal self. There was perspiration on her brow. She held Venu's hand and slowly came up to the road, where the mother waited.

"We escaped death, Venu. Why visit this dark hole, of all places?"

Venu was silent.

Prasuna excitedly told the mother about the incident and praised Venu for his courage and presence of mind.

Prasuna could not forget her own reaction and she reverted to it again and again during their return journey. She felt ashamed of herself. She started speculating what Venu might have thought of her behaviour. Was his noticeable silence a consequence of the contempt he felt for her? She could not bear his silence, and put out a casual query : "Why is man so much scared by the cobra?"

"Its poison is sure death", said the mother.

"There are other creatures equally poisonous. One cannot account for the kind of fear a cobra arouses."

"Well the cobra is indeed unique. It is a wonderful combination of beauty and power, life and death. Of mutually contradictory things. The human mind cannot conceive of the contradictions coexisting. Can we think of beauty and terror, life and death with equanimity in mutual juxtaposition? The cobra signifies the unusual juxtaposition and impinges on the mind in an extraordinary manner. We experience it as fear, because it is something unknown to the mind. Our tradition has therefore identified the *kundalini* power with the cobra...."

"Venu has a penchant for bizarre explanations," thought Prasuna. But she could not lightly dismiss his steadiness in the presence of the serpent. There was something special about him, and possibly, the story of his previous birth too was something more than an idle fancy. She had no way of assessing it. She recounted to her husband every thing that had happened during the trip. He laughed and said : "Crazy fellow. He must have fancied some girl in the college, who finally disappointed him. We should arrange his marriage soon."

*　　*　　*

On the eve of his departure to Delhi, Prasuna asked Venu a straight question, whether he was in love with any girl. He looked askance for a moment and then said : "Ah, yes, the flower-girl!"

"No joking, please. I am asking you a serious question," said Prasuna.

"My answer is serious too. I'll confide in you. There is an affinity between my mind and the story that came up at Hampi. I see it now clearly. Sita wanted the golden deer. But what foolishness. The arrow kills it. A dead deer cannot be the same thing as a live one! When you think of grasping or possessing beauty, it is the sure way to lose it. The moment Sita saw the deer and enjoyed its sight, that was the golden moment! The perception of beauty and the restless desire for it balanced each other in perfect juxtaposition. The very next moment the desire prevailed. Sita expressed it to Rama. Well, the events followed. Time is a matter of sequences. Reason is nothing but cause and effect. Time and reason cannot hold beauty. Truth and beauty lie beyond them; in the perfect juxtaposition and balance of contradictions Truth and Beauty can be experienced. In the story, the flower-girl is beauty and the mother is dharma, the two standing in contradiction and in juxtaposition on that rainy night. The *sardar* failed to realize immortality."

"You mean restraint of desire is preferable to its fulfillment."

"It is not like that. The restraint should be devoid of dissatisfaction; and the desire should not lose its power. It is action in inaction, and inaction in action, as the Gita puts it. It might strike one as meaningless. Because thought and language cannot reach forth to this experience. The experience we know is like a wave moving up and down, desire to fulfilment, fulfilment to desire. Its constant movement is life, which is perceived as time and its movement. Man is unique in trying to transcend time. He wants to be free. There are two ways : either you move with time accepting life in its totality, or you transcend it by the juxtaposition of dualities. Then you get out of the circle of births."

Prasuna became thoughtful. Venu was an enigma to her. She gave up the attempt to understand his philosophy. Apart from his philosophy, Venu was lovable and charming. His philosophy, understood or not, was a part of that charm. He talked beautifully. What kind of a wife would suit him? That was her concern.

"Venu, perhaps you expect your wife to be a thinker, or at least capable of discussing philosophy with you! And then she must be beautiful too, as you are after beauty and truth."

"She must be like you."

"Oh, I am useless," Prasuna said in puzzlement.

*   *   *

Venu's mother was unwell after her trip to Hampi. There was no question of her going to Delhi with Venu. He went alone.

Venu's viva voce was over. He informed his brother that he had done well, and would return in a fortnight after visiting Kasi and Hardwar. A fortnight became a month. There was no further news of Venu. Two letters addressed to Venu by a friend of his, who had also appeared for the examination, were received at Bellary. Then came the communication that he was selected for the Civil Services. His brother inquired through various channels. Venu's friend informed the family that he had last seen him proceeding to Hardwar. An advertisement was placed in the newspapers. And a report to the police was already there. Venu's disappearance remained an unsolved mystery. Venu's mother firmly declared : "Venu is not dead. He must be in the Himalayas. He will certainly return one day." Prasuna agreed with her. The hope rekindled her desire for life....

Twenty years! The jasmine is in full blossom.

"I am going for a walk," says Venu and disappears in a hurry. This Venu is Prasuna's nineteen-year old son! Prasuna is knocked out of her reverie. She mumbles : "Venu did not die!"

Blood – Red

The sky was sick. It vomited blood. Gradually the red was absorbed by the blackness of darkness. A lamp was lit in the hut situated in the yard opposite. The little lamp won't last very long. Afterwards it would be absolute darkness. Nothing would be seen by the eye.

From seven o'clock to ten in the morning, Sarathi sits in the back verandah of his upstairs apartment and watches her, the woman in the hut, going about her daily chores. While cooking the lunch, she moves in and out of the hut. There is an improvised bath-room of bamboo screens, into which she darts often to cleanse a vessel, or to take some water from there into the kitchen. Sometimes she feeds the chicks scattering grain before them.

All her movements are of interest to Sarathi, who observes her with fascination.

She appears on the scene again in the evening at four o'clock. Sarathi is punctually on the watch. She cleans the front of the hut with a broom, and then sprinkles water on the ground to settle the dust. The next thing she does is to enter the bath-room to take a bath. She takes a clean sari with straight folds twisted like a rope and throws it across the bamboo screen to her left. Then she proceeds to remove the sari she has been wearing, and puts it across the screen that faces Sarathi. At the precise moment she does this and stands naked, her hand, her face and her shoulders disappear quickly after affording Sarathi an exciting glimpse. It is something of a climax, and like a poem replete with hidden meaning, it gives him something of an ecstatic and aesthetic experience.

After the bath, she quickly wraps the clean sari round her naked body and runs into the hut, but in that sight, Sarathi finds no pleasure. An unknown sadness and melancholy fills his heart.

At about half-past five, arrives a man in khaki uniform. Her husband. Arranging a string-cot for himself at the door-front, he settles down and sips the tea she brings him. He makes conversation, and she talks to him moving about, or standing for a while at the door in Sarathi's full view. Though words are not distinctly audible, Sarathi enjoys her occasional laughter. He believes that she is aware of his presence, as he is aware of her's.

The husband is absent for some days. It may be three days or five days or even a week. It is likely that he is a truck-driver. Sarathi hasn't made any inquiries and doesn't know for certain any information about the couple, not even their individual names. He has no interest in finding out. Direct experience is enough. What one sees with the eye, isn't that enough? Why hanker after names and information? To what purpose? There is no pleasure in information as such.

In a life bereft of all physical pleasure, this is the only aspect of 'sex' experience that has been left for him. The doctor has prohibited all sexual indulgence by the body. Five months ago he vomited blood. He was frightened, when it was diagnosed as tuberculosis. He was mentally depressed. The doctor assured him that the disease was yet in early stages, and it won't be necessary for him to join any sanatorium. He has been under treatment.

Sarathi's wife left for her parents' home. She knew nothing about Sarathi's illness. The diagnosis and her journey coincided. There was hardly any time to tell her. Sarathi finally decided not to as, she was going for confinement.

After her departure, Sarathi slowly grasped the big change that had overtaken his life. When the doctor said that sex was prohibited for him, the implications of that did not dawn upon him immediately. The mind's separation from the body was becoming a reality and the implications of that separation, he was in the process of understanding now. Many a truth was revealed to him now.

The woman's talk and laughter with her husband, as Sarathi watched her, appeared like deliberate teasing and mocking directed at himself. In the beginning, Sarathi used to suffer from jealousy and would run indoors. He would lie on his bed and thoughts would besiege him. The man in the khaki uniform appeared to be the luckiest man in the world. Sarathi would imagine himself in the position of the khaki-clad person, and would live his life. Then new aspects, hitherto unsuspected, came into his perception. To acquire intimacy with the woman, to possess her and enjoy the pleasure of her body, was no doubt the most desirable thing in the world. But in actuality, he would miss many other things, when he become her husband in real life. For instance, he would miss the sight of her taking a bath. At that moment, he would be driving a truck and looking at the road ahead. He might talk to her at length sipping tea in the evenings, but he would get his chance of possessing the woman only in the darkness of the night.... Then with the little lamp out, what would the mind see and enjoy? The present ecstatic and aesthetic experience won't be available then. In the darkness all will be one! In that darkness what difference would it make whether it was she, or some other woman, or his own wife, whom he had already known as a woman. Would there be any difference? What kind of difference? Any difference depends on sight, on the discriminating mind; and in the case of the body and its touch, there would be no differences to make out. If that is so, why should one feel jealous of the truck-driver?

The basic question is : whether sex pertains to the mind or the body? When he looks at his wife, she is indeed most attractive as a woman. But in the role of a wife, when she talks about family politics, and about relatives or money-matters, the attraction is gone, and she becomes a bore. Only indifference remains towards her. While in bed with her, what provokes him is a sort of memory of having seen her and felt drawn to her at other moments. And that provocation might excite but would not sustain him to the end. And the end would leave him cold and depressed. The end was death. It was a void! This had not been so in the early days after the marriage.... Sex turning into a habit lost its meaning. The same habit brought in the touch of death in the shape of tuberculosis, is Sarathi's guess.... Therefore, he is willing to forego physical sex and follow the doctor's prescription both in letter and spirit.

"What are the conditions conducive to tuberculosis?" he asked the doctor. Doctor Ramam was an old friend. He spoke at length and set forth a variety of reasons, but none of them would apply to his case. In environmental conditions, or in the matter of nutrition there was nothing to cause tuberculosis. But for quite some time there had been a psychological dissatisfaction, the result of a partially realized struggle between his mind and his body. First he thought it was a simmering discontent of his inability yet to produce an heir. Five years after marriage, he was going to be a father at last! But then the tuberculosis too made its appearance! The simultaneity of the two events brought home to him the absurdity and the illogicality of life.

To separate the mind and the body in respect of sex, on closer examination it did appear a tenable proposition. What is seen by the eye (whether the eye is closed or open) is categorized as 'mental.' And all other sense-experience is categorized as 'physical' or pertaining to the body. Is that logical? When the eye and the other sense organs are all parts of the same human body, all sense-perception, whether that of the eye or the other sense organs, should be reckoned as body experience, as 'physical' only. If by definition all experience is to be finally attributed to the mind and mind only, then all kinds of sense-experience should be called 'mental' experience only. That would make touch, smell, taste and coition things of the mind, and not of the body. If that is so, what difference does it make whether a man enjoys a woman with the eye or with a tight embrace? Metaphysically it makes no difference whatsoever! But socially it makes a lot of difference!

There is a link between the eye and the other organs of perception and their enjoyment. What the eye perceives constitutes a provocation for the other senses as in the case of food or woman. What the eye perceives is sought after to be grasped, to be made one's own; and that is at the root of all anguish and sorrow. Isn't something 'real' unless one grasps it in one's hands and possesses it? Is the rainbow not 'real'? The rainbow is not 'there' spatially. One can journey to the moon but cannot go to the rainbow! The rainbow is a reality for the eye only. Is it less enjoyable than the moon?

The appearance of the moon is sweet like an 'ice-cream.' One would nibble at it. Man fancied many things about the moon across the ages. But when the moon actually came into man's grasp, the experience was but ordinary, if not one of disillusionment. Hills, valleys, craters and dust, nothing much else! The moon has now become 'real' to man, but what is he going to do with it?

The separation of the body from the mind, which amounts to the separation and containment of what the eye perceives and enjoys from what the other senses would desire to enjoy in tandem, is a matter of will and practice. It leads to pure joy; it is true freedom. Therefore all thoughts of possessing a woman should be banished, decided Sarathi.

The sunrise was a joyous spectacle in the morning. Later in the day when he visited the doctor, the same sun tortured his body. From a distance, the spectacle of human beings in their variety of activities, in their speech, gesture, laughter and anger, in their animation presents a fascinating experience. But only as a spectacle. When one goes near them, it is a different matter. It appears to him he is in love with humanity only from a distance.

When he tries to engage a rickshaw, or when he approaches the fruit vendor, the bargaining, the delay the little complications they indulge in, the cheating practised by the milk-man and the vegetable vendor, cause not only vexation but generate revulsion towards humanity. Actually he is indifferent to the fate of humanity in mass. He is capable of personal relationships with individuals. There is compassion, love and affection in him for individuals.

Sarathi prefers to have his regular injection from the nurse, Nirmala. He prefers her to the doctor. She takes an X-ray of his chest, and bestows a sweet smile on him. She is always fresh like a jasmine. With a full breast and neat curves, Nirmala is attractive, but for some reason, her eyes are dull; there is neither a sparkle nor an invitation in them. One searches in vain for any personal communication in them. Sarathi reads only helplessness and escapism in her eyes. Moonlight in a desert, is the expression that comes to his mind, when he thinks of Nirmala.

Today Doctor Ramam said : "Your X-rays shows that almost all the spots are gone! Remarkable improvement, Sarathi! You may get back to work in another month. Of course, you should continue to observe all the rules without exception."

"Oh, I don't know how to thank you, Ramam. To you and to nurse Nirmala, I'm very much beholden. Can I have a word with her, just to say thank you?"

"You haven't spoken to her yet, all these days?"

"No, she doesn't appear to be that type at all. But she has been uniformly courteous to me. I want to thank her personally."

Dr. Ramam smiled and said : "Well, I have warned you. Keep off women!"

"Does it mean I cannot take interest in her even as a person?"

"There is danger in that. To begin with, every thing is innocent. Temptation lurks behind all such moves."

"Well, I am a little curious. You know I have been trying to figure out what I have lost because of tuberculosis, and have been cultivating resignation towards my condition. What I want to learn is how a person like Nirmala manages to be without sex, when she is a healthy woman?"

Dr. Ramam laughed, and cast a glance of suspicion at Sarathi.

"Sarathi, what is it you are talking? Are you really a greenhorn to be taken in by appearances? In matters of sex she is a free-lancer, to borrow an expression. She has her price, a little on the high side, no doubt. But she is accessible. You can have her, but it won't suit your health. Doctor's orders, you know."

Sarathi was shocked.

"Why do you employ a woman like that in your nursing-home?"

"A woman like that suits my set-up. She is businesslike and scientific. She is immune to romance and to any afflictions of the heart a woman may be prone. Being immune to fanciful desires, she avoids any head-ache for herself and for me too."

The discussion ended there, and Sarathi never spoke to Nirmala. Returning home he scrutinized his impressions of and feelings towards Nirmala. He discovered that his feelings towards Nirmala were not affected by the information that Ramam had provided about Nirmala's amoral sex-life. The affection he had felt for her now turned into compassion. It is a pity, that the social system, and the people around created circumstances which forced Nirmala to live in the way she did. But pity, why pity? Is it because she could not acquire respectability? Tied to some man in wedlock, if she had become a bond-slave, would that have been well with her? Whether her style of life pleases her or not, how could anybody, how Sarathi himself, judge? It is a make-believe world, we accept, as though society lives by a single moral code even in personal matters. In truth, one individual differs from another in choosing his morals. Man in society has two faces : one turned towards society and another inwards. Every man wears a mask and lives as he pleases. The mask worn by Nirmala, as an unmarried nurse, is quite workable and appropriate. It might be a satisfactory thing for her. Who is

Sarathi to question it? He should be pleased with her courtesy, her service, and her manners, which are true indeed and not false! Any assumed attitude of pity or criticism merely destroys that pleasure, which her association professionally gives him. The moon should be looked at from the earth, from a distance. There is no point in landing on the moon. Your pity and interference are unwanted by your fellow-men.

This new perception of people holds good in the case of the woman in the hut too. No need to inquire after her particulars!

* * *

Sarathi went to the railway station to see off his friend Viswam. Viswam an engineering graduate worked at Nagarjun Sagar for four years, but he was not made permanent in his job. He couldn't get employment in spite of his best efforts. He didn't have the money to bribe his prospective employers. His parents were poor and entertained high expectations. They had spent everything they had by way of property for his education. Viswam and Sarathi hailed from the same village.

Viswam brought a camp-cot and a wooden box full of his books and entrusted the two to Sarathi and told him that he was leaving for Srikakulam.

"I am glad you landed a job at last," said Sarathi.

"No, not for a job."

"Why Srikakulam?"

"There is nothing better for me to do now."

Viswam explained that he had decided to join the revolutionaries (1969). The present social system denied justice, denied opportunities to the talented and deserving young men. The social order was in ruins ethically and politically. It had to be overthrown. There was no way to reform it. Srikakulam had started the movement, and Viswam was going to join it. Viswam was emotional, thought Sarathi.

"Well, what is your role in it?" asked Sarathi.

"I want to see blood. I want to strike at the pillars of this social order. I want to put bullets into the people's enemies."

"Have you identified who they are?"

Sarathi tried to explain that he (Viswam) would be turning into a machine, and would be simply obeying orders, not acting on his own. Individuality and freedom ought not to be mortgaged to power-hungry ideologists.

"Where are the individuals you speak of? I see only greedy vultures. On the other side are the hunters. I join the hunters to avoid being gobbled up. I'll be a soldier in a just war. A soldier cannot be a commander. He has to obey first. There can be no independent thinking or individual choice in a situation of war."

"All this is an illusion. Running after a mirage. In the new order you are going to establish, would human relationships move like wheels in a well-lubricated machine? I have no faith in that. For, the leaders who dictate to make the revolution, will not be able to get over their habit of exercising power and would enslave the people. What would happen to your dream then?"

Viswam argued vehemently in support of revolutionary Marxism. Bold action and risks were unavoidable. Finally he said : "Look Sarathi, is there any other way open for me? All speculations aside, I am for immediate action. I cannot bear the despair of my parents. This is the only way for me. Let me go with hope and confidence in the future. I have a few friends there...." It meant he had no friends here.

Sarathi could understand Viswam's state of mind. He went to the station to see him off. The guard gave the whistle and the train moved. Viswam's compartment moved on. After a few minutes, the train stopped abruptly. The station staff and others rushed to a spot ahead of Sarathi. Sarathi followed them The mangled body of a twelve-year old boy was lifted from the railway track. The train resumed its onward journey. The passengers were unaware of the accident. The boy had lost both his legs.

The boy was a tea-vendor, and had tried to get off the moving train.

As Sarathi turned back home, the gory scene was fixed in his mind's eye. Would the boy survive? Even then, what would be his life like, with both legs gone?

* * *

Sarathi rejoined work. He was again in the company of men, after a period of enforced loneliness. He tried to follow his old routine of watching the woman in the mornings. In the evenings he would either miss the watch, or be too late to see the woman leave her bath-room. He was firmly entrenched in the theories and conclusions he had arrived at during the period of this illness. But his mixing with colleagues in the office and his visits to the cinema brought forth a subtle change in him. He could perceive physical desires and the urges of the body reasserting themselves. The mind desired to encompass all the beauty the eye perceived, and that sometimes turned into a body-ache. The smallness and the weakness of the body with its proneness to disease made the enormity of his mental aspiration an absurd and ridiculous thing. Would it ever be possible to quench one's infinite thirst for beauty with the finite body? Physical sex might be a small anodyne! No, not even an anodyne. But temptation was growing strong, as the fear of death, which had restrained it hitherto, receded. It was getting insistent.

Man, which means the mind, is a great opportunist. Renunciation has been categorized for men and women respectively as that of the burial ground, and that of the delivery room! Men take a dim view of ambitions, witnessing death; and women resolve to give up sex, unable to bear the pangs of delivering a child. But such a renunciation is soon forgotten. Any metaphysics, or political ideology, or social regimentation, howsoever powerful cannot determine man's being, or deflect the urge of his life. They only serve to justify and interpret his need and his purpose. In the case of Viswam revolutionary politics came in handy. For Nirmala, a scientific attitude to life and perhaps feminism provide an intellectual justification. And as a patient suffering from tuberculosis, pure mentalism sustained him. But he isn't yet out of the woods. He is still a patient under doctor's orders. To forget that would be dangerous.

"The woman supplies eggs for us, she wants an advance of ten rupees. She plans to buy a pair of hens, as the present ones are hatching. She is a reliable person and we might as well advance the money," said the cook to Sarathi.

"Who is that woman? Where does she live?"

"Here in the hut down below." The cook Venkayya said with a grin. Sarathi didn't relish his grin. He innocently queried : "What hut do you mean?"

"It is there opposite, where you sit in the rear verandah."

"Oh yes, who is she? What does her husband do?"

"He is a truck-driver. Not really her husband. He brought her here as his mistress."

"Where do they come from?"

"Chilakalapudi."

"Near Masulipatnam?"

"Yeah. A very nice woman, very reliable. She would personally make the request. She wants to request you for a sweeper's job or a water-woman's job in your office, if it may please you to recommend her for employment. She wants to have an opportunity to see you and represent her difficulties."

"Well, she can see me. You may give her the hen she wants."

The next night, as Sarathi sat with the pan-material by his side soon after his dinner, the woman came in introduced by Venkayya.

After Venkayya's exit, Sarathi looked up.

She was holding out her hand with the ten-rupee note towards him, and said : "Not necessary. I got the hens. I don't require the money."

She appeared to be more refined than he had expected. At close quarters too she was attractive in a different way, and Sarathi was pleased. She came a step nearer and held out the note with deliberation. Sarathi received the note and remarked: "Why did you say that to Venkayya?"

"Unless I mentioned money, Venkayya would not have arranged this meeting...."

Surprised at her clever initiative, Sarathi was dumbfounded for a while. She took the pan leaves and applying wet lime, she prepared pan for him and handed it to him. Their fingers touched.

"Why look at me so intensely? You keep a watch throughout the day. How can anyone bear those looks?"

"How did you receive them?" Sarathi took her hand in his and continued to hold it.

"Please let me be...Venkayya may be coming in."

"But it is Venkayya who brought you here!"

"Let me go now."

"What is the hurry? You have to tell me yet the purpose of your coming to see me."

"To return your money. And then to see you at close quarters. Now it is up to you to be kind."

"What is your name?"

"Rajamma. Rajalakshmi."

"Well, Rajalakshmi, what is the job you want? And what are your qualifications?"

"I passed the fifth class long ago. At your feet, any job you may be pleased to offer. I'm your slave, "She said in mock-seriousness.

"That last expression of feudal submission reveals that you have been to Telengana too."

"Of course, my lord. We spent one year there."

"Share the pan, Rajalakshmi."

"Is that an offer?"

Sarathi got up and closed the door and bolted it. He took her into his hands.

After that she was a regular visitor.

Sarathi offered presents. Saris and things like that. She refused them outright. She said she was not indigent, and didn't want any thing in return. She requested Sarathi to pay bonus to Venkayya and keep him happy.

That physical sex could never reach forth to the mind's quest for beauty, which had been Sarathi's earlier conclusion and despair, was proved to be wrong with what Sarathi realized from his relationship with Rajamma. What the mind alone could not attain to, the perfect union of mind and body accomplished. Sarathi was now rid of all speculation, all thoughts and philosophy. Waiting for her and for the exquisite moments was the sole purpose and meaning of life for him now. The experience transcended the mind and the body and could not be categorized by the intellect.

A month passed by. During nights Sarathi had bouts of cough. Rajalakshmi's visits became few and far between. He had to send word through Venkayya and invite her on some occasions. When she arrived, she would advise him to see the doctor and not neglect his health. Sarathi never visited the doctor and felt curiously reluctant to do so.

A telegraphic message was received that Sarathi had become a father! Rajalakshmi advised him to go and get his wife and child, which would relieve him of his loneliness.

Sarathi became thoughtful at her suggestion, but did not respond. Then she added : "Next month we are also leaving."

Sarathi queried : "Where to?"

"Why do you want to go? Let him go, if he has to. I'll rent a house for you. You won't be a burden to me. I can afford it."

She laughed, and gave him a kiss for his offer.

"An excellent proposition. But my husband won't let me go like that. He has rights. He will kill me."

"Your husband? What rights? You ran away with him, didn't you?"

"Not so. In god's presence he wedded me, and tied the thaali round my neck."

"Then why did Venkayya tell me differently?"

"That was a part of the strategy. Otherwise Venkayya would not have approved of my behaviour. I had to resort to many tricks to reach you."

"Living in amity with your husband, why did you think of this affair with me?"

"He is a husband the world gave me. You are a husband I gave myself!"

"Then why don't you remain with me and leave him?"

"Well, that is that. I must tread the path approved by society."

Sarathi pleaded with her. He gave her many promises. He was angry with her. He offered to transfer some property in her name. Rajalakshmi was firm in her refusal to stay.

That night, after she left, he vomited blood. He simply turned on the tap, flushed it out and washed his mouth. He lay on the bed and could not sleep.

He sent for Rajalakshmi four days in succession but she didn't turn up. Finally, when she came, she informed him that her husband would arrive in the early hours and they would quit the place the very next day. They won't stay till next month.

Sarathi cut the apple into small pieces. The sharp knife drew a drop of blood from his finger, and it stained one of the pieces. Rajalakshmi said half in jest : "I want to eat that piece marked with your blood."

In the course of the night, when she forgot herself and slept in his arms, the sharp knife descended down her throat.

Sarathi surrendered to the police.

Viswam was shot dead by the police in an encounter.

From death unto immortality, says the Upanishad.

"Mrityorma amritam gamaya."

The Clone

As I wriggled out of the swarm of coolies and rickshaw-wallahs soliciting me when I got off the bus, I was confronted with the jingling tin-box from a beggar asking for alms.

"Get away," I said in disgust.

"Ten paise please!"

Who is this fellow, speaking English?

A wrinkled face and a white beard showed him up as an old man, but there was a twinkle in his eye, which intrigued me. He was lean, but not bent down with age. A staff in his left hand, and the tin-box in his right hand, a half-sleeved shirt and an upper cloth slightly torn. But he was clean and looked healthy. With a Gandhian loin-cloth coming down to the knees, he was respectable but for his seeking alms.

As I paused and looked at him, he said : "You will pass the exam, and will get a first class too."

His words hooked me. He must have guessed. That was very clever of him. But I valued what he said, even if it amounted to flattery. I needed that kind of assurance. I said : "I won't offer you money, but I would get you a cup of tea, would you have it?" He followed me to the nearby tea-stall.

The previous day I had written the last paper in my M.A. Examinations. I had not done well to my expectations, and since then was in doubt whether I would get the first class I required. My future career depended very much on that first class. Through the bus journey my mind had oscillated on the issue and I could not set it at rest. The old man's pronouncement had clinched the issue somehow. I felt thankful to him. Though I happened to be a rationalist, I was not beyond certain things that afforded satisfaction to the mind and gave it peace for the moment.

While sipping the tea, I asked him : "Do you know anything about astrology?"

"No, Sir."

"You predicted something for me."

"I say what comes to my mind."

I was disappointed. Whether he was an astrologer or not, he could have at least maintained the pose and talked something to please me. But he was too honest.

After I paid for the tea, I turned to him to say good-bye.

He suddenly said : "Please don't trust astrology."

"Why?"

"It is my personal experience," he said in English.

I became inquisitive, as he appeared to be an educated man.... I asked him whether he would accompany me to my home which was near the public park. He agreed. As we walked on, I inquired :

"You seem to be an educated person. Don't you have some-one to look after you?" He didn't answer.

"You referred to your experience. What is it?"

He was silent till we approached the park. "Let us go and sit in the park, I'll tell you," he proposed.

"My home is nearby," I said.

"No. Let us sit in the park for a while."

I was intrigued, and went into the park led by him. I sat on a concrete bench. He remained standing facing me.

"You asked me about astrology. Unless you learn the secret of creation, you cannot understand the nature of astrology."

"I don't want to discuss the Vedanta. I want to listen to your personal experience only."

"I will come to that. But you should first permit me to mention a few things. Without the introduction, you will not make any sense out of my experience. Rama and Ravana, epic characters like that, exist always. Circumstances, environment and manners may change, but personalities don't. For example, the cinema and the TV have replaced the stage drama. Old actors are dead, but new actors come up playing the same epic roles. Even so in creation, countless human beings are born and they die. But you don't have as many personalities as the physical bodies that appear and disappear in time. The number of personalities is limited and finite. Each man thinks he is unique, his life is unique. That is an illusion. To realize that he is acting out a role, which many have filled earlier, and he is only repeating it, is true knowledge...."

"Population has increased many-fold. A great variety of life-styles have emerged. I cannot believe in you theory of limited personalities. Please go on to your experience."

"The increase in population doesn't affect what I way. A film that used to be released in ten centres earlier is now released in twenty centres. The picture is only one, the number of copies has increased. The variations that are apparently new are not truly so. They are superficial. The personalities at play are a limited number only."

"If that is so, then astrology must be an exact science."

"Of course it is. One who has grasped the secret of creation does not require the aid of astrology. For the one, who has not been let into the secret, astrology is like a mirage."

"Well, I want to listen to your story."

"What is my story? Who am I? There is no answer to these questions. I can only tell you something of which I have been a witness, or a role-player, and you could judge its usefulness for your future."

The man narrated the following :

"In this town, some years ago, there was an officer in the Commercial Taxes Department. He had a daughter, who was studying medicine at Madras. He had great hopes of her. He expected to rise in social status when she became a full-fledged doctor. When she was doing house-surgeoncy, she married a colleague, who was a *harijan* by caste. The officer went to Madras, disowned her in grief and anger, and returned home. When he got down from the bus, he was accosted by a beggar, an old fellow like me.

"Where are the family relationships? Who is indebted to whom? Give charity to a beggar," he said to the officer. He was taken to the tea-stall, just as you did in my case. The officer asked him to tell his story. The man belonged to the vysya community. He had a grocery store. His only daughter eloped with a young man of *ediga* (toddy-tapper's) caste. When she ran away, she took with her all the gold and cash, he had saved. Being a widower, and losing face among relatives he resorted to begging and became a sannyasin. Hearing the beggar's story and noting the parallel event in his own life, the officer went home.

Six years later, the officer was posted in a different town, and he was senior enough in the department to expect promotion. He made a trip to Hyderabad to see the higher-ups. He had made himself rich during those six years by fleecing merchants. Reports and complaints had gone to the head-quarters. His promotion-file was therefore kept pending. The officer, during his trip to Hyderabad did his best to influence by all kinds of means, the people who mattered, and was confident of his success. On his arrival back home, he was again accosted by the same beggar, who had met him six years ago. "Something for your good will happen." The officer couldn't recognize him immediately. But when he did, he was pleased and took him to his house. He asked the beggar to predict the future.... "There is nothing more to say," said the begger and repeated his words : "Something for your good will happen and there will be a change in your life."

"Where have you been all these years?" queried the officer.

The beggar gave the names of the four towns, in which the officer had worked during the preceding six years. The officer asked him why he had not met him earlier in one of those towns. "You saw me several times, but you didn't recognize me." That was his reply.

The beggar left, but the prediction did not come true, as the officer had hoped. Promotion was denied to him. Charges were levelled against him and an inquiry was ordered. He had to spend a large portion of his ill-gotten money. Finally, he lost his job. He forfeited all retirement benefits. He came back to this town. As he owned a house here. With great difficulty, he saw his son through college. The boy being brilliant in science, landed a job in Trombay, near Bombay as a scientific officer. He became the chief support and sent money to the parents. His father went to Bombay to discuss a marriage proposal that had come up. The young man went to the beach for sea-bathing in the company of friends. He was drowned. The father, who was still in Bombay, collapsed, but he survived to perform the obsequies of his son. He returned home. And the beggar was there!

The man's anger knew no bounds. He wanted to thrash him on the spot. On the three occasions of his great loss, the beggar had accosted him, and he appeared to be an embodiment of the cruel and relentless fate that had pursued him through life. When he jumped at the beggar to beat him, he stepped on his own dhoti, and fell flat on his face. The beggar as well as other passersby helped him to get up, and brought him into this very park.

After that he used to frequent the park every day and sit with a vacant mind. He wouldn't speak to anyone. He shunned company. The beggar moved at a distance, and the man saw him and ignored him. One day he beckoned the beggar.

"Who are you? On three important occasions of my life, you met me. You brought me ill-luck and tragedy into my life. Why don't you leave me alone?"

"Sir, my meetings with you did not precede your misfortunes. I saw you only after the event each time! I might have said something to bring you peace. Was it my fault?"

"Your predictions were misleading lies. You said I would get promotion. I lost my job. You said that something good will happen, but disaster overtook me."

"Sir, I never professed to be an astrologer. I said something *for* your good would happen. How can we mortals judge what is really good for us? The results of karma, of our past actions have to be borne. Isn't it good that the account is settled here in this life itself? Life consists of both pleasure and pain. Our disappointments match our desires. Astrology is an elusive thing. It is a mirage. For the moment it strengthens hope, as we see it, and not as things actually are destined to be. What man wants is peace. Man doesn't get it by attachments and acquisitions."

"An unfortunate fellow like me, how can I hope for peace? Do you know some mantra or tantra to attain it?"

"Only if you ask...."

"This is strange! Who are you? What am I to you? What is this relationship between us over all these years?"

"We cannot find answers to those questions, let us not bother. I'll give you a mantra. It will reveal to you the secret of creation, and you will find peace of mind."

The man agreed, as he had nothing to lose. The beggar took him to a corner to the park, where a few trees provided cover from public gaze. He was asked to sit in the lotus posture, and shut his eyes. Then the beggar whispered something in his ear. He forgot himself, and didn't know how much time had passed. He didn't know whether he went to sleep, or went into a trance.

When he opened his eyes, it was dawn. Without his knowing it, the night had come and gone. A mantra was revolving in his mind. There was no one around. The beggar had disappeared. The mind was at peace, and he had no inclination to question or reason anything. The staff and the bowl of the beggar lay before him. Without hesitation, he took them as his own and walked to the bus-stop. He boarded the bus to Tirupati. He never went back to his house. And it is the same person who stands before you now!

"What is the secret of creation? That beggar and this person lived the same roles differently. The differences are only apparent."

"In a hall of mirrors one person is seen as many, and with differences too, because of the differing angles. You will realize this if you enter the Hall of Mirrors at Tirumala. This world is God's Hall of Mirrors."

The story was over. I asked him : "What happened to your wife?"

"I have nobody, nothing. It was quite a few years before I returned to this town. I am not concerned with anything. My coming here was with no specific purpose. It was His will. And what I said to you at the bus-stop as well as what I have narrated to you, these have just happened. Till now my story, if you call it that, has not been narrated to anybody. Why did I tell you? Well, that I don't know. It is His will."

I thought over the matter and commented :

"I don't see anything miraculous, but I do see symmetry and coincidence in your story. You have made it into a theory and call it the secret of creation. Is there no other solution to life's problems except sannyasa and beggary? I don't approve of this tradition. I want this tradition to go. Your experience and your theory are of no use to me?"

"My dear Sir, peace of mind is not linked with sannyasa and beggary. In our country this is a life-style, for those who have lost everybody and everything. This profession or life-style is not important. Please do not be misled by the externals. One who grasps the secret of creation will attain to peace, whatever might be his profession or life-style. Whether you are an officer or a beggar, or change from one to the other, that is not important.

That is only role-playing. One should get one's release from dissatisfaction, pain and restlessness."

"If there is no connection between sannyasa and mental peace, then what is the way for attaining peace?"

"I will give you the mantra. That is the way."

I flinched. I was not ready. I didn't believe that any mantra could bestow mental peace. The transformation of the former officer into a beggar, and the disappearance of the first beggar leaving his legacy behind, foreboded a risk in my own case.

"What will you gain by giving me the mantra?"

"It is God's will."

I was not satisfied with the answer. He was evasive.

"I am young and fresh. There must be a lot of people, who are tired and old, who desire peace of mind and would gladly receive your mantra. Why don't you approach them?"

"It is God's will."

"I am not ready."

"It is God's will."

He went away, and I turned homewards. His story and his theory were a matter for cogitation. If his theory were to be valid, then this must be my first meeting with my clone! Would that imply that I am destined to be a beggar at the end? Can I not escape that fate? In playing a role God has assigned to me, have I no freedom? What is the meaning of free will?

Where are the answers? Only my life can provide them.

The Sea

Puri beach. The morning ten o'clock sun enriched the sea's blue. The white-crested waves kept running to us as we slowly walked on the sand listening to the dirge. Lakshmiprasad stopped near the water and a wave washed his feet and receded.

"The sea has bowed to me" declared Lakshmiprasad.

"Oh yes, if your are careless, he would pull your loges too, and sweep you off your feet," said Sangamesam. Joining his two palms into a cup, he took the sea-water, lifted his hands towards the sky and offered the water in a devotional gesture.

"Is that a *tarpon* to someone dead?" I asked him.

"Why someone? It is for myself!" replied Sangamesam.

Opposite to the beach, across the road, stood in a row guest-houses and tourist lodges.

"We have walked quite a distance from our place. There is some temple across the road. Let us have a look at it and then return. It is already getting warm," proposed Sangamesam. We voted approval and crossed the road.

It was a temple for Lord Gouranga.

The priest, a *goswaml*, spoke to us about Krishna Chaitanya known as Lord Gouranga. The legend is that Sri Chaitanya went into the Jagannath temple and disappeared. The priest said it was not so. Sri Chaitanya had walked away into the sea, at the same spot where we had stopped a few minutes ago. And the temple was built just opposite to that spot.

As we walked back to our lodge, a discussion ensued.

"If he had walked into the sea, his body should have been washed ashore," I expressed my doubt.

"It is quite possible that the sharks made a feast of him! Everything grown into a mystery or a miracle. That's what our countrymen do. Most unscientific fellows on earth," remarked Lakshmiprasad. By profession he is a physician, and has been well-favoured by the goddess of wealth, Lakshmi.

"What do you mean by science?" Sangamesam joined issue with him : "Science is what you think, is it? Well, what does your Einstein say? If an object approaches the velocity of light, it disappears. And what is a human body? It consists of atoms, or say electrons or even smaller particles, whatever it is. As we see the formation of water drops as a cloud, so the human body is only a formation of these fundamental particles. When these vibrate to attain the velocity of light, the human body will become a flash of light and disappear. There is nothing unscientific about it."

Sangamesam has long been a traveller on the path of knowledge and enlightenment. He has no profession, no job. He has inherited property, and his wife works as a lecturer in a Madras college. He owns a house. He has two children. Sangamesam has dabbled in many things. Poetry, philosophy, the arts and archaeology along with Yoga and spiritualism have engaged his mind off and on; he would spend days without end in the Thanjavur Library or in the Madurai temple of Devi Meenakshi forgetful of everything else. On this occasion, it was he who had come to Visakhapatnam and brought me and Lakshmiprasad on a visit to Puri. We happened to be childhood friends and classmates at school.

"Theory is O.K. But is such a thing ever possible? What is the 'light barrier?' It is impossible for a physical body to attain the velocity of light. That is a barrier set by nature. How can Chaitanya or anybody else cross that barrier? Can you show another case like that of Chaitanya?" said Lakshmiprasad.

"My dear Prasad, I speak as a materialist. The human body is a machine. It is like a generator. The mechanical and chemical energies generated by it, we use them all the time. It produces electrical energy; the experiments on the brain establish it. Now is it impossible, if properly worked by the brain and the nervous system, that it should generate light? A rare few have accomplished that. They have attained to bodies of light, and have continued so for an long while, after their physical bodies mingled with dust. There appears to be a time limit even for them. There is nothing impossible about Sri Chaitanya converting his body into light, into pure energy and disappearing from the sight of men." That was Sangamesam's explanation.

"Please don't try to obscure the dividing line between science and the *Puranas*, Sangamesam, and throw the people of this country into darkness again; you will be doing a disservice," said Lakshmiprasad.

"Today's science-fiction will be tomorrow's science-achievement! Our thought and imagination must be bold and adventurous, Prasad! What would you say, brother?" Sangamesam turned to me for support.

"That may be as you say. But who is interested in the manner or mode of death? We should rather project our thought towards letter ways of living. Whether one dies and returns to dust or becomes pure light, it is not going to help humanity to live, and hence all research into it is useless." That was my opinion.

"You are mistaken," said Sangamesam. "The mind and the body go together. Death is the conclusion to life. They too go together. In Sri Chaitanya's life, devotional ecstasy was the most distinguishing trait : by mere touch he was able to impart it, transmit it to others. The culmination of that ecstatic state of mind must have transformed his mundane body into light. And it appeared as death to ordinary people. He walked into the sea, he had to, as the sea alone could receive safely that immense energy. His walking into the sea is not a legend but a fact."

Lakshmiprasad has a large nursing-hospital at Kandukur. He came to Visakhapatnam to attend a medical conference. Sangamesam had arrived from Madras four days earlier. I live in Visakha being employed as Reader in the University. It was a rare meeting of three old friends and we decided to take a holiday visiting Puri. We exchanged notes about our personal and family affairs without reserve during the trip.

Lakshmiprasad has two daughters, no sons. That is one disappointment in his life.. The first daughter is a doctor and has been married to a doctor. Both of them work in this hospital. The match for the second daughter is settled. She will marry an I.A.S. officer in the coming *Sravan*. Lakshmiprasad is now looking for grandchildren. He is planning a tour abroad. He is also ambitious, and would even enter politics, when the opportune moment arrives. That is what he gave us to understand about himself.

Well, the month of *Sravan* arrived and the marriage of Lakshmiprasad's daughter was duly celebrated, attended by Sangamesam and myself. Within a week of our return from the celebrations, we received the thunderbolt of a message that Lakshmiprasad was dead.

How did it happen? The newly-married couple returned to Lakshmiprasad's house after the customary sojourn at the bridegroom's place. Lakshmiprasad planned a picnic to a nearby sea-side resort called Ramayapatnam. He asked two of his doctor colleagues to accompany him; his wife daughters and sons-in-law and a few servants constituted the picnic party. In the early hours of the morning, the male members of the party left in a vehicle, and the female members with two servants were to follow in another vehicle at 9 a.m. with lunch-baskets. After bathing in the sea, Lakshmiprasad was standing on the beach very close to the water. His tow sons-in-law and a doctor colleague were still in waist-deep waters. Suddenly a mountain-like wave came up and swallowed the three bathers, whom Lakshmiprasad had been watching. Lakshmiprasad fell down unable to bear the shock, as he believed that both the sons-in-law were gone and his colleague.

When the wave touched the shore, it swept Lakshmiprasad's body into the sea. The son-in-law and their companion, however, ducked and reached the shore, though the senior son-in-law had to be brought unconscious to the shore by the other two. The second doctor colleague, standing at a distance, had observed the fall of Lakshmiprasad. When he ran to the spot, the body had already gone into the sea. When the unconscious son-in-law revived, all of them started looking for Lakshmiprasad. Then his body was washed ashore and restored to them. But Lakshmiprasad was dead. It wasn't death by drowning; he had died of shock.

We, Sangamesam and myself, were present for the obsequies. We condoled his death in the appropriate manner. We too were in a state of shock. As we waited in mournful silence for our respective trains at the Singarayakonda railway-station, Sangamesam said : "You remember our Puri trip, and what you spoke about life being more important than death. The manner of death is a commentary on the individual's manner of living. Mahatma Gandhi, a great votary of non-violence, died a violent death! Lakshmiprasad's death demonstrates how much he was attached to money, ambition and his family. His absolute identity with them is seen in the manner of his death. In a way he was lucky. If his sons-in-law had died, as he imagined, and he had lived to mourn the loss, what would have been his life hereafter?

"Then, is death the opposite of our attachments in life?"

"Yeah, death is the other side of the coin."

"What about the man who develops non-attachment to the things of life?"

"He becomes triumphant over life and death."

"Do you mean to say he won't die!"

"He will die in the body. That is not important. He will not *experience* death. As he has attained to a state beyond duality, he sees death as continuous with life. Spiritually ambitious men by *sudhana* may even succeed in building a body of light, which may last after the earthly one is gone, but even that will not save them from death, unless they have attained to non-attachment and non-duality to experience life and death as one. So there can be ambition and attachment even in spiritual *sadhana*. An ordinary man too survives with his subtle body for a period of about 15 days, according to the *Tibetan Book of the Dead*. That is why ceremonies are performed and the dead are fed ritually. Some, no doubt, develop the subtle body and continue to survive to help others. But helping others is also a manifestation of life's desire."

As Sangamesam continued to speculate, my train arrived on the platform and I had to take leave of him.

An year passed by. I fell ill with dengue fever. I was recovering, but felt a terrible weakness both in the body and in the mind. It was the full-moon night of *Sravan*. I had a dream. Sangamesam was there. Standing a little away from my bed, he was asking me to get up and join him. He was in a joyous mood and was urging me to get up. I tried but my extreme weakness prevented me. "If you want to get up, you can do it, come on, my dear fellow," said Sangamesam and put out his hand towards me. I tried to reach it, but failed. But I touched something and my dream was gone. I was groping against the wall :

When I had got up from my bed three days later, I received a letter.

"Dear Brother,

I have been going round and round for a long while. Forget what I told you about Einstein's theory, or about developing a body of light. All that is meaningless. Except joy, *ananda*, serene joy, everything else in meaningless. The sea of joy in me and the joyous sea outside me are one and the same. Separated from that joyous sea of consciousness, we gather sea-shells on the beach like idiots. There is neither meaning nor meaninglessness to life. Mind-body, mundane-body ethereal-body these are not separate. Tradition, religion, knowledge, science, everything is void. They are the curtains of illusion to be brushed aside to meet the sea, my sea of joy. If there is joy in life, in the small things like getting up, drinking coffee, contemplating nature, soaking in rain, and os on, it is measuring out in small tea-spoonfuls the joyous sea of consciousness. Day after day. Life after life. No, the sea is my beloved. The sea is my all. The sea is my consciousness, my joy. I am the sea. No *maya* can separate me hereafter. I am the sea. The sea is I and I am joy...."

Sagara Sangameswara Sastri.

I couldn't make anything out of that letter. In his quest, Sangamesam had become mystic, his mysticism bordering on loss of reason and madness. A few days later I received the news. The sea had washed ashore Sangamesam's body on the Edward Elliot's beach, which he used to frequent. Whether it was natural death, or suicide, I could get no information. No one could know. After all this, after I lost my two friends to the sea, the secret of life and death still remains a mystery to me. Whatever little understanding I had about it was washed away. I sit silent and dumb, dumb even in my mind, staring at the sea from the sands of Visakha beach.